EVERYTHING HAPPENS IN AUGUST

EVERYTHING HAPPENS IN AUGUST

JOHN BUDDEN

Matador
5 Weir Road
Kibworth Beauchamp
Leicester LE8 0LQ, UK
Tel: (+44) 116 279 2299
Fax: (+44) 116 279 2277
Email: books@troubador.co.uk
Web: www.troubador.co.uk/matador

ISBN 978 1848762 633

Front cover photograph: David West

British Library Cataloguing in Publication Data.
A catalogue record for this book is available from the British Library.

Typeset in 11pt Sabon MT by Troubador Publishing Ltd, Leicester, UK

Matador is an imprint of Troubador Publishing Ltd

Printed in Great Britain by the MPG Books Group, Bodmin and King's Lynn

For Sally, Georgina and Beatrice

part one

chapter one

Jefferson Tweedy had had better days. By the time he sank into seat 13A on the slightly delayed flight from JFK airport to London Gatwick, he was in a state of sweating dishevelment. It had all happened in the blink of a socially excruciating eye and now as he stared out of the window, he took a moment to reflect on life's cruel irony and also to have a furtive look at his trousers.

He had been late for the flight and spent a rather fraught half an hour softly whining abuse at the knot of traffic just outside the airport. He toyed with the idea of abandoning the hire car in the unmoving traffic but chose instead to sit impotently whilst contemplating the prospect of missing his flight. Towards the end of the half an hour he decided that this was probably all Ailsa's fault.

Once inside the terminal he lost further precious seconds searching for a packet of pear drops. A friend's father once told him his one simple rule for flying: if he had not answered a clue from *The Telegraph* crossword by the time the stewardesses finished their 'in case of emergency' routine, then he would pick up his hand luggage and get off the plane.

It was the same for Jefferson only with pear drops. He had to have finished a pear drop – sucked not crunched – before the flight was ready to depart or else he too would up and leave. He had been plied with the sweets by his mother on childhood flights to see Aunt Joan in Belgium. The flights to Belgium stopped the day his 'Uncle Gert' ran away with the whore from Antwerp (confirming his mother's suspicions about men with moustaches); by which time the young Jefferson equated pear drops with safety in the skies and so the habit remained.

Having secured the sweets, he hurtled towards the boarding gate where he didn't quite barge an elderly couple into the rope that cordoned off the boarding area, although his actions were enough to elicit a loud tut from the air steward who was guiding the couple down the 'nasty slope' to the plane. Jefferson, hand luggage bouncing, threw an apology over his shoulder and ran on towards the plane. Later on the flight, he allowed the same old man to move ahead of him in the queue for the plane's toilet. This was a gesture he was to regret somewhat after the gut wrenching discovery he made on the old man's departure. Having overcome the first wave of nausea, Jefferson reflected that there was probably some kind of natural justice in all this, before taking a deep breath and reaching for as many paper towels as he could lay his hands on.

Boarding the plane, Jefferson swiftly spotted the potential difficulties of seat 13A. It was the window seat as requested, but ensconced in seats 13B and C was a mother and child. A mother and child of gargantuan proportions. The child was in the midst of destroying a family size packet of crisps whilst the mother gently grazed on a travel bag of sweets. Jefferson himself had never been svelte and lived by the benefits of a favourably cut suit, but now the heat rumpled linen of his present model would be severely tested by the approach to seat 13A.

He never relished this sort of situation and envied the confident manner in which he'd seen the Americans deal with such moments; he knew decisive action was the key, possibly accompanied by an authoritative smile. This was how Ailsa (although Scottish) did it when they went to the theatre, although her father (also Scottish) in similar situations chose to dispense with the smile relying rather on a combination of clear purpose and superiority.

Jefferson began the journey to 13A with a weak smile directed towards the heavy boned mother. She responded with a teeth radiating, my sweet Jesus it's the man of my dreams, ten year old in her first school musical, beamer of a smile. Sweat broke onto Jefferson's brow. He felt obliged to grin a little wider, hoping that his eyes would convey the necessary social deterrent, before pressing on towards his seat. It seemed at this early stage of the manoeuvre that the mother was going to stay seated, so Jefferson fixed his eyes firmly above her and shuffled into the first foot space. As he planted his right foot on the vacant patch of floor he felt the shift from beneath him and looked down to see the rise of the behemoth. She rose to eye level with a breathy 'room for a little one' and a mouthed 'hi', opening her eyes a little wider to heighten the effect. Jefferson felt a fresh dampening of his forehead but pressed on. As he shuffled away from the mother a dart of liquid splashed his ear and he thought for one terrible moment that she was licking his ear lobe. Horrified, he looked to his left and saw the fat son's hand squeezed tightly around a cartoned drink, the still dripping straw peeking through between fat index finger and fatter thumb. In response to this the mother was now pressing herself against Jefferson in an attempt to reprimand the son and it was at this point that Jefferson felt the undeniable twitch of arousal in his trousers. Horribly proud, he pushed roughly past both mother and son and lurched into his seat.

It couldn't be denied. The very thing he'd longed for two hours ago had arrived when squashed between an obese mother and her son. He looked down at his trousers, uplifted and stained with blackcurrant cordial. He decided to stare out of the window and visualise drowning puppies.

Jefferson Tweedy had never been over endowed with attention from women, so when Ailsa McLeish approached him one night in the student union bar of the University of West Wales, he suspected that she was probably fulfilling some drinking game forfeit imposed by the women's hockey team. His suspicions had dulled somewhat by the time Ailsa took him back to her room and freed him of his long resented virginity. He hadn't known a great deal about it but he felt he had acquitted himself reasonably well and Ailsa's post-coital feedback was largely positive. She later claimed to have 'had her eye on him' for some time and although Jefferson found this improbable he replied with a worldly 'likewise'.

Their parting earlier in the day, ten or so years after that fateful night in the union bar, had been the cause of Jefferson's lateness and the source of no little consternation on his journey to the airport.

Late the night before Jefferson had asked Ailsa to marry him and on reflection he was pleased with how it had gone.

In keeping with the other important moments in his life Jefferson had not prepared the event particularly carefully. Rather he had felt in recent weeks that Ailsa was expecting something of the sort and since he felt no great revulsion towards the idea he had decided to propose. Ailsa for her part had answered 'yes' with pleasing speed and all had seemed very jolly. When they returned from dinner, Ailsa had whispered that she was 'popping to the bathroom' which Jefferson knew was his cue to make the necessary preparations. He had never been very keen on the idea of lying atop the bed in all his glory, ready for Ailsa's entrance (as recommended in 'Lover Man – the considerate bedfellow' a slim volume Ailsa had bought him a few Valentine's Days back) so his preparations more usually took the form of a stifled breaking of wind somewhere away from the bed before creeping under the covers and considerately warming her side with his feet. Ailsa then returned with something of a flourish and things had progressed swiftly (the image of rattling through an agenda had crossed his mind briefly but he managed to quell it). Indeed at one point Jefferson had gone as far as to engage in some unison moaning; he wouldn't have dreamt of singing a solo, so to speak, but since it was a special occasion he thought it would have been churlish not to join in. He'd watched Ailsa carefully for his cue and when the moment arrived he joined in with as much gusto as he could muster.

On returning from the bathroom, Ailsa labelled him 'magnificent' and although Jefferson thought this owed more to her getting carried away with the occasion he was pleased none the less. They then talked of their plans for Ailsa joining him back in London and there was some tentative discussion regarding the wedding. She was due to return from her placement in New York in August and thought that if they both got on with the preparations they could get married in late August or early September. At that point he gallantly promised to 'take care of things' and contentedly went to sleep.

He was awoken at 7 o'clock the following morning by Ailsa doing something that he thought his mother probably wouldn't know the name of. She had continued gamely for some time but to no avail; the long and the short of it as he had explained to Ailsa was that he simply couldn't manage it – Ailsa had replied rather cuttingly that it was 'probably just the short of it.' He went on to explain that he'd had a lot on his mind and that first thing in the morning wasn't his preferred work pattern but none of these justifications seemed to appease Ailsa and in truth none of them rang true with Jefferson; this sort of thing had never happened to him before and now didn't seem a very good time to start. The recriminations began, the inquest raged before Ailsa finally put it down to some deep seated fear of marriage. Jefferson nodded gravely and promised to 'do something about it', since he was aware of the time and didn't want to be late for his flight.

With the plane airborne and the fasten seatbelt sign off, Jefferson gave up the charms of the window and unearthed his laptop computer from his bag. He decided to set about looking for wedding venues; figuring that a conspicuous show of wedding enthusiasm would not go amiss in the difficult next conversation with Ailsa.

As he waited for the machine to load he absentmindedly turned to his left and fell into the full beam of the fat mother's smile. Trapped in the headlights of her teeth Jefferson felt the panic rushing into his eyes. He jerked his head back towards the screen and began to tap maniacally at the keyboard. Had he detected a certain knowing in her look? Had she felt that fleeting pressure on her skirt? He stole another glance to his left and now the son was smiling, that same conspiratorial smile. Jefferson managed a sickly grin before theatrically falling asleep over his computer.

chapter two

J.P.P. Montgomery's fingers barely touched the wheel as his immaculate powder blue BMW ate the miles of the M11 and headed serenely for Newmarket race course. He contemplated the beauty of the late morning sun and whistled softly. His head was full of the races and he aimed to be at Newmarket in plenty of time to savour the occasion. He would meet the governors for lunch and a few drinks before slipping away on his own for twenty minutes to the paddock. This was a favourite part of the day, standing alone amongst the crowd and listening to the punters as they oohed and aahed in admiration at St George's Blue. She excited comment from novices and experts alike and he never tired of hearing their praise. He loved the look of her with her grey/blue colouring and black mane. Lib had commented right from the start that he enjoyed the ritual of the races as much as the race itself and he knew she was right. He found the colours of the horses, the lushness of the grass and the colours of the silks irresistible.

Montgomery pushed his hair back before dialling the number for home. He thought a call might be a good idea after this morning's slight altercation. He waited a moment before Lib's voice came on the other end of the line; as always she answered the phone as if she had been interrupted from her favourite pursuit.

'Yes?'

'Hello pussycat. How are you?'

There was no response.

'Listen I'm sorry your tiger bared his teeth at you this morning, silly old cat didn't think what we was doing did he? All het up before the big race – took it out on pussy. Well your big cat's calling to say sorry and see he if he can't make it up with a spot of dinner tonight.'

'I might have something on.'

'And if you have my darling I shall wait for you to return home and I shall bow and scrape before you to plead for your forgiveness.'

He paused and listened to his wife's silence before continuing.

'Half past eight? Siegfried's?'

'Perhaps. What time's the race?'

'The three thirty.'

'Best of luck.'

'Thank you pussycat. Half past eight at Siegfried's then? I'll book our usual table.'

'If you must.'

'I must, I must. You're a darling.'

The phone went dead and he smiled.

He looked out towards the horizon and breathed deeply. The weather and the going were perfect for St George's Blue and he couldn't see one earthly reason why she shouldn't continue her glorious run of form. All very satisfactory he thought as he turned the radio on; there would be champagne at Siegfried's tonight.

'Thank you Sarah and so back to our major story; the government's announcement this morning of the creation of a single Examinations Board for all British schools. We go now to our Education Correspondent, Emily Board. Emily, what can you tell us about this announcement?

The announcement comes James in response to the increasing pressure the former Examinations Boards, and indeed the government itself, found themselves under due to the catalogue of mistakes and errors that have blighted the public examination system in recent years.

I was told by a source close to the launch, that the final straw came with the misplacement of the GCSE Biology papers for three schools in Nuneaton; an incident that caused such embarrassment for the then head of SuperEd, Roger Weaver. This capped a catalogue of embarrassing incidents for the board including: examination papers finding their way onto an internet website, the Cornwall marking scandal of 2003 and the recent story of two examiners found marking A Level History papers in a pub in Croydon, and the combination of these events have led the government to decide enough was enough and to create the new system that we've seen unveiled today.

This is what Lord Mcleish of Dunblane had to say at the press launch earlier today.

'It's time for parents and pupils to trust in the service we offer them. We must reclaim the gold standard of the British education system. We must offer a service that employers can trust, one that is a reliable indicator of a student's suitability

for a course or for employment. StanEd will restore the public's faith in a system that has become a laughing stock. We will provide a public service ethos combined with the clear sightedness of business...

Montgomery turned the voice off with a flick of a steering wheel lever.

He breathed deeply and spoke to the horizon,

'We live in a world of grey men and bespectacled women.'

With that he lowered the sun roof, pressed the accelerator to the floor and motored on towards the waiting bliss of Newmarket.

chapter three

Emma Carr sat in her four wheel drive jeep, half listening to the radio. She was stuck in traffic two streets away from St George's Cross school and was later than she liked to be.

There had been problems with Luke again that morning, so she was late to leave and now here she was. She watched three boys walk past her car, and thought of Luke and his convulsive sobs – heels dug in like a dog refusing to enter the vet's surgery. She had presumed wrongly that it was a phase that would pass but now most days were the same and she had run out of ideas about how to deal with it. She just couldn't shake the feeling that this shouldn't happen with a teacher's child; a head teacher's child. The school refusers ('truants we used to call them didn't we?') were a group she'd had nothing but contempt for up until she realised that her son was one; and still the contempt had not altogether passed. These children were supposed to come from dysfunctional families with parents that were complicit with their child's behaviour. The sort of parents that let their children take the day off for their birthday and then wrote letters to form tutors describing their child's bogus ailments.

Yet now she watched her nine year old son turn into a sobbing wreck at the thought that it was time for school.

Again last night she had listened to her mother's thinly veiled accusations;

'No-one likes walking to school with a stranger do they duck?'

'He's walked with Abby since he started school, mum.'

'That's what I mean.'

Emma could almost hear her mother crossing her arms.

'All of his friends go to school with their nanny, mum and they don't have problems getting out of the house.'

'Do you think it helps then?'

The three boys had stopped on the corner to Emma's left. They were St George's Cross boys but she only knew the tallest one of them by name. He was called Cornelius Evenett and Emma knew him because she'd removed him from a Science lesson the previous day. When she arrived at the classroom she had found Cornelius repeatedly screaming 'batty boy minge' at Mr Wells the Head of Year 10. It was only when Emma had asked Mr Wells to leave the room for a moment that Cornelius had stopped shouting and walked with her to her office. She asked him on the way why he was so angry and the boy replied, 'I'm not, he's a prick.' She warned him that this was not an acceptable manner in which to address a member of staff before seating him outside her office and beginning proceedings to internally exclude him for the rest of the day.

All three boys wore trainers, baseball caps and hoods with their grey St George's Cross blazers either over their 'hoody' or poking out of the top of their bag. They watched the road and Emma sensed they were looking over her car;

she bent down to adjust the volume of the radio and then looked straight ahead. As the traffic began to creep forward she turned towards the boys and smiled warmly before grinding to a halt a car's length further forward. She looked straight ahead and tried to look at ease.

When the lights changed, she edged through the junction to find she was stuck in a throng of cars similar to her own. Enormous cars, most of them silver, parked in zigzagged areas of the road from where beautifully coiffured mothers smiled cleanly down on their departing young ones, from the heights of their military sized vehicles. This was the arrival of the day boys for St George's College. The boys, and only boys, that attended the prestigious and long established public school that resided imperiously in the road parallel to St George's Cross. 'A street and a world away,' as Mrs Bastic Styles said when Emma arrived for her first day at St George's Cross. The boys smiled back at their mothers before striding the four yards to the school gates. As a group they sported the distinctive British Racing Green blazer of the College with some of the younger boys in shorts. Emma looked in to the grounds and through the windows of the dormitories to see the boarders preparing themselves for the day. She knew that beyond the dorms lay the quad, complete with peacocks and gargoyles. Then on to the endless fields for rugby, cricket, football and hockey, all with fluttering corner flags decked in the green and purple colours of the school. To the left of the fields stood the building that housed the Olympic size indoor swimming pool that had produced a bronze medallist at the previous year's Commonwealth Games and beyond that were the twelve tennis courts which Emma could see from her office window, dull orange with rigid green nets and bright white lines.

She watched as Cornelius Evenett and his boyz slouched and bopped their way past the College entrance, headed for St George's Cross. She recalled that under the previous Head a deputation of boys from the College Prep School had come in to a St George's Cross assembly to plead their humanity and show that they were just like the boys that so mercilessly bullied them on the way to, from and sometimes during school. She'd also been told of the time when a pack of St George Cross boys had walked through the College's lower school eating area during lunch, 'looking threateningly at the diners' according to an eye witness. The same witness went on to say 'they didn't do anything, they just…sauntered.' The college had tried to press trespass charges but the boys were unidentifiable on the CCTV footage due to their hoods and an identity line up produced no conclusive results. Each new report of an attack on a College boy seemed to split opinion in the St George's Cross staffroom. For some it was confirmation of their 'they're all animals' attitude whilst others seemed to take a curious pride in the attacks; as if they'd beaten them at football.

The traffic eased after the entrance to the college and Emma followed St George's Road round to the right and arrived at St George's Cross school.

The school stood before her, a condemnation of sixties architecture. Discoloured panels soiled the main building whilst prefab huts sat around it like draughty, illegitimate offspring. There was a large blue sign near the entrance that had St George's Cross in large black letters and above the name in smaller white letters was written 'We're proud of'. Emma had commissioned the sign in the name of improving the self image of the school and to help the pupils and community to feel an affinity with their local place of education.

The front section of the main school was fresh from its monthly clean but the rest of the buildings were covered with graffiti and 'tags' as Emma had learnt to call them. She could rarely make out what the tags were meant to say but she had recently appointed a member of staff to catch the perpetrators of this graffiti. She had also sent a letter home to every pupil saying that those caught would be dealt with in the severest possible way. They hadn't caught anybody yet.

The school was in its second year of 'Special Measures', enforced after its last OFSTED inspection and Emma Carr had become its head teacher six months ago. The previous head teacher had left through 'mutual consent' after an incident in the playground where it was alleged that he stripped down to his underwear and ran around flailing his arms and shouting, 'Look at me, look at me.' The head teacher's defence at the hearing was that he was trying to break up a fight through diversionary tactics but this was not considered enough for him to retain his job. Emma was the only applicant for the post and secured the position after a half day interview in which she presented two power point presentations and outlined her vision for the future of the school. The governors produced the contract there and then and after signing it Emma drove to the girls' school in Cheam where she worked and handed in her pre-written letter of resignation. She began work as head teacher at St George's Cross that Easter.

Pulling into her allotted parking space, she looked once again at the picture of the beaming Lord McLeish on the front page of her newspaper, before carefully folding the paper and tucking it under the front seat of the car. She lifted her briefcase from beside her, stepped down from the car and strode purposefully towards her office.

chapter   four

Jacob Haliwell was also a touch late into the office. The night before had followed what was an increasingly familiar pattern and its after effects had prevented him from making it into the office anywhere near his designated start time of 9.30am. Not that anyone in the office appeared to care when he arrived at 11.15am and he himself certainly didn't care since he now prided himself on the fact that nobody cared less than Jacob Haliwell. He knew it didn't matter that he was late since he couldn't start 'work' until the photographs arrived and they didn't generally turn up until twelve-ish.

As he saw it the job he now did held no resemblance to the one he signed up for and so the person he was now need bear no resemblance to the person he had been when he started. He occasionally looked back on the young and idealistic journalist that he once was and felt a withering contempt for his naïvety. He'd come into the profession with his head full of John Pilger and the glories of campaigning journalism and now here he was, reduced to producing fifty words every few hours on the latest media whore his job had helped to create. It hadn't always been like this.

Prior to the arrival of Dickie Gittens, he'd enjoyed working at The Express. He'd been second on the Foreign desk and he'd had moments, such as covering the rise of Le Pen in France, when he felt that if the great Pilger should happen to walk into the office at that moment, he would probably approve of his work. It wasn't central to the paper's ethos but they had covered it and he'd felt that if *The Express*' readership was in anyway 'despairing at the rise of fascism in Europe so soon after the horrors of Nazi Germany' then he himself had played some small part in this. Indeed this was the final sentence of his piece on Le Pen that had made page 7 of that day's edition and which he now kept in his bedside drawer.

Then Dickie Gittens arrived.

The takeover was done in typically cavalier fashion and *The Express* quickly joined King Dick's (as the other papers called him) roster of publications. Jacob wasn't familiar with his entire body of work, but he took the time to acquaint himself with 'Fat Dutch Sluts', which he considered to be something of a masterpiece of the genre and he remembered 'White Hot Blacks' with some fondness from his school days, arriving as it had from the sweating palm of Vincent Penfold, the self titled 'purveyor of porn' from the year above Jacob at school.

Dickie Gittens' first editorial meeting at *The Express* had now taken on near mythical status amongst Fleet Street staff. It had lasted just under ninety seconds, in which time Gittens eyeballed every individual in the room before issuing the following call to arms.

'Fuck China, fuck France, fuck Nicaragua, fuck Germany, fuck all those little countries that used to be Russia (no one chose to interrupt), fuck Israel, fuck Palestine ('impartial,' as Belle later observed), fuck Italy, in fact fuck 'em all. We're an English paper for English readers and that's what we're all about. We're gonna sell papers, tits 'n' talent and they'll be English|tits or my name's not Dickie Gittens. Now if you don't like it you can fuck off. Come and see me and I'll sort you out and I'll get people in who want a bit of it. Thank you and God Bless.'

The following night in the 'Coach and Horses' Belle, Jacob's best friend at the paper, decided that she would be taking Mr Gittens' kind offer and was handed a cheque for £8000 the following day.

'How can he afford to do this? He can't do it for everyone can he? The place'll go bust.'

'He won't get staff in will he. It'll be Reuters and a few desk staff. He doesn't need staff for what he wants to do.'

Jacob went the following day to speak to Roy Downes, Dickie Gittens' number two, about the future of the Foreign desk.

'You can have Entertainment, she fucked off yesterday.'

Jacob's subsequent enquiry about the future of the foreign desk was greeted with a derisory laugh and he was told that he had until tomorrow to let them know about Entertainment.

He went home that night and tried to invoke the spirit of John Pilger; he failed and the next day he accepted the role of Entertainment correspondent for *The Express*.

That night in the 'Coach and Horses', when he told her of his decision to accept the post, Belle raised an eyebrow but kept her counsel. He tried to explain his reasoning to her, but failed. On reflection it appeared to comprise of two motives, neither of which he was proud of. The first was cowardice; he was terrified of having to look for another job. He hated interviews and he didn't want a change of career (Belle informed him that she was going to train to become a teacher, an idea that filled him with abject horror).

The second factor was far darker and not something he would ever admit to Belle or anyone in polite society – he had enjoyed Dickie Gittens' speech. He had never heard anyone speak like that, least of all to a room of experienced journalists, and he had found something thrilling in it. To Jacob it had been a little like one of Dickie's magazines – a dirty pleasure. He dressed this up to Belle as an attempt to subvert Gittens' regime from within, 'better to be in the tent pissing out and all that…'. Belle simply nodded slowly.

It had been six months since she and most of the rest of his colleagues disappeared to pastures new, leaving Jacob to man the Entertainment desk with a picture of Pilger blu-tacked above his computer. What was left of the Foreign desk was now handled by a girl that came in one day a week and covered stories about Scotland, Ibiza and occasionally Wales. The girl had once come over to his desk to borrow a pen and seeing the picture of Pilger had asked if that was Jacob's dad. He'd said yes and she'd said 'Ah bless,' before returning to complete a story about an HIV infected Spanish waiter who was targeting 'easy' English girls.

The rest of the press loved the arrival of Dickie Gittens at *The Express*. Their coverage was filled with euphemisms like, 'Gittens has brought a swashbuckling approach to Fleet Street' and 'he has brought new blood to the paper'; whilst it became clear to Jacob that his first impression of Gittens had been right – he was an arsehole. A charismatic, hectoring, moneyed, philistine of an arsehole. He sacked people on the spot, he humiliated people in meetings, he pervaded the paper entirely and the sales went through the roof. *The Express* was selling a third more papers a week than it had before the arrival of 'King Dick' and he had simultaneously slashed the cost of running the paper by a third.

'Tell me I'm fucking wrong,' he would scream as each set of new sales figures were announced and nobody could. This challenge would often be followed by Gittens running around the room waving the paper in the faces of anyone who was in his vicinity and repeating the cry 'Tell me I'm fucking wrong.'

'So what do you do on Entertainment?' asked Belle at their bi-monthly lunch.

'Well, I come in hungover and I wait for the photos. Then they arrive and they decide which one to give me and I write about it.'

'Ooh how exciting.'

'Absolutely; they work a strict rotation policy. When you left it was Jordan, Robbie, Posh and/or Becks. Now it's Jordan, Peter, Cheryl, Posh and/or Becks. Oh and sometimes Martine, they like her as well – even though she hasn't been in anything for ages.'

'And what do you write?'

'Twenty five to fifty words…'

'Really?'

'Remember Dickie's words, Belle. 'These cunts don't want to read' – quote.'

'Jesus.'

'Absolutely. So I write about how gorgeous Jordan looks

and if I can tell from the photo I might write about where they are and that's about it; top level, investigative journalism.'

'Pilger-esque some might say.'

'Pilger-esque indeed. And how's teaching?'

'Well we're just about to start our first placement but so far it's been great.'

'Please tell there's still time for it all to go horribly wrong so I can gloat and feel good about staying with King Dick?'

'Theoretically yes.'

'Thank God for that.'

'But I don't think it will.'

'Cheers.'

Whilst Jacob awaited the arrival of the day's photographs he flicked through the stories from Reuters. He made a point of reading the foreign stories first before moving on to domestic matters. After following the developments of the revolution in Chad, Jacob came to the following headline:

'Government Creates Single Examinations Body.'

He couldn't put a name to the smiling man beneath the headline and checked to find it was a Lord McLeish of Dunblane. He laughed at the title before reading the rest of the story. He made a mental note to mention it in conversation the next time he saw Belle.

As he finished the story, Fat Nick arrived with the day's photograph. It was another of Jordan and Peter's break up – this one featuring Jordan standing hatchet faced outside their joint shop, only opened the previous month.

'The closing of the shop Jacob.'

'Ah yes, don't tell me – JordAndres – brilliant, brilliant.

'Selling everything from…'

'Everything from sex toys to puppies.'

'Lovely. What page is this Nick?'

'Might be front page, definitely page three.'

'Did we manage to get a picture of her holding *The Express* yet?'

'Not yet but she promises she will next time.'

'Thank you maestro, a pleasure as ever.'

Nick left and Jacob settled at his computer and began to write:

'The monstrous Jordan and her pea brained prick of a former husband, who represent everything I despise about modern Britain...' He deleted and paused to think. He contemplated Jordan's handkerchief of a dress and wrote the headline:

Jordan's Puppies For Sale.

'Brilliant Jacob,' he muttered, 'absolutely brilliant.' He continued to write with one hand whilst covering the eyes of John Pilger with the other.

chapter five

Having touched down safely and waited for his admirer from seat 13C to leave (with only the briefest of love lorn glances over her dimpled shoulder), Jefferson picked up his luggage and made his way to the train station. It was here that he saw the picture of his father in law to be on the front page of a discarded copy of *The Times*. He read the accompanying article through twice before reflecting that he felt almost no surprise at seeing Gordon (as he never called him) McLeish splashed across the front page of a national newspaper.

Jefferson had what could best be described as an uneasy relationship with his future father in law. He feared that the tone had been set on their very first meeting when, keen to make a positive impression, he had strode forward to shake Lord McLeish's hand in a business like fashion without seeing the family's beloved terrier Hamish come streaking out of the bushes to greet him. As Jefferson's right brogue impacted with Hamish's left foot (with what some would later swear was a crunch) the dog's yelp of pain was only upstaged by Lord McLeish's roar as he pushed Jefferson away from the squealing dog. Jefferson had ended up in a well tended herbaceous border whilst Ailsa and her father whisked Hamish off to the kitchen for immediate medical attention.

The dog died two months later at 'an unnaturally young age' as Lady McLeish pronounced at dinner and her mournful post mortem was accompanied by a muttered 'never the same' from Lord McLeish. Ailsa had assured him that he was not held responsible for the early demise of young Hamish but Jefferson feared the die had been cast.

After this unfortunate beginning he strived to ingratiate himself into the McLeish's affections by every method in his repertoire: the reassuring laugh after every mildly humorous comment, the early raising of favoured topics of conversation, the earnest listener, the enthusiastic agreer on all points made, the hard drinking bon viveur, the Spartan abstemist, but none of these things could thaw the frost at the heart of their relationship. He had only been alone with his future father in law once or twice in this time and the over riding memory of these encounters had been of unease and constant conversational wrongfootedness. The root of this was the fact that he found it utterly impossible to predict the responses of Lord McLeish ('you should call popsy, Gordon') to any given question. Regardless of the topic chosen 'popsy' would unerringly find a way to take it down a conversational cul de sac, leaving Jefferson nodding his head inanely as he frantically scratched around for a suitable response. During these times of conversational dead air, Lord McLeish would fix him with steely blue eyes and wait. He was a man who used none of the conventional conversational fillers – the oh yeses, the reallys, the mmm, the reassuring smile – techniques that Jefferson never appreciated until they'd gone. And into the subsequent silence Jefferson would stumble, armed only with a deeply inane piece of drivel that would be greeted with a raised eyebrow and a non committal 'yes'.

He'd been told at one Sunday dinner that Ailsa's father had been given his title of 'Lord McLeish of Dunblane' for services to New Labour. A couple of hurried glasses of wine later he had asked Gordon what these services were, to which the reply was 'aiding New Labour's links with the business community. I'm a safe pair of hands for them Geoff.'

His future father in law insisted on calling him Geoff and in public this became Geoffrey. Jefferson had corrected him once and his father in law had replied 'Yes Geoff.' He never raised it again.

During the course of these torturous conversations Jefferson had never been able to ascertain exactly what it was that Ailsa's father did for a living; only that he'd started out as a 'tax advisor' and that he was an internationally renowned expert in 'tax avoidance'. Ailsa was at pains to point out that this was a very different thing to tax evasion and was completely legal and of real benefit to the business community. Jefferson had no reason to believe that it was anything other than legal and told Ailsa that it sounded 'very good'. Later that same day he raised the subject of the title again.

'It is a bit unfortunate isn't it – Dunblane.'

'What do you mean Jefferson?' peered Lady McLeish over her half moon glasses.

'Well, what with that nasty business.'

'Are you referring to the incident, Jefferson?' Lady McLeish's Scottish brogue became markedly more pronounced.

'Yes.'

'It isn't Gordon's fault, the death of those poor children you know Jefferson.'

'No I wasn't for an instant…'

'No.'

The discovery of the picture of his future father in law in *The Times* coincided with the arrival of a text message from Ailsa.

Hello hubby to be!!!!!!!!!! Call popsy urgently. Big Kiss xxxxxxxxxx

Why an otherwise perfectly sane and intelligent young woman should constantly resort to the language of the over indulged day girl when referring to her father (and it only applied to her father) was beyond him. He had mentioned it once, but the response was so fearsome that he pretended she'd misunderstood what he'd meant and the subject was dropped for ever more.

Looking at the message, Jefferson wondered what on earth his future father in law could want with him. The prospect of a one to one telephone conversation was horrific – what would he address him as when he answered the phone? His brain ran through some possible topics for small talk. Jefferson was not interested in sport but he had picked up enough to maintain one side of a conversation, 'Did you see the footie? What about that referee!' That sort of thing but Lord McLeish seemed utterly uninterested in such matters. He didn't seem to read as a past time, indeed he'd once said that since he dealt with two to three hundred e mails per day the thought of reading in his spare time simply made no sense to him. Besides, the very fact that Jefferson was considering it as a possible source of conversation was damning, since Jefferson last completed a book on his summer holiday three years ago. He'd rather enjoyed it but he didn't want to risk disappointment by reading another. Still he had a stock of phrases to hand should the subject ever arise, 'God I'd love to read more, I'm just too busy', 'I only see the film versions these days!' – the latter delivered with the knowingness of the well read man playing down his knowledge. Still the likelihood of needing such phrases with Lord McLeish was slim indeed.

His musings were interrupted by his phone ringing. He heard the refined Edinburgh accent of Lord McLeish of Dunblane.

'Geoff, it's Gordon.'

'Ah hello Lord McLeish.'

'Listen can you meet for some dinner tonight, I've something I'd like to talk over with you.'

'Certainly, Lord McLeish.'

'Shall we say 8 o'clock at Shepperd's.'

'Great.'

'Do you know where it is? Just the down from The Stafford; ask for my table.'

'Absolutely, sir.'

'Good, see you there.'

'Yes thank you, see you there. How are things with yourself and Lady McLeish…'

The line went dead.

With his attempts at familiarity smothered at birth, Jefferson headed for the taxi rank.

And so it was that Jefferson Tweedy found himself on the night of his return from America, in Shepperd's in St James's at ten minutes past eight, waiting for Lord McLeish of Dunblane.

He'd had time to pop home to Balham, drop his luggage off and change into a lightweight linen suit that he was rather fond of, and that he thought to be particularly sympathetically cut. He had got a degree of colour from his stay in the States and all in all felt himself to be in pretty good shape. He couldn't help feeling that this rare moment of physical self belief was somewhat wasted on the steely eyed McLeish of Dunblane, but he did suspect that as he ordered a gin and tonic the attractive young waitress's eyes lingered a touch longer on him than might usually have been the case.

Shepperd's was the type of place that would traditionally have been home to Conservative politicians and sympathisers alone, but now it seemed as if along with the policies, the political lines between restaurants were blurred as well. Jefferson was reminded shortly after he arrived – in the most discreet way possible – that diners did not remove their jacket in Shepperd's; he nodded keenly and slipped his jacket back on immediately.

The restaurant itself was laid out with a mixture of small tables and dark wooden cubicles. The cubicles could seat four people at most and were clearly there to provide the privacy necessary when dealing with matters of state. Jefferson recognised one middle aged man with dark wavy hair who was talking rather louder than the rest of the diners but couldn't put a name to him. He thought he might ask Lord McLeish who he was but then decided that he probably wouldn't.

As he scanned the restaurant again he saw Lord McLeish being greeted by the maître d. The two of them exchanged a few words before laughing warmly at their shared joke. Lord McLeish shook the maître d's hand with a double handed grip and Jefferson could see the glint of his cufflinks beneath the navy blue suit. Lord McLeish left the maître d with a pat on the shoulder and made his way towards the table. Ten feet away from the table he announced 'Geoffrey,' and proffered both his hands. Jefferson felt it was probably time to stand up and offered both of his hands. Reading the body language it seemed as if his future father in law might be about to hug him, and as unlikely as that seemed he felt that in the name of familial goodwill, he should go with it. Mid way towards a hug though it became clear that Lord McLeish was not about to hug him, forcing Jefferson into a hearty laugh and an extravagant, customised hand shake.

They sat down and Lord McLeish began to pour the sparkling water for both of them.

'So how was the States?'

'Oh, excellent.'

'And Ailsa's staying out there for another six months?'

'That's right, great job she's got.'

'So I understand and what about yourself Geoffrey?'

Had Ailsa told them about the proposal? Was this some kind of assessment of his future prospects? She had promised to wait for a couple of days before letting her parents know and now he was being subjected to a check on his ability to keep their daughter in the manner to which she was accustomed.

'Well I'll start to look around for things immediately. Although I hear things are still quite slow in the world of accountancy. I'm sure I've still got a few contacts who can get me an opening or two.'

'I think these sabbaticals are an excellent idea. Not something we had in my day of course.'

Lord McLeish began to laugh as Jefferson wracked his brains for their final conversation before he left for America. He was sure he had told him that it was a redundancy package that Mycroft, Pigott and Welch had given him, 'slow market Tweedy, chance for you to make a fresh start somewhere else.' He looked into the steely eyes for clues and found none.

'So are you set on a return to accountancy?'

'Well I'd rather presumed…'

'Only I've a new project that I think would suit someone with your qualifications and at your stage in your career.'

'Really?'

Lord McLeish paused and adjusted his cuff links.

'What do you know about education Geoffrey?'

'Well not a great deal really, other than that I went to school.'

Jefferson laughed to signal that he had cracked a small joke but Lord McLeish pressed on, unmoved.

'Perfect. We need someone from outside the system. The thing's crying out for someone who can cast a cold eye over its failings and effect a change. The whole system's been in the hands of the 'herbal tea brigade' for as long as anyone can remember and naturally they have made a complete horlicks of it – as inevitably they will Geoffrey, as inevitably they will.'

Lord McLeish paused to sip at his sparkling water, presumably to rid his mouth of the taste of the 'herbal tea brigade'.

'These people wouldn't know how to run a bath Geoff. They've lost papers, they've set the wrong papers, they've not marked papers, they've marked papers wrongly, they've destroyed new papers and kept the old; everything you can imagine could go wrong, has. Year after year they cause embarrassment through their ineptitude. The system's an absolute shambles and we want to do something about it.'

Jefferson knew from previous conversations that when Lord McLeish referred to 'we' he meant the forces for good and light within the government, amongst whom he naturally included himself.

'Is this what I was reading about in the papers?'

'That's it – 'StanEd – A new horizon for education'.

Lord McLeish paused to allow the splendour of the words to hang in the air. After a longer pause than Jefferson would have dared to leave he continued.

'We need to inject some business sense into the thing. Reorganise and adapt the running of it and make sure that they do the basics right. I don't know if you know but there are dozens of these examination boards at the moment, all doing their own sweet thing and it's been nothing short of a shambles. So we are going to reduce that to one board, one board that can actually do the job. It makes sense doesn't it? So there will be one examination board with all the kids sitting the same paper for Maths, the same paper for English and so on.'

'It certainly sounds sensible.' Jefferson took a sip of his water to show his agreement. Lord McLeish fixed him with his icy blue stare, 'And we need someone to run it.'

'Oh.'

'And that's where you come in Geoffrey.'

'I see.' Jefferson paused. 'You want me to find somebody for the job?'

Lord McLeish smiled briefly.

'No Geoff, we want you to run it.'

Jefferson took a moment to control his sense of rising panic.

'The problem is sir, I'm not really sure I'm terribly well qualified.'

'Answer me this. If I ask you whether losing exam papers was good practice for an Examining Body, what would you say?'

'I'd say it was a bad thing.'

'And so would we. And if I asked you if putting exam papers on the Examination Board website two weeks before the exam was a good idea, what would you say?'

'I'd say it was a bad thing.'

'And so would we. The difference is that you know how to make sure it doesn't happen and they don't.'

'Do I?'

'It's common sense man and that's precisely the quality that they have been missing and that you will bring to the job. It appears so obvious to the likes of us who have been schooled in the world of business, but to these people it's a mystery. They have not the first idea about how to run a business effectively and it's crying out for someone in charge who does.'

Lord McLeish sipped again from his glass of sparkling water and thanked the waiter for the arrival of the menus.

'The role on offer is Chief Executive of StanEd.'

Lord McLeish looked closely at Jefferson.

'You've also to think about the future Geoffrey. It goes without saying that the package that accompanies the job is highly favourable and would give any young couple a wonderful start in life, the sort of thing that any responsible young man thinking of his future would be a fool to turn his back on.'

Lord McLeish fixed him with a stare.

'Order your dinner and then I'll tell you all you need to know.'

chapter six

Emma Carr's PA knocked on the door to her office. She waited, before receiving the usual distracted 'yes', from within. She entered and stood just inside the door. She waited to see if Mrs Carr would look up from her computer screen but it quickly became clear that she wouldn't, so she began to speak.

'I called the College.'

'Oh yes. What did they say?'

'That Mr Montgomery wasn't in school today; that he was working from home.'

'But he's got a house in the grounds hasn't he? How can he be working from home? Can we be put through to his home line?'

'Oh no, they don't do that. He absolutely insists that he isn't interrupted. He has important work to do on the budget apparently.'

'Well who do we speak to regarding their parents' cars? Honestly Janet it's like a car park out there at dropping off and picking up time.'

Janet nodded and paused before her next comment.

'His secretary says that his car's not there.'

'Whose car?'

'Mr Montgomery's car.'

'Why would he be out if he's working from home?'

'Well I think that's what his secretary's getting at.'

'Perhaps his wife's got the car. He is married isn't he? Poor woman. By the way, can you cancel my assembly this afternoon or see if Vikram can do it. And could you ask Valerie to come and see me? She's put together this new Key Stage Three data and I want to really unpack it with her and talk about the bigger picture.'

'Certainly Mrs Carr. What's the assembly on so I can tell Mr Syal?'

'Raising achievement.'

'Very good.'

'Oh and Janet, can you let all the cabinet know that I want them here for three o'clock Wednesday afternoon and let them know it might be a late one.'

'Certainly Mrs Carr.'

As she shut the door slowly, Janet listened carefully and heard only a heave and sigh from Mrs Carr amidst a shuffle of papers. The door closed and she reflected that she was still waiting for her first 'thank you' in her dealings with Mrs Carr. The manners duck, as her husband had christened it, remained unbroken.

When the door closed Emma Carr went back to the multi coloured spreadsheet in front of her. Heavy sighing was interspersed with occasional frantic jottings on the pad in front of her.

There was a knock at the door and the tousled head of Valerie Bastic Styles popped around the door,

'Oh hello Emma, you wanted to see me?'

'I did Valerie, come in.'

'What are you working on?'

'That data that you produced for me. '

'Oh I hope it's useful.'

'It's terribly useful actually. Come round and have a look at this.'

Valerie moved behind the desk and looked over Emma's shoulder at the screen.

'I think that what we have here is the very key to this school's under achievement. Now take for example Raymond Baxter in Year 9. He is a good representative of our student intake. All the tests shown in the white column tell us that he is a boy of above average intelligence. This data predicts that he should be achieving at least six A*-C grades at GCSE. Now if we compare his present grades – building in two grades improvement with maturity and development – then we get the red column, which tells us that at present he is on course for only two A*-C passes at GCSE; one in English and one in Art.'

'I don't know if you know Raymond, but he's not an easy boy.'

'But in English he is on course to get a B grade at GCSE whilst in History he is working at an F grade. Now surely if someone is capable of passing English GCSE then they are capable of passing a History GCSE, or at least doing rather better in it than an F grade. And I'm afraid that the discrepancies lie between the teachers. Why is he on course for a B with Mr Harris in English and an F with Mr Wells in History?'

Valerie Bastic Styles shook her head earnestly and Emma Carr continued.

'Now this only needs to be happening to Raymond Baxter in three subjects and then he falls below the magic 5 A*-C grade boundary and when he falls, our figures drop with him; and at the moment it is happening to him in at least four subjects. So how can we stop this happening?'

To Valerie Bastic Styles relief, this last question proved to be rhetorical and the head teacher swiftly continued.

'Now this is how I see it. It seems to me that for too long teachers have blamed the pupils for all the problems. You hear it in every staff room in the country: there's no support at home, they won't listen, they don't want to learn, there's nothing you can do with kids from round here etc etc. But the point is that some of the teachers *are* doing it. Now Mr Harris has his flaws, he is difficult and contrary as we know, but I'm afraid Valerie, one cannot argue with his results.'

'You're absolutely right Headmistress; it's so easy for teachers just to blame the pupils.'

'And this is why the school is failing. We have students who can and should be doing better and they are not. So for these pupils to achieve their potential, which in turn would mean that the school would achieve its potential, it is the teachers who must do better.'

'Very good Headmistress, absolutely.'

Emma Carr paused for a moment and then looked directly at her deputy head.

'They're going to do things my way. They've tried it their way and it hasn't worked. OFSTED told us that and all the data tells us that, so there has to be change and that change means that they are going to do it my way. There will be a raft of new initiatives, that I know have worked at other schools and the staff will follow those initiatives to the word. In addition to this there will be a strict disciplinary code: verbal warning, written warning, followed by dismissal proceedings for anyone who we don't feel is meeting the required standards. You and I, along with the rest of the Senior Management Team, will carry out rigorous and regular observations of lessons and there will be follow up measures for any practice that we believe to be unsatisfactory. And this will apply to all staff. There will be no special favours; we are all failing together and we must all succeed together. And if there are any complaints, I'll simply show them the data.'

'Very good Headmistress.'

'Please call me Emma, Valerie.'

'Very good Emma.'

chapter seven

J.P.P. Montgomery was whistling a snatch of 'Bye, Bye Blackbird' when he entered his office the following day.

'Morning Rosie, how are we this fine day?'

'Very well head master, yourself?'

'Chipper, chipper. St George's Blue romped home and all's right with the world. And what is more Rosie she led from the front against a very decent field. I then followed this with a top class dinner at Siegfried's with the divine Libby and now I have the privilege of seeing you in full bloom – so yes Rosie things are very well.'

'I'm very pleased to hear it head master.'

'And how did the first XV get on yesterday afternoon?'

'I believe they won very comfortably over at St Jude's head master.'

'Excellent. And what do you have in store for me today?'

'You have assembly for the lower school this afternoon and there is the lower school Drama Production this evening.'

'Jolly good, although I do hope that Mr Percival hasn't chosen another one of his worthy eastern bloc specials for our delectation. There is more than enough time for misery and oppression in the later years, don't you think, and a dash of song and colour does so help the little ones along.'

'Also head master, Mr Castle has been in to see me two or three times.'

'Oh that wretched man; what can he possibly want this time?'

'He seems very exercised about the launch of this new Examinations Board.'

'STINK is it?'

'Er, StanEd sir.'

'StanEd! Bloody priceless isn't it Rosie? Are we alone in a sea of lunatics?'

'Well Mr Castle seems to think there ought to be a meeting about it.'

'Rosie, do you know the mistake I made when appointing Mr Castle? I allowed Celtic sentimentality to colour my vision. I have always had a healthy respect for all things Welsh, especially the people, which in the main has stood me in very good stead but I made a fatal error with young Castle. It was clear throughout the interview that he was a rancid little turd of a man and yet I appointed him due solely to his Welshness. How wrong can you be? The man is singularly charmless and as far as I can ascertain moves through life without a single redeeming feature.'

Montgomery flicked idly through the post on his desk before continuing.

'So now he wants to busy himself and waste the rest of our time over this latest government initiative does he? Does Mr Castle run any clubs for the boys Rosie? If he doesn't, suggest to him that this might be a better way of expending his dreadful energy.'

'I think you might want to pay some attention to these developments head master. There is an awful lot about it in the press.'

'It's your New Labour mates Rosie. I saw the pictures of that pompous arse McLeish. Have we not had enough of being told what to do by uptight Scottish Presbyterians? The place is riddled with them. A friend of mine met your Lord McLeish one night at The British Overseas Club, dreadfully dull man by all accounts. Knighted for services to New Labour? I have it on good authority Rosie that he swallowed a festering pile of shit for them and then donated an obscene amount of money for the privilege.'

'Well they're going to unveil the Chief Executive on Wednesday afternoon; I don't think Lord McLeish is directly involved.'

'Ah, his kind never are directly involved Rosie, are they? Well give Mr Castle his moment in the sun and call a senior management meeting for Wednesday afternoon. We shall see what Lord McLeish and his lot have up their sleeves for us.'

J.P.P. Montgomery then performed a miltary about turn and set off on his morning tour of the school, stopping to pick up a handful of grain for the peacocks as he went.

chapter eight

Jefferson read the text again:

Congratulations to my clever husband on his big job. Big Kiss xxxxx

Jefferson marvelled at the swiftness with which the news had travelled to Ailsa; perhaps there was something in the time differences to explain it.

He had accepted the role Chief Exceutive of StanEd since he had no other plans and he knew it would make both Ailsa and her father happy. Naturally, when accepting the job from Lord McLeish, he dressed it up in with a few suitable phrases; 'a real challenge', 'a chance to put something back' and this had been received with a hearty double handshake and a cry of 'welcome on board' from his future father in law. Jefferson rather enjoyed this and whilst being slapped on the back happily put to the back of his mind the gnawing doubt that he had no idea what vessel he had just boarded and also the fact that, despite his mother's best efforts, he had never learnt to swim.

The following day he accompanied Lord McLeish to meet Sandy, 'a man to offer some guidance with your speech to the press'.

Jefferson was surprised to see Lord McLeish so quiet in the company of this small man, who carried a smell of sweetness with him, but he enjoyed the attention that Sandy paid him and found him to be very complimentary. He advised him on his choice of suit – 'dark and English', the colour of his tie 'something primary' and requested an assurance that his shoes 'would be black'. Jefferson was reminded of going to have his school uniform bought for him in Hewitts in Bromley and liked it. Sandy then spent a considerable amount of time discussing what ought to be said at the press conference. He informed Jefferson that he must convey 'a sense of authority' and there were certain things that he, Lord McLeish and all the other interested parties would like him to say. It was this list that Jefferson consulted now.

Time for Change

Time for Accountability

Time to reclaim the public's trust

(Sandy had underlined the above point with two vigorous squiggles and looked Jefferson in the eye whilst stating that 'it wouldn't disappoint me if you mentioned this more than once')

With immediate effect

Business sense with public service ethos (three squiggles 'tremendously important')

Raising of standards

No re-marks

Each pupil achieving their unique potential with an Examination Board they can trust ('finish with this')

Sandy had then outlined the way the press conference would work.

'Lord McLeish will introduce you, and then you'll have a few minutes for your speech. Now feel free to write your own speech built around the phrases that I have suggested, but if you'd feel happier on this first, rather daunting occasion you could follow this speech that I've prepared for you.'

He produced a sheet of paper from his breast pocket with a flourish and another waft of scent. 'It won't take you long and this would cover all the areas that I'm sure you feel are important for the press and public to know about. What do you think? Would you like to use mine?'

Jefferson thought that this was probably a good idea and nodded his head. 'Excellent.' Sandy placed the pre-prepared speech in his hand. 'After that there will be a few questions from the press which I will manage. Rest assured there will be no rogue questions allowed through my little net and then it's big smiles and back out to the wings. Exit stage left you might say. Remember: purpose, efficiency and common sense.'

That Wednesday afternoon, whilst Jefferson Tweedy was being made up by an effete boy called Leigh, J.P.P. Montgomery and Emma Carr simultaneously began their meetings in St George's College and St George's Cross schools.

'Before we tune in to see what the government has got in store for us this time…'

Emma Carr raised her eyebrows in her well practised 'why can't they leave us alone' pose that never failed to raise a knowing laugh from any gathering of teachers (her cabinet of senior teachers duly obliged), 'there are a few things that I think it is vital that we cover today.'

She paused to look around the table before closing her eyes and beginning her speech. The Cabinet members knew that the closed eyes signified a long and heartfelt speech was to follow.

'As you all know, I am passionate about teaching and learning. I believe that is where the real change occurs. We can spend all day unpacking the data that falls on our desks, not that I'm saying it hasn't got a place, but it's teaching and learning where the real change is effected. And this school needs to start dong things differently. OFSTED have been in and they have told us in no uncertain terms that we are failing. The teachers in this school have had the chance to do things their way and they've been found wanting, so now they're going to have to do things our way.'

She handed out a hefty pack of papers.

'This is quality assurance. It is a series of termly checks to monitor the achievement levels of all pupils and teachers. If you could read this pack and then cascade the information down through line managers to all the relevant parties. Friends of mine in business have assured me of its effectiveness and it has already been implemented at a number of forward thinking schools. I want St George's Cross to be on that cutting edge. I want our students to be getting the same as the students next door. Why shouldn't they? Tell me why they shouldn't?'

A mumbled 'they should' came back from the assembled cabinet. Emma Carr looked directly at the deputy head Valerie Bastic Styles,

'Tell me why they shouldn't.'

'They should,' came the firm response.

Down the road, Bryn Castle was addressing the St George's College senior management group.

'Take for instance our close neighbours, St George's

Cross, their head is implementing no end of interesting and progressive initiatives. The Key Stage Three strategy for example has been shown to have excellent results throughout the country and I have it on good authority that St George's Cross have already run a number of twilight sessions to implement this change, yet we make not even a cursory nod towards it. And our use of data bases is simply non-existent. How are we tracking our pupils' achievements during the course of their time here? We should see each pupil as being on an educational journey which has begun before they arrive with us and continues after they have left us. Our question must be how far have they travelled in their time with us at St George's College? Data bases can help us to do this. To quote the research by Jenkins and Allthrop 2008 'we have a lot of inert data it is time for it to become ert.'

Castle looked expectantly around the table for a response to his carefully prepared witticism but was met with a sea of indifference. He pressed on swiftly.

'If we could combine the data and initiatives being employed by schools such as St George's Cross, with the students and facilities that we enjoy here at the College, then there would be no stopping us. Nobody wants us to be left behind.'

A hush fell around the table. The assembled senior managers of St George's College looked guardedly towards the head master and awaited his response. Mr Castle had been tentatively raising the subject of initiatives and change for a number of meetings now but this was his most explicit speech yet. J.P.P. Montgomery opened his eyes and looked around the table.

'How many of us are sympathetic with Mr Castle's speech?'

The question was met with silence.

'Well? How many of us are sympathetic with Mr Castle's speech? Have I appointed a chorus of weasels and yes men? Speak up. How many of you feel that Mr Castle has a point, that his ideas and initiatives are the way forward for St George's College?'

Susan Williams, teacher in charge of timetable and former Head of Mathematics raised her hand. Montgomery's gesture encouraged her to speak.

'I can't see how cherry picking the elements that suit us could hurt. No one says we have to do them all do they?'

She looked towards Bryn Castle who jumped in immediately.

'Absolutely, Susan. We are in such a privileged position; we are not required to follow anything. Look, I just think if you keep on doing the same thing you've always done then you keep on getting what you've always got and I can't see how that can be a good thing?'

Montgomery stirred in his seat and fixed his eyes on Bryn Castle.

'Even when it's been rather good, Mr Castle?

'But all the other schools are going this way, head master.'

'The point that you are missing with such unerring accuracy Mr Castle, is that the parents that send their children to St George's College, and indeed pay large amounts of money for the privilege, are not looking for us to be like all the other schools.

Now I have listened with some consternation over the past few weeks to you continually raising the ugly topic of data and the like and I'll tell you something that you appear to have forgotten. We have always had data and there have always been initiatives. The key is that we have chosen to use it as a reference point rather than the only point. I believed and continue to believe that educating the whole boy was rather more important than poring over his data. Do we not know our pupils well? Where their strengths and weaknesses lie?'

'With respect head master, I'm not for an instant…'

'With respect Mr Castle you'll find the previous questions were of a rhetorical nature and I remind you that I am the head master and when I am talking you will listen. Now we find ourselves with a generation of teachers that seem determined to put the cart before the horse. Tell me this Mr Castle, where does being a member of a triumphant first XV show up on your data? Where does being in the cast of one of Mr Percival's excellent, if somewhat obscure, drama productions show up on your data?

I grew up surrounded by a generation of men, teachers Mr Castle, who flew Bombers over the Ruhr Valley before they entered the world of education. Now what were we to tell them about the need for Key Stage Three initiatives and the need to spend your nights studying data? I stand for education in the richest, most glorious and most old fashioned sense of the word. Now when I am dead and gone you and your type may pick over the bones of this antiquated philosophy but I tell you now and for the foreseeable future that as regards data, 'that way madness lies'.

The assembled staff around the table had heard the speech before, or at least a variant on it, and now stole glances at a stony faced Mr Castle and a crestfallen Mrs Williams.

'Now Mr Castle, if you'd be good enough to turn on the

gadget in the corner, I believe they call it a television do they not?'

'Yes head master.'

'And we'll see what your pals, the grey men and the bespectacled women, have got in store for us now.'

chapter nine

Jefferson Tweedy was ushered from the make up room by a young woman who introduced herself as 'Bex with an x'. She led him through a brightly lit corridor until they reached a metallic coloured door. She pulled it slightly ajar and through the gap he could see his Lord McLeish addressing a large gathering of journalists. His words drifted through to Jefferson.

'…man with a background in business. Experienced in the efficient running of companies, the perfect man to run the new board for Examinations and bring some much needed order to a system that remains central to the success of today's students – tomorrow's work force.'

He glanced towards the door and received the thumbs up from Bex.

'Ladies and gentlemen – Jefferson Tweedy.'

Bex ushered Jefferson forward into the room. After the introduction he was expecting a round of applause, instead there was a low murmur which was only interrupted by the occasional click of a camera. Halfway between the door and the podium Lord McLeish greeted him with a smile that showed his teeth and the customary double hand shake. When he finished the hand shake he patted Jefferson on the back and ushered him towards the podium. Jefferson felt for the speech in his pocket and then in his other pocket. He became aware that his mouth was dry and the act of swallowing was starting to hurt. As he failed to find the speech the thought ran through his head 'don't start patting your pockets' so he began to furtively slide his hands around his torso searching for Sandy's speech.

'Wet palms or self love?' murmured Jacob Haliwell to Belle as they watched on the T.V. in her lounge.

'He doesn't look very promising does he?' she replied.

Jefferson finally found the speech in his top pocket where a handkerchief would have been if he had worn one. He briefly struggled to remember how it had ended up in there but decided that that wasn't a good use of his mental energies.

'Grey men Mr Castle, grey men – oh for a dash of colour from any direction,' said J.P.P. Montgomery in the meeting room at St George's College. His colleagues nodded, laughed in agreement and never took their eyes off the television.

Jefferson laid the speech on the podium and glanced up at the cameras. A flashlight blinded him and as he looked back to the speech, a chorus of spots danced and sang before his eyes. Slowly Sandy's words made themselves visible through the glare and with a deep breath he began.

'For too long our children have had to put up with a confused and second rate examinations system. We constantly remind them of the vital importance of educational achievement and success and the need to fulfil one's potential yet how do we repay their vigilance and effort?

Through an examinations system that makes us a laughing stock throughout the rest of Europe.'

Jefferson paused and took a sip from the glass of water that sat on the podium. As he did he remembered Sandy's words and looked directly at the cameras before continuing.

'How would we feel if we had spent thirteen years preparing for an examination, only to be told that our paper had been lost? How would we feel when a friend sends their paper off for a re-mark and receives a mark three grades above the one originally awarded? How would we feel if our paper were discovered to have been marked by a man in a pub, who last taught in 1972? How would we feel when the examination that we had worked hard for appeared on the examinations board website two weeks before the exam itself? I dare say we would feel cheated and let down; and that ladies and gentleman is exactly how our children feel every year under the present examinations system.

This government has watched on for long enough and now we must act. Enough excuses, enough blips. So I am here today to announce the setting up – with immediate effect – of the new board for standards in Education – StanEd.'

Jefferson saw that Sandy had written PAUSE on the sheet and so he took the opportunity to look around the room before he went on.

'From today every school in the country – regardless of entry policy, religious affiliation, specialist status, private, public or state sector – will sit the same examinations. These are examinations that will be set by StanEd and marked by StanEd; professionally set and professionally marked. There will be no more re-marks. With a trustworthy system no more time need be wasted on the countless appeals and re-marking of papers. This wasted manpower will be re-directed into more productive areas. This will give schools and students a system they can trust and believe in whilst providing a level playing field for all educational establishments to perform on.

These will be examinations for the general public to trust. Let the parents see which schools are performing and those which are not; let us promote informed choice for all.

This is a radical departure for the British education system but the British education system needs a radical departure; and what we are promising is radical change underpinned by business and common sense.

PAUSE.

An information pack will arrive at all schools tomorrow morning, informing them of all they need to know about the changes and how they will affect them.

It is time for a change. It is time for the public service to enjoy the efficiency of the business world. It is time for transparent accountability and it is time for the British education system to regain the status it deserves. And above all it is time the children of Britain got the examinations system that they deserve.'

Jefferson took a moment to let his words sink in before sweeping the speech from the podium and striding purposefully towards the metallic door. Remembering too late, he addressed the press pack over his shoulder,

'Sandy will answer any questions,' and with that he pushed through the door.

Emma Carr could barely conceal her delight at the conclusion of the speech.

'A breath of fresh air. An even playing field and a

professional administration, that's all we've ever asked for. Now we can really get to work on improving that value added for each student. Mrs Bastic Styles, go and see if the information pack has arrived.'

J.P.P. Montgomery was less impressed.

'Write down every last word that you're going to teach the boys tomorrow and have it on Mr Tweedy's desk by the morning; you might as well because that's where we're heading. Every pupil being taught the same thing at the same time and then sitting the same exam. The inability to accept difference and the mess of humanity – the surest indicator of a limited mind. Oh dear oh dear, we are being led by the lowest common denominator, lions led by donkeys. This is what your pals are interested in Mr Castle, taking away every last vestige of professional judgement, any whiff of creativity, any notion of rounding the child. They long for one huge homogenous mass, making it all the easier to fill in one of your spreadsheets no doubt. Battery chickens Mr Castle. Leave the teachers out of it, they can't be trusted.'

J.P.P. Montgomery paused.

'Mr Rose, ensure that you are in school early in the morning then ambush the postman, relieve him of that information bundle and throw the wretched thing in the bin.'

'What do you think this means then?' Jacob asked Belle.

'Don't know really,' she replied.

As Sandy Dalziel finished answering the questions from the press, Lord McLeish of Dunblane stood unseen at the back of the room, deep in conversation with a figure whose face could not be seen for shadow. Lord McLeish was restricted to a series of nods as he listened to the man's words. A departing journalist, who had decided that he had heard all he or his readers could possibly wish to hear from this rather dull gathering, only heard the final words of Lord McLeish,

'I understand you completely and rest assured it will happen.'

These were words which the journalist paid no attention to either then or at any date in the future.

The following day Emma Carr looked at the mammoth bundle of paperwork in front of her.

'I don't think we can over estimate the importance of this documentation.'

As she spoke she ran her hand back and forth over the bundle.

'I feel entitled to request that we all stay here tonight until we feel we've got a handle on these developments.'

'Absolutely head teacher,' piped in Valerie Bastic Styles.

The rest of the table remained silent.

'Good, let's get cracking then.'

chapter   ten

The following day, Jefferson Tweedy was picked up by a dark blue Jaguar car at 9.00am precisely. The previous night he had called Ailsa three times and got happily drunk on a bottle and a half of Bulgarian wine whilst flicking through the channels to catch clips of himself on the news. Ailsa said that she couldn't wait to see the clips and that popsy had already called her to say how well he had done. As he opened the second bottle of Chateau Sofia, he reflected on the undeniable prick of pride he felt at this reported praise from his father in law to be.

Half way though the previous day's speech Jefferson had realised that he had never enjoyed anything more in his life. He had never thought of himself as a man who would enjoy power and fame but now he realised that was simply because he had never experienced them. He had loved the whole business; the make up, the female assistants, the attention in the room full of press, the speech itself and best of all how people treated him after the speech. Comments of 'Excellent speech Mr Tweedy,' from people he had never met and even a 'well done sir,' from a smart looking man in a suit. He was also rather pleased by the way he had handled theses tributes; striking just the right balance between graciousness and distance.

The television clips had also been a treat. He had feared that he may suffer the childhood cine film syndrome; the hero in one's mind replaced by the gibbering, gurning wreck on view, but he had been relieved – and on repeated viewings delighted – to see that he looked just like everyone else that made that sort of speech on television. He had hovered over the television during the six o'clock news on BBC1, the 6.30 news on ITV and the seven o'clock news on Channel 4 pressing the record button with delight as each feature on the syllabus began. Then for the next three hours, interrupted only by calls from Ailsa, he watched and freeze framed himself continuously, analysing every intonation and gesture to his heart's content. On reflection he thought that his additional weight actually leant his performance a certain gravitas, whilst the haircut that Ailsa had pushed him towards in the States struck just the right chord of youth friendly establishment.

He had intended to record Newsnight at 10.30 on BBC2 but by then the Chateau Sofia had taken hold and he fell asleep on the sofa with dreams of Kirsty Wark and press conferences.

Lord McLeish told him about the chauffeur driven car just before he left the press conference and Jefferson had a fleeting sense that things could not get much better; a feeling that hadn't altogether left him by the time he got into the car at five past nine. The driver greeted him with a 'good morning sir,' and Jefferson waited a few moments to convey the air of the pre-occupied executive before replying, 'Yes, good morning and your name is?'

Ronald then proceeded to drive him in a very competent

fashion to the other side of London, finally dropping him outside a building in Russell Square.

'Call me when you wish to leave sir, or be so kind as to let me know if you won't be requiring my services; much obliged. Here's my number sir.'

'Jolly good, Ronald,' nodded Jefferson as he stepped out of the car and looked up at the imposing building before him, 'jolly good.'

The building was a tower of dirt stained concrete that Jefferson had to strain his neck to see to the top of. Most of the windows were impenetrable with grime and one particular section of the building was almost white through the weight of waste deposited by the massed rank of pigeons perched on the scaffolding above it. As his eyes worked their way back down the building they reached the bottom and fixed on a dapper little man with neatly parted ginger hair making his way swiftly down the building's steps. The small man began to talk excitedly before he reached the pavement.

'Mr Jefferson, what a delight to see you. Your reputation goes before you and your speech, oh what a speech. Our entire staff was gripped, gripped Mr Jefferson. Forgive me for saying so sir but the entire building positively erupted in cheers at the end of it. You are the very man that we have been waiting for; a man of action, a man of purpose. Welcome to you Mr Jefferson.'

Jefferson felt his hand being clenched in a slightly clammy but surprisingly strong hand shake before the small man turned and almost skipped up the steps, gesturing for Jefferson to follow him without looking back.

Jefferson strived to retain a purposeful stride and followed the dapper gentleman through the swing doors into the building. As he entered the building the dapper gentleman was waiting with his hand outstretched once again.

'Welcome to Copperfield House – home of StanEd. In all the excitement I have forgotten to introduce myself, how very rude of me. Kenneth Andrews at your service Mr Jefferson, helping you to, what was it?'

As Kenneth Andrews conjured the words from his memory he stood poised with his finger in the air, 'Give the children of Britain the examinations system they deserve?' Ah yes that is what I am here for. You'll soon find out that I know the old building pretty well and anything you need Mr Jefferson, anything at all, just ask away and I'll do my utmost to see that it happens.'

He started off again down a corridor at a pace sufficient to force Jefferson into a trot to keep up with him.

'I thought we'd start at your office Mr Jefferson, the nerve centre as they say.'

He turned as he said this and simultaneously thrust his left hand out and pressed a button to call the lift. He looked Jefferson straight in the eye and Jefferson felt obliged to say something to break the moment.

'About time we got the whole system working eh Kenneth.'

'Absolutely, Mr Jefferson. The lift sir.'

Kenneth stepped aside and ushered him towards the lift with an extravagant wave of his right arm. Once inside he pressed the number nine and began to hum. It wasn't a tune that Jefferson recognised, in fact it wasn't any kind of a discernible tune but Kenneth maintained it all the way to the ninth floor where the lift stopped and he stepped out spryly and led the way to a room marked 9/11. On the door was a plaque bearing the inscription 'Chief Executive' and below it Jefferson was surprised and delighted to see another plaque bearing his name.

'To your liking sir?' inquired Kenneth.

'You must work jolly fast to have all of this ready,' replied Jefferson to which he simply inclined his head and swept into the room. Before them was an enormous space with a vast desk at its centre. To the left was a large sofa that faced towards a window that occupied the entire wall opposite the door. Jefferson walked over to the window and looked out on a panoramic view of the city.

'Spectacular isn't it sir?' came the voice from behind him.

'It certainly is.'

Jefferson turned from the window and watched Kenneth Andrews brushing his hand across a plasma screen the size of a small car that was placed on the wall opposite the sofa.

'So important to keep up with breaking news, don't you think Mr Jefferson?'

He watched the small man run his finger across the top of the screen before wiping his finger on a brilliant white handkerchief that he pulled from his trouser pocket.

'Tell me Kenneth, the man before me...'

Kenneth continued to inspect the screen closely as he answered.

'Mr Roger, sir?'

'Yes.'

'Barely here sir. Shall we say 'other commitments' kept him from his duties.'

Kenneth turned and fixed Jefferson with a gaze on the word commitments before continuing, 'And it's the children that suffer isn't it sir?'

'Quite right.'

There was a moment's pause before Kenneth folded the handkerchief and placed it neatly back into his pocket. He turned again towards Jefferson,

'Well I'll leave you to settle in sir and I'll ensure that you are not disturbed. I'm sure there are a million and one things you want to be getting on with. We have such hopes Mr Jefferson, such hopes.'

Kenneth Andrews stood in front of Jefferson Tweedy and inclined his head forward in a stunted bow before turning sharply on his heels and leaving Jefferson alone in the office.

part two

chapter one

Belle only had 'a college day' tomorrow so Jacob had little trouble persuading her to join him in a few drinks. She explained that her course was split into teaching practise and college days. On the first she was in school and actually did some teaching whilst on the second she and the other trainee English teachers met at college to compare stories from the front and learn a bit more teaching theory from the lecturers that had formerly been teachers. These were the easier days and so she was happy to spend the Tuesday night with Jacob on a tour of the Clapham drinking establishments.

She invited along a few friends and their partners from the course and they in turn invited along a few of their friends and it had ended up with a gathering of fifteen or so people. Attractive people, Jacob thought on the whole and intelligent and socially adept, the sort of people that Jacob had always imagined he would be working with – only wasn't. Yesterday's story had been a real scoop: Posh and Becks caught kissing in one of their old haunts in Madrid. He toyed with his choice of headline for some time before settling for 'It's Still Real love.' He was unsurprised to see that two other tabloids had settled for the same headline and Dickie had called him into his office and called him 'a cunt.'

Belle then asked why he continued to work for 'that monster' and Jacob asked if she wanted another drink and disappeared to the bar.

The evening began with a few quickly finished beers and by then he had already decided that he liked quite a number of the people that he had met tonight. He was particularly looking forward to spending more of his time with a selection of the English teachers. In the past few months his reading habit had become voracious; the more advanced his brain stem death at work the more literature he consumed at home. Increasingly the offices of *The Express* were not a place where it was deemed appropriate to discuss the topic of books and Jacob had taken to smuggling his latest novel into the toilet with him and grabbing a ten page fix under the noses of the philistine guard. A small act of subversion that he felt he could use as some form of justification when in a parallel universe John Pilger quizzed him about his career in journalism at *The Express*.

The English teacher that he bought vodka and tonic for, and one for himself, was a bright eyed intelligent looking woman called Georgie. She asked him a few interested questions about being in charge of the Entertainment desk at *The Express* which he answered in a dismissive manner. He then ordered himself (the teacher politely refused) another pair of double vodkas, one by himself and one through Belle, and quickly turned the conversation around to books. Georgie named her favourite author (at his request) as Graham Greene and the latest book she had read as a late period Muriel Spark. Jacob told her that he thoroughly approved of both of these choices and that as an English teacher she was 'the keeper of the knowledge for the children.' He then proceeded to ask if she had read any H.P. Lovecraft which she replied she hadn't and Jacob went scrabbling in his pockets for a scrap of paper. He found his travel card and scribbled 'The Mountains of Madness' on the back before thrusting it into her hand. He told her it was brilliant and then took it back and wrote 'A Confederacy of Dunces' – O'Toole.

'I can't remember his first name, but it's brilliant.'

'Are they both American?' Georgie asked.

'Yeah, it's the only writing of any worth at the moment. Who have we got? Martin Amis? Jesus.'

'Have you read any crime?' he took the travel card back from her and scribbled Pelecanos 'The Big Blowdown' on it. 'Terrific.' He expounded for a few minutes on the unexplored story of the Greek American immigrants before Georgie was asked by Belle to tell a friend's boyfriend the story of the boy at her school who howled like a dog whenever he got a question right in lessons.

Jacob excused himself and went to the toilet.

He closed the door of the cubicle and unearthed a pill from his inside pocket. He looked closely at it for a few seconds before swallowing it with the help of the vodka. He looked at himself in the mirror, said 'so early nineties' and pushed his hair away from his eyes. He had always been a weekend drug taker but in recent times he had taken a certain pride in his level of inappropriate midweek drug consumption. He had made a conscious decision that he had no obligation to be bright eyed and beady to do his work on the Entertainment desk at *The Express* and when questioned claimed that 'anyone would need an e to do the job that I do anyway.'

He made his way back into the bar and catching Belle's eye asked her if she had a piece of paper on her. She produced a piece of plain A4 paper which he then took towards a long necked boy called Tim that he had been chatting to earlier. Tim seemed pleased to see him and Jacob started writing as he asked the question,

'Have you read any Jim Dodge?'

At just gone eleven o'clock as the rest of his group left, Jacob was gyrating enthusiastically on the makeshift dance floor at the end of the bar. When Belle said good night to him he kissed her sweatily and told her she was 'an adorable girl' before she wriggled out of his clutches and waved at him as she walked away. Jacob smiled widely at the girl next to him, before unsuccessfully trying to perform the 'caterpillar' on the dance floor in front of her. From the floor he looked up to see Belle waving him towards the exit but he smiled and shook his head at her before making his way back to the bar.

chapter two

Jefferson Tweedy did not consider himself to be a lazy man, but he was aware that he had a propensity not to actively seek work out. During his time at Mycroft, Pigott and Welch he had realised reasonably quickly that he liked to be given instruction, clear instruction that he could then carry out to the word. Left to his own devices he was quickly distracted and rarely if ever completed a work based task.

He had a few preferred ways of spending the time. He enjoyed reading the paper (*The Telegraph* by choice, but he wasn't particularly fussy) and could amuse himself on the internet for hours on end. The internet had been a revelation to Jefferson and his only regret was that it hadn't been invented early enough to help him through his difficult teenage years. He would investigate anything from real crime sites to photographs from the Dutch korfball leagues. He frequently went into chat rooms and over the past couple of years had created two different chat room personas. The first was Rory. Rory was a private aide to the Prime Minister and despite being witty and in possession of a mind like a vice (Jefferson had alluded strongly in a communication with a girl in Strathclyde that this last compliment had been paid to Rory by the Prime Minister himself) he was so busy with the minutae of his peculiarly demanding job that the internet provided his only source of social interaction away from ministerial circles. Rory had been Jefferson's persona of choice, until in a mischievous mood one Tuesday afternoon he suggested to Valerie in Worksop that Rory enjoyed the painful pleasures of self flagellation and would she be interested in forming a 'mutually flagellating' group for people of a similar disposition. The enthusiastic response from Valerie and a considerable number of her friends prompted Jefferson to lie low as Rory for a while citing 'the pressures of government work' as his reason.

His second creation was Jessica, a teenage girl from the Isle of Skye who longed to see the bright lights of the city and earn her living on the West End stage. So far he had received two marriage proposals as Jessica and offers from three prospective accomplices to murder the Prime Minister as Rory.

When tired of the chat room Jefferson would turn to the dubious charms of 'The Hun.' 'The Hun' had been recommended to him by a colleague at Mycroft, Pigott and Welch at an after work drinks do and on investigation Jefferson discovered a free to access German porn site which he had guiltily investigated for a week or two. Ultimately he found that he preferred the jokes that they ran on certain pages to the endless pictures of European house wives. Besides for Jefferson the internet was a thing of beauty and wonder and accessing 'The Hun' was to him a betrayal of these ideals. He felt a profound sense of relief when he gave up the unseemly visits to Olga and her shaved comrades and returned to regaling boys in London with details of Jessica's recent success as Tzeital in the Skye Operatic Society's version of 'Fiddler on the Roof'.

So it was that after two days of employment as the Chief Executive of StanEd, Jefferson Tweedy had not as yet completed any StanEd related work. He wasn't entirely sure what StanEd work consisted of but he had not as yet knowingly encountered any. He spent a lot of time sending e-mails to Ailsa in which he described in intimate detail the plush office that he found himself in and she had replied how impressed she was with him and how she wished she could see him in his swivel chair. Naturally he told Ailsa that he was very busy and 'finding his feet' in his new role and she had said once again how impressed 'popsy' was with him.

The thing that did preoccupy Jefferson most in his first few days at StanEd was the idea of developing and nurturing the role of being a chief executive. He had watched the likes of Mycroft, Pigott and Welch very carefully during his time working for them and he had decided to employ some of their preferred methods with immediate effect in his new job. On his first day he wrote on a bright white sheet of A4 paper 'Being a Chief Executive – the rules for ruling.'

Rule 1 – never leave the office unless in the event of an emergency.

The word emergency had until now meant going to the toilet. He felt that too much exposure of the top brass to the underlings was a recipe for contempt, indeed a chief executive's aura and reputation grew in direct relation to the rarity of their sightings. When he was forced to leave the office he relied upon two simple techniques. The first was to always carry a bulky folder under his arm. This was designed to give the impression of the executive on the go, to suggest a man on top of developments and with a clear sense of purpose. The impression on encountered underlings should be that he was just on his way to a high powered meeting on which the future of several companies and their job may well depend.

The second came about after an early appraisal of his surroundings. There were two toilets on the ninth floor; one was ten yards to the left as he left the office and the other was a sixty yard walk the other way down the corridor and involved two sets of doors and a sharp corner. His policy was as follows; whenever he needed to pay a visit to the toilet he would turn sharp right and stride at a furious pace down the corridor. When he encountered a set of doors he would crash through them as if on his way to surgery in an American hospital drama. This pace would be kept up until he reached the toilet at which point he would consult the folder under his arm and then about face as if something even more important had just crossed his mind. He would then complete the same journey in reverse before checking both ways and sliding into the toilet nearest his office. Once inside he would unfurl *The Telegraph* from inside the folder and read it from cover to cover, beginning with the sport section.

These were the rules for his brief and rare forays outside his office but Rule 2 involved an equally strict code of conduct towards visitors within the confines of his own office.

Rule 2 – treat all visitors with fury.

This rule was most strictly applied to the first visitor to his office in the morning and the first visitor after lunch. He would not respond to their knock on the door and then when they poked their head around the door he would scream at them to 'get out' and as they shut the door he would follow it up with a roared 'Ceeerrrhrist'. This technique had been a particular favourite of Mr Mycroft at Mycroft, Pigott and Welch and ensured that he was regarded with due awe and reverence by staff and customers alike. Jefferson found this last rule difficult on the first morning but felt that these were the type of difficult decisions that came with being management and had thrown himself into it with gusto. Whoever was at the door left never to return and from then on his door, although only occasionally knocked at, was knocked with due deference and restraint giving him plenty of time to come out of whichever internet site he was investigating and before calling 'enter', replace it with the half full spreadsheet that he had created on his first day.

It was late on Thursday morning that Kenneth Andrews slid his head around the door after leaving a duly deferential post knock pause.

'Mr Jefferson?'

'Ah Kenneth.'

'Busy as ever I see sir.'

'There is much to do, Kenneth, much to do.'

Kenneth slid inside the door and addressed Jefferson.

'I have just returned sir from a comprehensive tour of the building and may I say sir, the improvement in staff morale since your arrival is tangible. There's a real spring in the step from the examiners right down to the tea ladies.'

'Excellent. It is so important don't you think? After all, an organisation is only as good as its staff.'

'So wise sir, so wise.'

Kenneth Andrews emitted a small cough before continuing.

'Now if I may address the business in hand, I come with regards the launch.'

'The launch?'

'Yes sir, the launch of the syllabus.'

'Ah yes,'

'As I'm sure you are aware sir, the examinations board is to throw what they are calling a launch party to help get the schools and their teachers, shall we say, onside.'

'Champagne and canapés, that sort of thing?'

'Absolutely Mr Jefferson. The teaching profession are so starved of glamour that we thought they might welcome the chance to indulge in a little finery.'

'As we are all aware Kenneth positive PR is so important these days. We're in a market and these people are our consumers, a little schmooze to oil the wheels for the new syllabus; it can't hurt can it.'

'Absolutely Mr Jefferson.'

'So what role do you see me in? Circulating, pressing a little flesh, talking to the people.'

'Up to a point Mr Jefferson.'

'Ah, go on.'

'Well it is our experience that when a group of teachers join together at functions such as these they can be, well, slightly fractious.'

'In what way Kenneth?'

'Well, they're not like other people sir. Most people wouldn't regard this type of event as work related. Most people would be quite happy to drink the free champagne and let their hair down a little; only it doesn't seem to work like that with the teachers.'

'Oh?'

'No sir. They will insist sir on talking about their work. They seem to see these functions as a chance to air their grievances and my goodness they do have a number of grievances.'

'Really?'

'Oh yes. There was a very unfortunate incident at one of these occasions with Mr Roger. He made the mistake of becoming trapped in conversation with a few of them sir and they positively mauled him. I had to take the unprecedented step of smashing a bottle of champagne on the far side of the room and feigning injury to create a diversion so to speak. Only then were we able to liberate him from their clutches.'

'Oh dear.'

'Absolutely. So as you can see sir a laissez faire approach to these matters is not to be recommended.'

'I see, this sounds very serious, so what do you suggest, Kenneth?'

'Well I have taken the liberty of writing down a few ideas for you sir. They are ideas that have come from my not inconsiderable experience at this sort of event. I like to term them examples of 'limiting small talk'.'

'Limiting small talk?'

'Yes sir, it's a phrase I created myself for situations such as these. It's a series of phrases, topics and questions that enable one to keep control of the conversation. As I say sir, given half a chance these teachers will twist the least promising subject and turn it to their own ends. We cannot stop them completely – that would be illiberal wouldn't it sir – but what I'm talking about is some discreet steering.'

Kenneth produced a sheet of A4 paper from his inside pocket on which was written a lengthy list of phrases under the heading 'Limiting Small Talk'. Jefferson glanced over the sheet as Kenneth continued.

'We did use this method before sir, with Mr Roger, but unfortunately Mr Roger would frequently drift off message and like I said sir, he rather paid for it.'

'I reserve the right to speak for myself you know Kenneth.'

'Oh absolutely Mr Jefferson, I wouldn't dream of putting words into your mouth – a man of your stature – rest assured these are simply suggestions for those awkward moments when the conversation may not be going the way we would like it to. As I say a pack of teachers are notoriously difficult company, but I'm sure a man like yourself sir will handle them with all the aplomb we've come to expect.'

'Thank you Kenneth.'

'I shall leave those with you for your perusal.'

And with that Kenneth Andrews slid backwards towards the door, never once turning his back on Jefferson and smiling as he went, before bending forward in an abridged bow and disappearing through the brilliant white door.

chapter three

On the 10.43 train to Victoria, Belle tried to raise the subject of taking ecstasy tabs on a weekday night. She began by broaching the subject in a deliberately jocular fashion which to her annoyance Jacob replied to in an equally jocular tone and the subject was dropped. She then struggled to avoid starting a sentence with 'No, but seriously' whilst inwardly regretting her enlightened stance of never offering people advice unless they asked for it.

'I don't think you should be taking es on a Tuesday night.'

'Really?'

'No.'

'I thought you didn't like me taking es, any night of the week.'

'I don't but Tuesdays are worse somehow.'

'Mondays?'

'Piss off.'

They paused. Belle continued, 'I just don't think it's right.'

'Neither do I.'

'Then why are you doing it?'

'Dunno.'

Another pause.

'Well I've said it now, I don't want to keep on like I'm your mother.'

'Thank you.'

'That's all right.'

They were on their way to the launch of the StanEd syllabus. To neither of their surprise *The Express* newspaper had not regarded the launch of a new Examinations board and syllabus as being terribly high on their list of must cover stories. There was after all the release of a former weather girl back into captivity after four scintillating days in an Outback reality show to cover. So after their shared viewing of Jefferson Tweedy's inaugural speech, Jacob mooted the idea to Belle that they go along to the launch together. Their entrance would depend on him hiding the Entertainment part of his press card and on her hiding the out of date year on her's. Jacob thought that this, coupled with the limited number of people trying to 'blag' their way in to such an event would ensure their entry.

He sold it to Belle on the grounds of increasing her knowledge of how the power brokers of her chosen profession went about their business, whilst he sold it to himself by reasoning that it was closer to real journalism than anything he might encounter during the rest of the day at *The Express*. He was happy with this pair of justifications.

Also aboard the 10.43 was Emma Carr. She sat facing forwards to ward off her travel sickness and was poring over a recent study on the disaffection of Afro/Caribbean boys within the state school system. The author, one Jean St Vincent, spoke passionately about 'the lack of a mirror that these pupils find to their own lives and culture in the systems of predominantly white run schools.' Emma underlined this section with a freshly sharpened pencil and nodded her head in agreement. The value added scores for black boys at St George's Cross had been shown to be 'below average' in the last set of data and in the margin on page 22 of Jean St Vincent's work, Emma Carr wrote INITIATIVE NEEDED and underlined it three times before closing the book. She looked at her watch to see that she had ten minutes spare to look at the latest budget figures; she reached into her bag for her luminous yellow marker and set to work.

J.P.P Montgomery joined the train four stops after Emma Carr and sat reading *The Times* in a first class carriage. He had contemplated taking the car to the launch but when Lib mentioned the congestion charge he thought better of it and set off for the train station.

He rarely missed this sort of event and could always rely upon an invitation due to his position as head master of one of the area's more prestigious public schools. He attended them now for much the same reason he used to attend the Teachers' Union Conferences in his younger days. Not due to any particular interest in the matters under discussion (although a brushing up on recent developments was never a complete waste of time he found) but more so he could cast a careful eye over the competition and keep abreast of teachers and teaching outside of the College. As the years passed he found himself increasingly depressed by the calibre of person the teaching profession attracted. They seemed to be either the likes of Castle, with his transparent ambition and distasteful attention to detail, or those insipid lumps too earnest for any other role except deeply uninspiring teaching.

It was after one of these conferences in the early 90s that Montgomery decided to apply for the role of headmaster at St George's. He had reflected that the competition was so woeful that not only should he apply for the post, but he should also insist that for the privilege of employing him the school help him to buy a racehorse and share the cost of training and running it for the duration of his stay in the job. Their willingness to do all of these things reminded Montgomery of the importance of knowing one's own worth.

At least in his younger days after a hard day's conferencing there had been the chance of encountering some young female teacher at the hotel bar, getting her suitably drunk on subsidised drink before coaxing her upstairs to the mini bar for a chat about classroom discipline and a grope. These days hardly anyone drank at these affairs; when discussing it with Lib, Montgomery compared it to 'Los Angeles, where apparently two drinks makes you an alcoholic.' This reflection came after a rhinoceros of a woman accused him of being drunk, 'mid-conference'. His retort of 'A man cannot survive on sparkling water alone madam,' provoked a snort of disgust and a very pointed flap of the conference agenda sheet in his direction.

Nonetheless he was rather looking forward to today's event and in particular the opportunity to cast an eye over the great Jefferson Tweedy. As he watched the approach of the Thames out of his left window the words of his old English master Reg Langton ran through his mind, 'Still we must make the best of the day boys, we must make the best of the day,' and Montgomery wondered what the great and much missed Langton would have made of Jefferson Tweedy.

chapter   four

As the head teachers and journalists arrived at the Grosvenor House's Jubilee Suite, Jefferson Tweedy sat two floors above them, intently watching them on a huge security screen. Beside him sat Kenneth Andrews, twiddling with an array of knobs that appeared to decide which camera angle and which part of the suite they watched.

'Is this really necessary Kenneth?'

'Preparation Mr Jefferson. It can help to ease your passage downstairs; a few well selected close ups and a little information goes a long way.'

'They all look perfectly normal. Surely I can just go down and mingle with them?'

'The exact same mistake Mr Roger made I'm afraid sir.'

'How many did you say there were of them?'

'Five hundred, sir; a range of the country's schools.'

'Best to worst?'

'Up to a point Mr Jefferson. We like to say achieving and improving sir. Terms like 'worst' tend to cause something of a fuss at affairs like these.'

'I see.'

'Now if you'd like to watch the screen carefully Mr Jefferson…'

Down in the Jubilee suite, Emma Carr was struggling to remember the name of the woman she was talking to. She was a head teacher from a school in the same borough as St George's Cross and they had met numerous times at the meetings that the borough held for local head teachers. She liked the woman but could not for the life of her recall her name. She could remember the name of her school which was St Stephen's Saviour, but the woman's name would not come to her. She was Scottish and of that indeterminate age between thirty five and forty five which Emma found almost impossible to place (which seemed odd to Emma since she herself was firmly in the centre of the same age bracket). The woman was wearing a pair of glasses that Emma's mother would have termed 'trendy' and clearly paid close attention to her personal appearance. The woman had eyes that crinkled when she smiled and a way of audibly breathing in when she agreed with a point that Emma made. Emma was unsure how to take this at first but had now decided that she rather liked it. It was as if each and every point she made literally took the woman's breath away.

Emma was talking with some passion about the move towards value added results for pupils and a number of other school based subjects when the Scottish head teacher raised an eyebrow and her eyes crinkled,

'So do you have many dealings with the great man next door?'

'Next door?'

'At the college.'

'Oh sorry, yes, Mr Montgomery.'

'How do you find him?'

Emma had a pre-prepared answer to this enquiry which was always greeted with affirming nods and noises at school, 'Oh he's a bit of a dinosaur isn't he?'

'Do you think?'

'Doesn't everyone think so?'

'You've heard the stories haven't you?'

'Well I'd heard something about his being a Conservative MP a long time ago.'

'Oh I think it was Liberal, great pals with Roy Jenkins and that crowd that set up the SDP; I was told that he was an important figure behind the scenes. Apparently this all happened after a career as a barrister, a lengthy spell of alcoholism in Australia – which involved two separate marriages to women of aristocratic descent – and a time as a chat show host on Australian television.'

'I didn't think Australia had an aristocracy.'

'No they were English apparently, although I'm not quite sure what they were doing out there.'

'Is it true?'

'I've no idea but then where's the fun in knowing for sure? And then of course there are the horses.'

'The horses?'

'Oh yes, everyone knows about the famous horses.'

'Well I don't, do tell.'

'My God, you don't know about them? Then I shall tell you. By all accounts our Mr Montgomery is a big one for the races and goes as much as he can; nothing wrong with that of course. So when he applied for the job at St George's College, ten or twelve years ago or whenever it was, the governors had offered him the job and as they're waiting for him to accept he tells them that he will only take the job on their agreeing to certain conditions. So they ask him what these certain conditions are and he says that he wants it written into his contract that he is not expected to be in school on the day of any of the big horse races that happen during the year.'

'You're joking.'

'No. I can't remember how many there are of them but it's a few a year; so anyway they agree to this.'

'How?'

'It's just, I don't know, but anyway that's not the end of it. He then says that a friend of his breeds horses and that there's a young horse that they think is going to brilliant and he asks the school to share the cost of buying this horse.'

'What and he won't take the job if they don't?'

'Pretty much.'

'God. And they agreed?'

'Yes. So they bought this horse together and he followed it wherever it raced and any time it won he shared the money with the school.'

'God it's just a different world isn't it?'

'Listen the details may be slightly out, but that's the drift of it. That first horse was called St George's Boy I think and when it got too old to race they put it in as a stud and there have been a string of them ever since. The one at the moment is called St George's Blue, you can see it in the papers and apparently this one's really good so they all do pretty well out of it.'

'I don't know how you can get away with it? The arrogance of saying that an interview...'

'Extraordinary isn't it? You should ask him about it some time, it's hilarious. It's impossible to get a straight answer out of him but it's always entertaining. He does bring a certain something to the whole business though don't you think? Oh I know a lot of people find him utterly loathsome but I've always found him to be charming. He always remembers my name even if we haven't seen each other for months and that's always charming isn't it?'

Emma looked carefully at the still crinkled eyes for any signs of sarcasm but after careful examination could find not a flicker. The woman's comments forced Emma to redouble her search for a name: Bryony, Beatrice, Brenda, Belinda none of them seemed right, before her agonies were ended by the arrival of an attractive woman and her boyfriend who greeted the Scottish head teacher with an effusive 'Sian'.

Sian? Emma looked askance.

The conversation between Sian and her companion continued.

'Belle, what are you doing here?' She turned to include Emma. 'Emma this is Belle Jones, our PGCE student in English.'

'Lovely to meet you,' said Emma as she panicked at the thought that she couldn't recall the name of any of the PGCE students at St George's Cross. She then remembered that they weren't taking any PGCE students until the following term; the teacher training college having recommended the school took time to 'refine their policy regarding students' before they sent them any more. She felt a wave of relief.

The PGCE student was explaining something about NUJ passes that Emma didn't really listen to, before she was introduced to the curly haired boyfriend. He was introduced to her as 'a real journalist' and Sian introduced Emma as 'the woman that is turning St George's Cross around'.

Emma replied with a 'well I don't know about that,' shook his hand warmly, wondering if she could get the school some positive press through this meeting.

'Whereabouts do you work?'

'*The Express.*'

'Oh they're doing very well aren't they?'

'After a fashion.'

'Oh well that's good. Do you cover much education news?'

'I'm on the entertainment desk.'

'Ooh you must meet lots of famous people…'

Over the journalist's shoulder she could see the unmistakeable figure of J.P.P. Montgomery making his way towards them. He stopped to kiss Scottish Sian on both cheeks before placing a hand on the journalist's shoulder.

'I do apologise young man but I must just say hello to the divine Miss Carr.'

Montgomery leant over and Emma felt a kiss firmly planted on both of her cheeks.

'And how are you Miss Carr?'

'Very well thank you and yourself?'

'One mustn't complain, everything appears to still be functioning.'

'Well that's good. Mr Montgomery…'

'Please call me J.P.P.'

Montgomery turned with a smile and heartily introduced himself to the PGCE student and the journalist. She watched the back of his well-cut suit and heard,

'Do you really Jacob? And how do you find working for Mr Gittens?'

Emma went off to find another glass of mineral water and came back to find the whole group laughing uproariously and J.P.P. Montgomery waving to a waiter to come and top up his champagne glass. He turned back to Emma.

'Well now Ms Carr and how are things at St George's Cross?'

'Well, Mr Montgomery, I'm pleased I caught you because I've been meaning to ask you about your parents outside the school gates.'

'My parents?'

'Yes. Must they drive their children right up to the school gates? It causes terrible congestion and our parents get stuck in it and that impacts on our attendance and lateness figures, which was something OFSTED highlighted as an area for focus. It really is an issue.'

'Ms Carr, I couldn't agree with you more. The whole business is a complete bloody farrago and of course they will insist on driving cars that bear a closer resemblance to military vehicles than family saloons.'

'Couldn't you perhaps put a sign up?'

'Miss Carr I don't know if this applies to the parents at St George's Cross, I sincerely hope it doesn't, but increasingly I find with our parents that they are utterly indifferent to what we suggest, ask or indeed tell them to do. Ultimately it appears they will take the course of action most convenient to them at that particular moment in time. So if that means driving their obese child right up to the school gates, I fear they will do that regardless of my writing a letter, putting up a sign or standing there waving a placard each morning resplendent in dress sword and spats.'

'I see, well if you could keep your eye on the issue.'

'They're all consumers now Ms Carr are they not? They can pick and choose the parts they wish to buy and those they wish to leave on the supermarket shelf. I can't begin to tell you how depressing I find it all but there you are.'

With her eyes crinkling Scottish Sian saw her moment.

'Mr Montgomery, just before you arrived I was telling Emma about your glorious past in politics. Liberal MP for where was it?'

'Ah Miss McLaughlin your mischief does you credit. Unfortunately I'm sure these good people have no interest whatsoever in my rather undignified past, be it in politics or anything else. Still your willingness to take us away from talk of the nuts and bolts of school life is welcome indeed.'

'Elusive as ever.'

'Suffice to say it's not all school halls and soggy puddings is it Miss McLaughlin?'

It was at this moment that the group's attention was drawn to the sound of a gong from a balcony that ran around the top of the Jubilee Suite. They looked around before seeing the face of Kenneth Andrews peering down at them, gong in hand.

'Good God it's J.Arthur Rank,' observed J.P.P. Montgomery.

The assembly of teachers took a while to silence and Kenneth Andrews felt obliged to give the gong another strike before beginning.

'Ladies and gentlemen,' came Kenneth's voice from on high, 'may I take the opportunity to thank you all for coming here today to help us celebrate the launch of StanEd – a new horizon for education. We do hope you will enjoy the new syllabus as much as you've enjoyed the champagne today.'

The crowd, necks craned upwards, laughed politely.

'Now it is my pleasure to introduce you to the man who will be taking us to this new horizon for educational excellence. A man who combines acute business acumen with the dedication to public service that connects us all. Please join me in welcoming, Mr Jefferson Tweedy.'

Kenneth banged the gong again and pointed down towards the huge double doors at the end of the suite. The crowd turned towards them and watched as the doors very slowly opened revealing the figure of Jefferson Tweedy, waving imperiously to the silent crowd.

'What are we supposed to do – clap?' murmured Sian McLaughlin.

It was Emma Carr who began the round of applause and the rest of the hall quickly joined in. Jefferson Tweedy allowed the applause to rise for thirty seconds or so, before bellowing 'Hello,' over the top of it and striding into the room. As he got towards the crowd he shook the hands of a few of the teachers nearer the doors and smiled brilliantly towards the rest of the hall.

Jacob Haliwell leant over to Belle as they clapped,

'What a thing, what a thing.'

Sian McLaughlin's eyes had been reduced to tiny crinkled slits as she watched Jefferson signal the crowd to be quiet. Once the crowd was silent Jefferson waited and looked around the room, making eye contact with as many people as he could before beginning. The crowd stood in an expectant hush. They waited a full thirty seconds before Jefferson lifted both his hands and pointed his index fingers towards the crowd. He jerked them towards the crowd with every syllable that he shouted.

'This is all about you.' Pause.

'Me, him (pointing up at Kenneth), this (gesturing around the Jubilee Suite), syllabuses, examination bodies – all these things mean nothing, nothing. It is all about you.' Pause.

'All I'm here to do is to give you an examinations system that you can trust, so you good people can get on with the job in hand, the job that you do best, the job of educating this country's children. God knows it isn't easy but any small thing I can do to make that job a little easier for you, then that's what I'll do. We've always got to remember that we're serving the children of UK plc.' Again he paused. 'Enjoy the champagne, you deserve it.'

With that Jefferson began pointing and clapping at the assembled head teachers. Unsure how to respond, the teachers paused before joining in with the clapping and before long the suite was filled with another round of applause. During the applause Jefferson waved and turned around before sweeping back through the double doors.

The applause lasted for a few moments after Jefferson had disappeared before being replaced by a buzz around the hall.

'Wow!' said Emma Carr.

'Wow indeed,' said Sian McLaughlin, 'what do you think of that then?'

All around them they could hear excited voices,

'Extraordinary.'

'Never seen the like of it at an Examinations meeting.'

'Like a breath of fresh air.'

'So charismatic.'

Jacob Haliwell and Belle looked at each other and raised their eyebrows.

'I don't know why you bother with Peter Andre and Becks, Jefferson Tweedy's your man,' said Belle.

'Absolutely,' said Jacob, 'teaching is the new rock 'n' roll. I may go and have a few words with your man Tweedy, see what he's got to say for himself. Coming?'

As Jacob and Belle made their way towards the huge doors from whence Jefferson Tweedy had departed, they left behind an animated Emma Carr, a crinkle-eyed Sian McLaughlin and a thoughtful J.P.P.Montgomery, whose eyes were fixed on the same door that they were heading for.

chapter five

In a room tucked away behind the Jubilee suite Jefferson Tweedy was loosening his tie and throwing a sheet of paper into a waste bin. He sat down in a comfortable red chair and stretched his legs out. As he did so the door burst open.

'Mr Jefferson, what can I say? So brave. To depart from the speech at the end like that sir – so brave – and to applaud the teachers themselves was nothing short of inspired, sir.'

'Thank you Kenneth, I thought it went rather well myself.'

'And I feel that your decision to dispense with the circulating and mingling was vindicated to the very highest degree sir. Keep them at arm's length sir and what happened? They were eating out of your hand sir. Oh and what will the press make of it sir? A day of triumph indeed, one for the annals.'

There was a knock at the door. Kenneth turned swiftly and glanced back at Jefferson before going to the door. He opened it a small way and there was a quiet conversation that Jefferson could not hear very well.

Kenneth closed the door with an 'if you'll just wait there for a minute,' before creeping back into the room.

'It's a gentleman from the press sir, a Mr Haliwell from *The Express*.'

It crossed Jefferson's mind that this was an odd first name but said nothing whilst tightening the knot on his tie.

'A very popular paper sir, I wonder if you might talk to him.'

'Of course I'll talk to him if he'll just give me a minute.'

Kenneth slid back to the door and spoke in whispered tones before shutting the door and returning to Jefferson.

'Now sir, you're looking very well and we do hope there might be a photo opportunity for us here. And do you have our list of 'desirable phrases'? These gentlemen do work in soundbites and we want to convey our message don't we sir?'

Jefferson felt in his back pocket before saying,

'You know I feel like I might do without the list this time Kenneth; I don't want to come over as a puppet do I?'

'Heaven forbid Mr Jefferson. If for one moment I gave the impression that that was what we were hoping to achieve I apologise most profusely. No, no, no that is no good at all, not for a man of your stature. They are simply useful phrases to have in the back of one's mind, lest you ever feel that the interview is drifting 'off message'.'

'Jolly good Kenneth, just so long as we understand each other.'

'Absolutely Mr Jefferson.'

Kenneth then slid back to the door and ushered Jacob Haliwell into the room. Behind him came Belle and Jacob introduced her as 'the photographer'. Noticing the small ginger man's glances at her lack of photographic equipment he added, 'She needs to check on the light etc. If it's all okay she'll go and get her camera in a minute.'

'Excellent.'

Jacob watched as the small ginger man settled himself into a seat by the door.

'I was rather hoping to interview Mr Tweedy on his own.'

'Oh no, it is very important that I am present; as a third party so to speak.'

'Well I'm sure that won't be necessary.'

'I'm afraid Mr Haliwell that this is how things are done at StanEd.'

Jacob looked towards Jefferson who nodded his head solemnly.

'Alright, I don't suppose it will make a great deal of difference.'

The interview ended ten minutes later after Jacob had asked a wide variety of questions that all received an answer including the words 'professional ethos', 'a system the public can trust' or 'time for accountability'. He had begun with StanEd related questions, before changing tack and watching in wonder as Tweedy managed to incorporate the same phrases into questions as diverse as 'Which football team do you support? What was the last film you went to see?' and 'Who do you consider to be your role models?'

The interview was terminated by an 'Excellent' from the small ginger man and he and Belle were ushered out of the room with thanks for their time and expressions that no doubt the article would be very positive and faithful to what was said in the interview.

'Outstanding Mr Jefferson,' said Kenneth Andrews as he shut the door after waving the journalist and his photographer off down the corridor, 'an excellent day's work.'

chapter six

The Year 9 cohort of St George's Cross wandered into the assembly hall. The few that were not trying to catch the eye of their friends saw a series of laminated pieces of paper conspicuously fixed with drawing pins to the walls. On closer inspection (not something many of the listless thirteen and fourteen year olds chose to do) the pieces of paper were found to carry words of unspeakable wisdom. Lest her charges had not taken it upon themselves to discover such pearls, Emma Carr stood at the front of the hall pointing energetically towards the walls whilst mouthing 'read them – they're about you.'

When the entire year group were finally in the hall and Mr Wells the head of Year 9 had silenced the audience, Emma Carr pointed towards Valerie Bastic Styles who was standing on the left hand side of the hall. Mrs Bastic Styles stood with a stick raised to the piece of paper on the wall beside her and in a manner reminiscent of a pantomime singalong pointed to each word as she pronounced,

'You've got to search for the hero inside yourself.'

She repeated this over and over until Emma Carr pointed towards the back of the hall. Here, Jamie Essex the young head of Geography was standing next to another piece of laminated card holding a similar type stick. He then began in the same way.

'In this life, long and hard though it may seem

Live it as you'd live a dream.'

He repeated this until Emma Carr pointed back to Valerie Bastic Styles and then back to him. They then began to chant in the round, reminding the more nostalgic members of the audience of renditions of 'London's Burning' at infants' school. Emma Carr then pointed to the right of the hall to Vikram Syal who got to work on,

'Weave your spell in life's rich tapestry,

Your passport to feel supreme.'

This was followed by another rendition in the round before it came to Mrs Carr herself. She pointed in an exaggerated manner at herself and pulled a 'the things I do for this school' face before launching into,

'And that's why you should keep aiming high,

Just seek yourself and you will shine.'

She then instigated an 'in the round' finale before bringing the four of them to a halt with the gesture that she had seen the conductor use on 'The Last Night of the Proms'. There was a moment's quiet in the hall before the applause (led by Mrs Bastic Styles) began. Emma let this go for a moment before bringing it to a halt.

'Now it's all a bit of fun and you get a chance to see us make ourselves look silly but there's a serious point here.'

She looked up to the back of the hall and signalled to the waiting Mr Abrahams in the sound box. The strains of

'Search for the Hero' by M People flooded the hall and over the top of it Mrs Carr shouted,

'Listen to the words, these are about you. Don't let your life slip by, fulfil your potential.'

The hall then settled into a slightly embarrassed quiet whilst the music played. Emma Carr began to sway gently with the music and briefly tried to clap slightly out of time before abandoning that and settling for a spell of shut-eyed contemplation, pondering the depth of the song's message. During the course of the song Mrs Bastic Styles had to remove Raymond Baxter for what she would later term 'making a mockery of the moment' and Josh Jackson was warned for laughing by Mr Wells. Mrs Carr signalled to Mr Abrahams to bring the song to a slightly premature end and she then looked around the room in silence. She waited in the silence before deciding she couldn't hang on for the hoped for thirty seconds and began.

'Year 9 is a vital year in your school life. You are moving towards being senior members of the school and before you know where you are you'll have begun your GCSE courses. Are you going to search for the hero inside of you or are you happy just to continue being what you are? So many pupils slip through this school without leaving any positive mark. Keep aiming high it's your passport to feeling supreme. I want you to succeed, all of your teachers want you to succeed, your parents want you to succeed, but (fingers pointing) this is all about you.' Pause.

'Do you want to succeed? Do you want to stand out from the crowd in a positive way? Not like the boys last week that I had to take out of assembly for making those disgusting noises. That isn't searching for the hero. Working hard – that is the key. Being brave enough to try and being brave enough to fail. Just keep the flame of truth burning bright. Work hard and you will be rewarded.'

She paused again.

'Thank you Mr Abrahams.'

The music began again and Mrs Carr strode down the central aisle in the hall pointing at the pieces of paper, before sweeping her arm to encompass all the pupils in the hall as she went.

Once outside the hall she headed towards her office quickly followed by Mrs Bastic Styles. The head teacher heard the call of her deputy head, 'head teacher,' behind and without turning motioned her towards the office. Once inside she pushed the door to firmly,

'Oh Emma, that was wonderful. Did you see them? They were rapt. I even saw some of them mouthing along with the song. Oh this is what being a teacher is all about isn't it, inspiring the pupils. Well done head teacher it was inspirational.'

'Thank you Valerie.'

The phone rang and Emma signalled to Mrs Bastic Styles to wait for a moment.

'Hello Janet. Oh yes and what did he say? He can, oh that's brilliant and for the 25th. He said that did he? Brilliant. Good. Have you put it in the diary? And on the bulletin? Right.'

She put the phone down and gave the thumbs up.

'He'll do it.'

'Oh wonderful. Who?'

'Andy Saville. Oh we are in for a treat on the 25th Valerie; this man is simply inspirational. He thought he might be on a motivational tour of companies in the South West, but that's been cancelled and he can fit us in. Honestly, he's just brilliant. He came to a friend of mine's work and they said he was incredible. Apparently he just changed the way that people do things there and they're always talking about him in the office.'

'Is he coming in to do an assembly Emma?'

'No, I've got him in to do the PD day on the 25th. Our staff need a shake up and he's the man to do it Valerie, he's the man to do it. Oh this is brilliant news.'

Emma Carr started to look breathlessly around for her diary and Valerie Bastic Styles smiled as she moved towards the door,

'Well that's all I came to say, well done head teacher. I've got teaching to do now,' and off she flew. As she left the office and headed down the corridor she might have overheard a snippet of the conversation and the snorting laughter of two of the younger members of the Drama department, but Mrs Bastic Style's head was full of inspiration, M People and Andy Saville and she swept on oblivious.

chapter seven

J.P.P. Montgomery's assembly to the lower sixth at St George's College started in more sombre tones.

'Gentlemen we are under attack. Not in the conventional sense of the word, there are no aeroplanes circling overheard waiting to bomb us, but in a more insidious manner and this of course makes it all the more difficult to repel and defeat. The attack I talk of is not from the outside, not from Islamic fundamentalists or right wing bully boys, but from within the ranks of our own society. Their light is bright and getting brighter gentlemen and I urge you not be blinded by it.

The people I talk of are cropping up in every part of our lives. These are not people of substance, these are not the people that made this country great. They are followers of a cult – the cult of naked ambition. Not the ambition that builds countries, the ambition that finds medical cures for the masses, the ambition that pushes back boundaries in knowledge and progress. No, this is the ambition of the individual for the individual. The great cult of me and I. They are the smoke and mirrors merchants, the deceivers, the dissemblers, the mandarins, the weasels, the grey men, the yes men. They are the colourless tiddlers living off the big fish.'

The mention of the word tiddlers had provoked some minor laughter in the middle rows and Montgomery eyeballed them.

'Laughter is a very powerful weapon Williams, Robson and you would do well to continue to employ it. It is one of the exact things that these people fundamentally lack, the ability to laugh either at themselves or at life. You are right to laugh at my pomposity but do not, I urge you, laugh at my message. Hang on to some magnanimity of spirit, hang on to some sense of what it is to be human and what it is to truly live. Sniff these cheerless wretches out, expose them to the light of humanity and above all laugh at them. Point at them and laugh at them, they are deserving of our scorn.

Invoke the spirit of Keats, Lawrence of Arabia, Churchill, Shackleton, Martin Luther King…',

'All men as usual,' whispered Susan Williams at the back of the hall.

'The great men who are ambitious for good, for life and for humanity. Pin your colours to the mast, be a thinker, have a view on issues, do not shirk our great responsibility, the responsibility to get involved in the messy business of life. Think beyond yourselves, 'no man is an island' – the maestro John Donne. Fight the self-interested, the people who have neither interest nor care for the greater good, who care only for the preservation of their shallow little worlds, for these are the very people that pervade our society at present. As I look around I see these values being rewarded and prized; gentlemen we are being run by charlatans and bluffers, it is up to the likes of you to stand firm in the face of such a tide. This is a great and glorious world we live in boys, never forget that, never forget that.'

Montgomery looked earnestly over the dais and removed his glasses and slipped them into the pocket of his gown.

'Thank you for your attention gentlemen.'

As he left the hall the boys stood and Bryn Castle leant over to Susan Williams and murmured,

'I think he's finally lost it.'

'Patience Mr Castle, patience.'

chapter eight

Jefferson Tweedy, still fresh from the triumph of the syllabus launch, span his executive chair round twice and came to face his computer. He had never realised how easy it was to be a chief executive. Already this morning he had barked at the tea lady and she had still come back later singing his praises for the 'wonderful speech' she'd heard about at the launch. If he'd have done that in his lowly position at Mycroft, Piggot and Welch he would have gone without biscuits for weeks on end. Now having read *The Telegraph* from front to back, he was readying himself for an extended spell on the internet. He had become increasingly enamoured with the wonders of eBay and was at that very moment waiting to see if his bid of £23 would secure him the services of an original Scaletrix set (mint condition) that he had already cleared a space for in the spare room. This on top of the £6 purchase of a 'Family Fortunes' computer game the previous night was keeping Jefferson in very high spirits as he opened up Outlook on the computer. He thought it only right that he speak to Ailsa on e-mail and tell her of his achievements with the wedding preparations thus far before allowing battle to commence on eBay.

In his former life at Mycroft, Piggot and Welch, Jefferson was used to an extraordinary number of e-mails every day. Thse ranged from appeals for lost keys through to rants about the hijacking of parking spaces and guinea pigs for sale. One particularly brutal and long running feud concerning the allocation of parking space 31a, prompted a group e-mail to be sent on the dangers of 'flaming e-mails'. These apparently were the sort of e-mails that people sent whilst still in a state of 'high agitation' and could cause great offence to both the receiver and any other people that happened to read it. The advice offered was: 'write a draft version of the e-mail that you wished to send and then come back to it the next day in a more reasonable and calm state of mind and decide if you are still happy to send it'. Jefferson wondered whether he ought to start sending a few 'flaming e-mails' himself to see if he couldn't stir the pot a little at StanEd.

As usual the only e-mail in his inbox was from Ailsa and read as follows:

Hi honey, hope you are well. Daddy tells me they were very pleased with you at the launch – you clever boy.

Did you get the wedding list sorted out? I've had a quick look through their online catalogue and have attached a list of things that look promising. Do the same and add your list to mine.

Speak soon.

A xx

Jefferson opened the attachment and was displeased but unsurprised to see that it extended over three pages.

'Christ.'

Scanning the page his eyes settled on: Silver Plated Toilet Brush £75. As he stared there was a knock at the door.

Caught unawares he called 'come in,' straight away and then kicked himself for his slip.

It was the tea lady on her afternoon rounds. He had asked her name a couple of days ago but now couldn't remember whether it was Maggie or Maddy. After a moment's reflection he decided that Maggie was the more likely name for a tea lady and called her in.

'Hello Maggie.'

'Aggy.'

'Sorry?'

'My name's Aggy.'

'And that's what I said.'

'You said Maggie sir.'

'No, no you must have misheard me, I quite distinctly said Aggy. Why you only told me your name a few days ago, how on earth could I have forgotten it already?'

Aggy the tea lady made her way towards Jefferson's desk and took the clingfilm off a plate of biscuits. Jefferson, keen to amend for his name blunder, beckoned her towards the computer.

'How much do you think is reasonable to pay for a toilet brush Aggy?'

'I beg your pardon sir?'

'A toilet brush, how much would you pay for one?'

'Well that's a funny question sir, if you don't mind me saying.'

'Indeed it is Aggy, but what would you say?'

'Well I get mine at the pound shop sir, so that's five for a fiver.'

'Really, so would you say £75 was rather a lot then?'

'Are we talking about a brush to clean a toilet with sir?'

'We are Aggy.'

'More money than sense.'

Jefferson smiled indulgently and feeling in expansive mood, pressed on.

'Do you have a family Aggy?'

'Oh yes sir. There's my husband Bill, the four boys and a girl.'

'Goodness quite a family. And what are their names?'

'Well Kenny's the eldest, then there's Ronnie, Sammy the girl, Leonard and the youngest is Raymond.'

By midway through the list Jefferson's attention had begun to waver but he managed to retort winningly with, 'Really, you don't look old enough Aggy.'

Aggy was unmoved.

'I feel old enough I tell ya. Great lump that he is, sits there all day he does.'

'Who's that Aggy?'

'My Leonard. I don't know where he gets it from because his father's always out grafting and I've never been afraid of hard work. He's on that stuff isn't he – Ritalin.'

'Sorry?'

'Ritalin. The school said he was a wrong 'un and I should take him to the doctor. Said he was misbehaving, couldn't sit still, so I took 'im and the doctor puts him on this Ritalin, said it'd calm him down. Now all he does is sit in on the couch watching that Sky.'

Without the first idea what Ritalin was or stood for and ruing the invitation to personal revelation, Jefferson responded with, 'Oh.'

'I wouldn't mind but he's not stupid and he's barely in that school now.'

'What, he doesn't go?'

'I tell him every night but I'm out by six and so's my Bill and well his brother's not going to get him up is he?'

There was a pause and Jefferson took his time in choosing a mint Viscount biscuit.

'I'm sorry if I've been a bit short with you before Aggy, put it down to the pressures of work.'

'Oh I know how it is with you types, it doesn't bother me. At least you're here, which is more than the last bloke.'

She gathered up the teapot and biscuits and put them back on her trolley.

'Right then I'd better be getting on. Mr Andrews'll be waiting for his hobnobs. He loves his hobnobs that one. Ta ta.'

Jefferson watched her leave and made a mental note to treat her appallingly the next time he saw her. In his position he couldn't afford to get too close to the staff.

chapter nine

PD days, or to give them their full title of Professional Development Days, were brought in to teaching under Mrs Thatcher's Conservative government in the 1980s. They were originally called Baker days after the then Minister for Education, Kenneth Baker and have taken on many guises since, the present one being PD days. The idea appears to be to give teachers additional time for professional and personal development, free from the burden of having children in the school. Children have long praised their introduction since it guarantees them an extra two or three days off a year.

The PD days at St George's Cross officially began at nine o'clock but coffee and croissants were available from 8.45 and staff were encouraged to partake of these. The croissants had been provided since the arrival of Emma Carr and as well as being popular with staff, had enabled Valerie Bastic Styles to tick the 'Making Staff feel Valued' box on the Investors in People form that OFSTED required the school to complete.

The staff arrived just before nine o'clock in rather jauntier mood than usual due to the absence of students. Huddled in their departmental groups they compared the list of terrible classes they had been spared by the blessing of the PD day falling on a Thursday.

'No Year 8 Wordsworth today, I can't tell you how pleased that makes me feel. The only disappointment is that Josh Jackson was suspended anyway and I feel like I'm using up my jokers.'

'Oh they're terrible after lunch aren't they?'

'Well I've got them twice after lunch and the other lesson's period 4, which is just as bad.'

Others chose to look at the PD day in a less favourable light.

'Bloody typical, I've got two frees on a Thursday and what day do they put the PD day – Thursday. Like last week, the fire alarm goes off in the middle of my free. I think she's looking at timetable.'

Two members of the science department had chosen to wear shorts despite the inclement weather conditions and both sported novelty T-shirts. One bore the words 'I learnt everything I know from watching Star Trek' whilst the other had a picture of Homer Simpson with his eyes turned towards the Starship Enterprise saying 'Beer me up Scottie'. Both men wore black trainers, black socks, shorts and T-shirts and their bare legs appeared to be sweating since the dark hair lay plastered to the skin. Whenever staff referred to the two science teachers the phrase 'they're characters' was employed in their description.

One member of the Design and Technology department wore a jumper emblazoned with reindeer. Other teachers speculated whether this was a laudable act of loyalty to the mother that had bought it, or a statement of defiance against Christmas starting earlier each year. Some feared it was neither.

Valerie Bastic Styles clapped at the front of the canteen and started waving her arms in a rather theatrical, we can all be a bit crazy without the kids here, type way before asking for silence.

'Good morning everyone. Can we all make our way into the hall please, the presentation will be starting in two minutes. Thank you.'

Once the staff were assembled, Emma Carr, still dressed in her usual work outfit, made her way from the back of the hall. Once at the front she waited for a few mutterers to quieten down before beginning.

'I always like to take the chance on days like these to thank you. To thank you for being the highly skilled and motivated people that you are. This school is nothing without you and all the hours that you put in for the good of the students. So thank you. Now it's always nice to have some time to ourselves and being good practitioners I'm sure you'll be taking the chance to reflect on your work so far this year. I spend a few minutes at the end of every week just jotting down a list of the things that I have done well and then I spend a few minutes on the things that I think I can improve on in the coming week. It's only a small thing and it doesn't take very long but I've found it invaluable over the years and I encourage you to do the same. We should all want to be constantly improving.'

Emma paused and took a sip from her glass of water.

'Now today we have a real treat in store. This is a man who has toured around both this country and the United States with his motivational talks and he specialises in helping people to get the best out of themselves and the rest of their team. He does normally work with business but I know that his lessons are going to be just as valuable for us today since we're all in the business of learning.'

Led by Valerie Bastic Styles, the staff laughed with varying degrees of enthusiasm.

'So without further ado, please welcome, Mr Andy Saville.'

The staff followed the head teacher's lead in applauding and waited for the arrival of the speaker. By the time the applause died out Andy Saville still hadn't appeared. The staff looked towards the door to the canteen but it remained closed. Emma Carr sat at the front of the hall smiling, enjoying the moment; her friend had told her about the way Andy Saville began his presentation.

Finally the double doors at the back of the hall opened and a suntanned man in a lightweight suit began to walk down the aisle. He was clapping very deliberately and looking around at the staff. As he reached the rows of seats where the staff sat he began to go up to individuals and stand in front of them, still clapping very slowly. As they began to laugh, or look away or fix him with their eyes he moved away and did the same thing to somebody else. The staff began to talk amongst themselves in the way a class would when their teacher was 'doing something different'. He clapped in front of about seven people, never once smiling or departing from the same fixed expression on his face, before he made it to the front of the hall. Once there, he stood completely still and looked at his audience. His suit was an immaculate light grey with a white shirt and a lemon-coloured tie. His shoes were patent leather slip-ons and on his wrist sat a huge chunk of gold watch. He then began to clap slowly again before stopping abruptly.

'I bet you've got two questions in your mind. The first one was is he going to turn up? And the second one is why is he clapping? I'll tell you why I was clapping, I was clapping you. My question is why were you clapping me? I was clapping you because you turn up every day and do a job that I, along with millions of others, could never do. We haven't got the patience, we haven't got the skill to deliver our knowledge to small people, we couldn't think of anything worse. So I want you to turn to the person next to you and congratulate them on the great job that they do and how well they do it.'

The degree of enthusiasm with which the staff took up the offer was varied but everyone did as they were told. Ironic slaps on the back and even a few hugs filled the hall.

'So tell me,' Andy Saville shouted over the hubbub, 'why were you clapping me? For turning up? Because your headmistress told you to?'

'Head teacher,' called out Valerie Bastic Styles, to laughs from the Maths department that sat around her.

'I'm sorry – head teacher. Well why were you clapping? I haven't done anything. What have I done this morning? I tell you what I've done this morning. I left my million pound house in Bexley and I managed to drive over here in my Porsche Boxster – big deal. And now I bet you're all thinking, flash bastard. That's right isn't it, you're all thinking you flash bastard.

Now let me tell you a little story. I used to be a professional footballer, but you won't have heard of me because I wasn't very good. I could stand here and tell you that I hurt my knee or the manager didn't fancy me but that wouldn't be true; the truth is I wasn't very good. Now I'd wanted to be a professional footballer all my life and then I got told 'Savo son, you're not going to make it.' Now it seemed to me that I had two choices at that point. I could spend the rest of my life telling everyone how if it hadn't been for my knee I'd have been a star or I could take the tougher option and start again. I took the tougher option.'

'Surprise, surprise,' whispered Rosaline Osborne the head of Music.

'I used that rejection as my motivation and do you know what registration plate I've got on my brand new silver Boxster. Do you? SAVO1. So every time I drive out of my million pound house the world can see that they didn't beat me.'

Some teachers took this opportunity to share their views with a neighbour on Andy Saville's rise from rags to Boxters. Emma Carr chose to nod vigorously whilst Valerie Bastic Styles' replacement as head of Maths chose to take some conspicuous notes at the elbow of his former master.

Andy Saville took a swig from his bottle of Evian and looked around the room.

'Now I want you to turn to the person on your right and look them in the eye. Then ask them their full name. When they've told you this I want you to give them a nickname. So to give you an example.'

Andy Saville walked to the front row where a group of Modern Languages teachers collectively cowered.

'Excuse me, what's your name?'

'Jonathan.'

'Your full name please,'

'Jonathan Edward Smith.'

'So I'm going to give you the nickname Smithy.'

'Genius,' whispered Michael Harris the head of English.

'Now when you have decided on your partner's nickname I want you to turn them around and start to massage their shoulders – like so.'

Jonathan Smith's eyes shot a glance to the rest of the teachers as Andy Saville got to work on his stress knots.

'Now once you've got the massage going I want you to start whispering in their ear, 'you're worth a million pound Smithy, you're worth a million pound.'

'He is taking the piss isn't he?' commented Tony Eaton the head of History.

'Don't be uptight about it, don't be all English about it; tell your work mate how much they're worth.'

Andy Saville broke off from massaging Jonathan Smith's shoulders and turned to the rest of the teachers and shouted,

'Go on, get on with it.'

The teachers turned to each other and exchanged embarrassed smiles. The less positive members of the group took this opportunity to swap opinions both on what Andy Saville could do with his Boxster and on how much they thought the person opposite them was really worth, before having their attention drawn to the girlish squeals of Valerie Bastic Styles as she was rubbed down by Ravi Zakhuddin the bright young thing of the maths department. They also enjoyed the sight of Emma Carr being massaged by Derek Sykes, the pungent smelling head of Site Services. One unreliable source later swore that he had seen Derek Sykes licking the head teacher's ear, but such reports remained unconfirmed. Each pair in turn settled to the task and began to whisper into each other's ears to the cries of encouragement from Andy, 'Anyone need any oil yet?' and 'there's a pair down here enjoying it a bit too much!'

And so the morning session passed in a wave of esteem raising massage and anecdotes.

The staff arrived back in the hall for the final session after a break for tea and biscuits. Those sitting at Emma Carr's table in the canteen made their way back in with slightly more haste than the rest, after listening to the head teacher repeatedly lecture them on the benefits of being 'challenged'. She even felt it necessary to send them off with a cry of 'go on and be challenged,' as they headed back to the assembly hall.

Once the teachers were assembled Andy Saville came back into the hall. This time he used the more conventional route of the door from the canteen before eyeballing his audience.

'So you've been talking over your tea. Yeah, yeah, yeah it's all stimulating stuff and a bit of fun but what's it got to do with teaching? How's it going to help me in the classroom?

Well here's how. I spoke to a friend of mine who is the head master in a tough school near where I grew up and he told me 'Andy, do you know the biggest thing that holds our kids back? Lack of self-esteem. Not a lack of resources, not a messed up home life, not poor teachers but lack of self-esteem. So that's what I've been talking about today, methods to improve self-esteem.'

As he said the word esteem, he removed his suit jacket and laid it carefully on the stage behind him.

'How often do we actually tell ourselves how good we are? And how often do we tell the kids how good they are? Use some of these techniques with the kids. Whisper in their ear that they're worth a million pounds.'

As he said the word pounds he removed his lemon tie and placed that on the stage as well.

As he placed the tie on the stage Valerie Bastic Styles put her hand up and called out,

'Could I just remind the staff that any physical contact other than the placing of a hand on the pupil's elbow could be mis-interpreted as physical or sexual abuse if allegations were ever brought before a tribunal.'

'Thank you Mrs…'

'Bastic Styles.'

'Mrs Bastic Styles. These kids will have felt rejection already. Not in the way I did from the world of professional football but in their everyday lives, from their parents and their family telling them you can't do this, you're not good enough to do that.'

On the final word of the sentence, Andy Saville unbuttoned his white shirt and as he placed the shirt on the stage turned his tanned back to the teachers. Mouths opened and the occasional snigger could be heard from the teachers whilst a few muttered words were exchanged. Andy Saville turned round to face them in his grey trousers and patent leather slip-ons.

'You're wondering is he going to go the whole way aren't you? You're damn right I'm going to go the whole way, because that's what I want you to do for the kids, go the whole way.'

There was an audible guffaw from one member of the audience at this point and it was later confirmed that it emitted from Tony Eaton the long time head of History. In discussion at a later date this was seen by the management as yet another example of Mr Eaton's unwillingness to move with the times and embrace new educational ideas.

Apparently impervious to the laughter Andy Saville removed one slip-on shoe at a time and then proceeded to toss each burberry sock over his shoulder on to the stage. The teachers sat staring at the events unfolding before their eyes. All were attentive, like teenagers in front of their first horror film and without saying another word Andy Saville removed his chunky gold watch and held it up in front of the teachers, swaying it like a hypnotist. He continued to do this for a number of seconds murmuring 'go the whole way for the kids, go the whole way for the kids,' before this too was placed on the stage.

'These kids need someone to tell them they can do it, they need their teacher to tell them that they can be someone. Don't be that manager that told me 'no', be the one that gives them their own personalised number plate.'

The removal of the suit trousers began on the word personalised and they were off and on the stage by the end of the sentence.

He stood before the audience in a pair of slightly baggy white pants and stretched his arms out sideways, echoing the posture of an unnaturally tanned Christ. After pausing to allow the teachers to savour this image, Saville began to talk slowly, nodding his head deliberately throughout the speech.

'Take a good look at me. Take away the Porsche Boxster car, the thousand pound Rolex watch, the eight hundred pound suit and the shiny pair of shoes – this is me. A normal bloke in a scraggy old pair of M & S pants. I've decided how I want to dress myself and I've gone out and got it.' He paused.

'You're the ones putting the clothes on these kids. How do you want them to dress?'

He waited for a moment before turning around sharply and sweeping up the clothes behind him. He then strode the length of the hall and departed out of the back doors. The teachers watched him go in silence and stared at the door long after he had departed. Valerie Bastic Styles began the applause from the front and slowly the rest of the teachers joined in. They turned to face the front and were greeted by a beaming Emma Carr.

'Isn't he extraordinary? I think we'd all agree that today has been a memorable day and I'm sure I'm not the only one who finds it invigorating to get some input from the world of business.'

Valerie Bastic Styles led the cries of agreement and even briefly tried to start another round of applause.

'Now of course beneath all of Andy's showmanship lies a very serious point and it is a point that I want to finish this session on and the point is about maximising the potential of our students. We are the ones in charge of the wardrobe and I want us to go away and think in our departments about how we can dress our pupils in value added shirts, self-esteem trousers and achievement of potential jackets.'

A very audible cry of 'Oh for fuck's sake,' went up from a member of the audience but Emma Carr chose to ignore it and thanked her colleagues for their attention before heading straight for the door to the canteen.

chapter ten

Jacob Haliwell checked his watch. He reckoned that he had two more minutes of reading time before his self-imposed toilet refuge must end. The book that he had locked the door of *The Express's* staff toilet for today was the new Ian McEwan. As a rule he avoided the recent McEwan novels, but as he completed the bogus flush of the toilet he contemplated whether this might be the best modern novel he had read that year. His fear was the ending, since he had yet to discover a modern novelist that could do a good ending; but so far, so good.

He briefly checked his image in the mirror and noted the milky colour of his cheeks. His teeth which had always been terrible, crooked and jagged, were now simply gruesome against the washed out pallor of his face. Friends used to compliment them as 'character teeth' but nobody did that anymore. As he left the toilet he wondered why he bothered to look at himself in the mirror since it was not something that he usually did. He wondered to himself whether the presence of the work experience girl upstairs had anything to do with it and he shook his head in despair.

She had arrived that morning, pristine in clothes evidently

bought for the occasion, and Jacob couldn't help but be lifted by her presence. She was enthusiastic and intelligent and she listened to what he had to say. For one brief moment he had idyllic visions of giving all this filthy journalism stuff up and becoming the sort of teacher you saw in old films. A copy of *The Great Gatsby* in hand, sitting on the edge of a desk whilst imparting his knowledge to bright-eyed girls called Eleanor and Abigail.

This bright-eyed girl was called Kathryn ('with a y') and was at *The Express* for a week of work experience. His heart lifted when she said how, 'she wasn't really interested in entertainment on its own, more in journalism as a whole.' He could have hugged her. She didn't even appear to want to secure a role on Children's television.

The day's photograph had arrived from Fat Nick twenty minutes beforehand. It was a picture of Martine McCutcheon; an awards ceremony statue in one hand and a copy of *The Express* in the other. Jacob explained to an enquiring Kathryn that she used to play Tiffany in *EastEnders* and then didn't turn up much in a West End show; but *The Express* still liked her because she was English and happy to hold *The Express* in a photo.

Jacob then left Kathryn to try and come up with a headline whilst he grabbed ten pages of the McEwan downstairs. When he arrived back he called over to her from the top of the stairs,

'How have you got on?'

He walked over and picked up the photograph from the desk.

'Ah, the lovely Martine. So what did you come up with?'

Kathryn picked up a piece of paper and said,

'It's not very good,' before preparing to read. 'Can I use her old soap name?'

'Of course. Go on then.'

'TIFFANY'S OUR JEWEL'

Jacob looked at the headline with an impassive face before slowly starting to nod his head.

'It's perfect – disgustingly good. God, how depressing. Are you very bright?'

'What do you mean?'

'In your class, in your year are you very bright?'

'I suppose so.'

'Good, I'm pleased because we couldn't have any old dumb arse being able to do this with such sinful ease could we?'

Jacob stood up from the corner of the desk where he had perched himself.

'Well that is our morning's work done. It's stressful stuff isn't it? And this afternoon we shall put together fifty to a hundred words of deathless prose to accompany this picture of national import and so keep the wheels of vital current affairs turning for at least another day. And so now my bright-eyed, pleasingly earnest Miss Kathryn, we are going to the pub for a well deserved long lunch, where I shall show you what it is to be a real journalist and to also prove that I am better than you at some things.'

Jacob headed for the door with a 'come on' before turning back to her and saying,

'You can't drink vodka like a Russian sailor as well can you?'

'I don't really drink.'

'Thank God for that. Let's go.'

chapter eleven

Emma Carr slammed the door into her office and threw her folder on to the desk. The door opened again behind her and Valerie Bastic Styles crept timidly into the office.

'Is everything all right head teacher?

'I will not be humiliated,' the head teacher screamed.

'Oh I didn't think the speaker was that bad head teacher and if he humiliated anyone I should say it was himself, stripping off like that. I'm sure it will not reflect badly on you.'

'Not Andy, Valerie, I thought he was brilliant, I'm talking about the person who shouted out at the end of the talk: I distinctly heard an 'oh for fuck's sake,' as I left the room. Now as you know I am as keen as anyone to foster good relationships with my staff, but this cannot be tolerated. I bring in a top quality speaker from the world of business, at no little expense I might add, and how do they repay me? Through humiliation, through a deliberate attack on my position and my authority; that's how they repay me. Well I will not stand for it, why should I?'

'Why should you Emma.'

'And incidentally Valerie, please don't call me Emma around the school. Obviously it is perfectly fine within these four walls but please never in the main school.'

'I wasn't aware that I had head teacher.'

'Yesterday during the fire drill.'

The deputy head took a moment to recollect.

'Oh, but surely no one heard?'

'That isn't the point, it simply isn't professional and God knows this place could do with some professionalism. Please, only within these walls.'

'Yes Emma.'

'Well I want these people found. I want to know who it was and I want them found, immediately. I cannot and will not be humiliated in front of the whole staff. This person or persons cannot be seen to get away with it.'

'Absolutely Emma, I shall get onto it straight away. I already have my suspicions; the English and Drama departments are always a good place to start with incidents like this – subversive tendencies.'

'Make sure you do, Valerie, make sure you do.'

As Valerie Bastic Styles stormed out of the office she almost ran into Gill Betts, a History teacher of many years standing at St George's Cross, who briefly waited for an apology from the deputy head teacher before realising that she wasn't going to get one and proceeded to knock on the head teacher's door.

'Come in,' came the reply.

Gill Betts entered the office to face the recently composed head teacher.

'Ah hello Gill. Do sit down won't you.'

'Thank you.'

'How did you find the speaker today?'

'Very interesting.'

'Wasn't he? Slightly quirky of course, but I do think we can learn so much from the way that business does things.'

'I agree.'

'So what can I do for you?'

'Well I need to ask a favour actually.'

'Ask away, we're here to help.'

'Well, it's about a week on Friday.'

'Charities' day.'

'Yes.'

'Go on.'

'Well as I'm sure you know the week after is half term…'

'How could we forget!'

'…and I've booked a holiday for me and Lily in Spain for the week.'

'Lovely.'

'And now here's the problem. There were two flights available; one that leaves at 1.30am on the Saturday morning and the other that leaves at 4.00pm on the Friday afternoon and I don't really want to take Lily on a through the night flight which will mean we'll both effectively lose a night's sleep.'

'Are there no flights on the Saturday or Sunday?'

'None at all, they were all booked up months ago. So what I'm asking is if you could excuse me from the afternoon of Charities' day, so Lily and I could get that flight at four o'clock instead of the all night flight.'

There was a pause as Emma Carr looked towards the ceiling whilst tapping her pencil on the desk. Gill Betts went on, 'Obviously with it being Charities' day. I won't be missing any lessons and I've already asked Michael Harris if he could cover my duties for that afternoon and he said that was fine.'

Emma Carr's eyes remained shut as she talked to Gill Betts.

'I'm going to have to say no Gill and this is why. I'd love to say yes but I simply can't set the precedent. If I say yes to you then I can never say no to anyone else, even if they haven't got as good a case as you.'

'I see.'

'I hope you do Gill because I just can't set the precedent.'

'Couldn't you just judge each case on its individual merits?'

'Believe me these are the hardest decisions to make as a manager but I have to make them and I think this is the right decision in this case.'

'So what if I had decided to be ill on that Friday and not tried to do the right thing by coming to see you? What would you have done then?'

'I know that being the conscientious professional you are Gill you wouldn't do that and it would be deeply disappointing to me if you did. But obviously we would require a doctor's note and all the usual evidence if that had have been the case.'

'Well thanks.'

'I'm sorry Gill, I really am but my hands are tied on this one.'

'And this is your final word on the matter?'

'I'm afraid it is Gill. The only other idea I can think of is that we speak to the bursar and calculate your wage for the hours that you are missing and then deduct that from your monthly wage.'

'Spare me.'

'I'm sorry you feel like that Gill, but I have to do what is best for the school. Anything else I can help you with please don't hesitate to come and ask me.'

Gill Betts stood up and headed for the door.

'I'm really sorry about that Gill, but have a nice holiday and send my love to Lily. I'm sure you'll have a lovely time.'

Gill Betts closed the door firmly behind her.

chapter   twelve

Kathryn the work experience girl had drunk an orange J2O and a glass of still mineral water whilst watching Jacob drink three pints of Stella and a pair of vodka chasers. Harry's Bar was now full with people who had taken their lunch break at a more conventional time and Jacob and Kathryn were sharing their large table with four thirty something men in brightly coloured shirts who were loudly discussing the merits of 'Virginia on the Far East exchange'. Jacob looked distastefully towards them before turning to Kathryn.

'So now you've had the old lie about journalism firmly exposed.'

'What's that?'

'You know the one; that *Sun* writers are actually really clever and probably more talented than all the other journalists because they know exactly who their audience is and they can pitch their work perfectly to that market using only words that an eight year old can understand etc etc. Well let me tell you it's rubbish, any monkey can do it.'

'You don't work for *The Sun*.'

'No but I wish I was; I look up to them now. That's how

far down the journalistic food chain I have fallen. They are a standard that I long to match.'

'If you don't like your job why do you do it?'

'You sound like Belle.'

'Who's Belle?'

'Belle is my beautiful friend who left me in this sinking shit to go and teach.'

'When was that?'

'About nine months ago. Nine months ago tomorrow actually.'

'So why don't you get out?'

'I'll tell you why – because I'm stuck in an abusive relationship. The more they beat me and humiliate me the less chance there is of me leaving. I'm worried if I fall out of this I might continue the cycle of violence and fall into porn or something.'

He took a long mouthful from his pint.

'Have you got a boyfriend?'

'No,' came the sharp answer.

'Oh Christ no I didn't mean it like that. Jesus that wouldn't do at all would it. No, no, no. No I was just interested.'

'I don't want to get one until my exams are out of the way.'

'Very wise, very wise. They're nothing but trouble anyway.'

'Really?'

'Well probably not all of them.'

'No.'

'I tried to kiss Belle the other night. I don't know what came over me really. She soon put a stop to it, said it 'wasn't a good idea, not with how things are at the moment.'

There was a long pause during which Kathryn looked intently into her mineral water.

'I suppose in hindsight it was a mistake but how are you to know?'

'I don't know.'

'No neither do I.' He looked closely at Kathryn. 'Well then, shall we head back to the seat of journalistic excellence? Are you ready to receive more teaspoonfulls of wisdom?'

She nodded her head and put down the empty glass that she had been cradling before following Jacob to the door.

chapter thirteen

Jefferson had arranged the wedding list at John Lewis and also contacted a number of churches in Oxted, the rather pleasant area of Surrey where Ailsa had grown up. Jefferson was not himself a religious man but he was happy to have the service in a church and Ailsa's mother had said that it would be better for the photographs if they had a church in the background. He was astonished by how busy all the churches appeared to be. One place in the village was booking for Saturdays in three years' time but the lady he spoke to had been very nice about it and assured him that she would put him on the reserve list because 'things do happen.'

It was nearly four months since Jefferson started at StanEd and on reflection things could not have gone better. All of his public appearances were generally considered to be triumphs and had resulted in some very favourable press. *The Telegraph* was particularly kind and Jefferson spent almost an entire morning in the toilet reading and re-reading the cuttings after the launch. He noted with some disappointment that *The Express* decided not to include his one to one interview in their edition but his disappointment soon passed when he noticed that *The Daily Mail* referred to him as 'commanding' in their editorial.

He was also equally pleased with the way he had taken to the role of chief executive. He felt that his status was appropriately high within the building, although he was starting to wonder whether his Mr Mycroft shouting techniques had not been a touch too successful since he saw next to nobody during his average day at work. Aggy would bring tea and biscuits in twice a day and on many days she was the only person that he saw; even Kenneth's visits were starting to diminish. When he asked Kenneth how things were going, Kenneth's replied 'supremely well Mr Jefferson, supremely well. The staff are working flat out under your inspirational leadership,' before scuttling away down a corridor. As he departed, Jefferson wondered aloud whether it would be a good idea for him to have a wander around the building 'to meet the troops'. Kenneth stopped mid-corridor, turned and replied 'up to a point Mr Jefferson, the staff are very busy at the present time' before Jefferson's phone bleeped with a text from Ailsa and the moment passed.

In addition to the lack of visits to his office he was also surprised by the lack of phone calls, post or e-mails that he received. In fact he had only received one letter since he arrived and that transpired to contain a photograph sent by Ailsa of him dressed as The Sundance Kid at a Wild West theme park that they visited just before he left. He had blu tacked it to his computer screen for that morning before deciding that it didn't convey the correct image for a young executive of his standing and so it was dispatched to the drawer of his desk never to see the light of day again. As for e-mails they too were largely from Ailsa, although Kenneth did send him an attachment containing photographs taken of him during the launch at Grosvenor House.

One phone call did come through to his office a couple of days ago and Jefferson was mildly surprised to find Lord McLeish of Dunblane on the other end of the line, but the confusion was soon cleared up when it became clear that Lord McLeish was hoping to speak to Kenneth. Lizzie on reception re-directed the call and Jefferson's line quickly went dead.

Now after watching back to back episodes of Baywatch online, Jefferson felt slightly at a loss as to what to do. He'd made inquiries about vintage Rolls Royce's (the topic of the diverting message from Ailsa) and felt that the wedding preparations were far enough advanced to divert any queries Ailsa might make in the next day or so.

His main aim on first arriving at StanEd was to ensure that his ignorance concerning all matters educational should not be exposed and he felt that that goal had been achieved. Now he felt that he could venture into the heart of the building and not fear the random questioning of a passing member of staff. Indeed if the worst should come to the worst he would simply 'Mycroft' them before storming off to the nearest toilet via the longest route available. Indeed he now felt confident enough to ensure that he was the one doing the questioning, since who amongst his staff would dare to initiate discussions with the 'commanding' Jefferson Tweedy?

Having convinced himself, he picked up a folder from his desk and made his way to the door of his office and looked both ways down the corridor. Having checked that all was clear, Jefferson strode purposefully towards the lift. It arrived immediately and Jefferson got in and pressed the number 2.

His plan as it stood was to start at Level 2 and work down. He had noticed that the lift had buttons marked LG and LLG and was keen to investigate these depths of the building and inspect the industry that he presided over from the heights of Level 9.

The lift stopped at Level 2 and he stepped out into the corridor. It was deathly quiet and stretched both ways as far as he could see. He decided to turn right and set off down the corridor. The left hand side of the corridor was all glass and made the corridor fairly warm even at this time of the year. He made a mental note that when he saw a member of staff he would comment that all their hard work was making it hot in here. The window afforded a view out onto another series of buildings similar to Copperfield House and the odd glimpse of London. Along the other side of the corridor were a series of doors at intervals of twenty or so yards. Each door was numbered with the floor and room number; the first on his right was 2/13 and Jefferson took a close look at the door, hoping it would reveal its secrets to him. Each door had a security code lock and at room 2/16 Jefferson decided to try one. He looked around him before pressing his ear to the door. He struggled to make out what he heard but thought it might be a fax machine receiving a message. He then looked blankly at the security lock before tapping in 123 – the door remained unmoved. He moved back into the corridor before returning to tap on the door. When he received no response he knocked more firmly and waited again. Having waited for thirty seconds, in which time he again pressed his ear to the door, he looked sternly at the security pad before moving on down the corridor. He reached a set of stairs after room 2/20 and descended them to the first floor.

Level 1 revealed more of the same; a length of deserted corridor and security locked doors. At occasional intervals on the window side of the corridor were potted plants in chrome pots and these seemed to be reasonably well tended, although Jefferson didn't know the name of the plant. He knocked at the door of room 1/15 and again received no reply, after which he tapped 007 into the security code but with the same result as before. He then went back to the stairs and made his way down to the ground floor and the reception desk. The receptionist turned as she heard him approaching.

'Afternoon Lizzie.'

'Good afternoon Mr Tweedy, what brings you down to these parts?'

'Oh just visiting the staff, making sure everything's ship shape.'

'An excellent idea sir. As you can see I'm hard at it; it's a very busy time of the year as I'm sure you know.'

'You know sometimes I wonder Lizzie if it could be any busier. Still we can only do our best can't we?'

'We do what we can sir!'

With a benevolent smile Jefferson moved off to the stairs to continue his inspection of the lower reaches of the building. As he got to the stairs Jefferson stopped and looked back towards the receptionist who had gone back to her work.

'Lizzie?'

'Yes Mr Tweedy?'

'You wouldn't know the codes to any of these rooms would you? Only I was doing some work on the second floor earlier today and I appear to have left some papers in there.'

'Oh I wouldn't know about that sir. Security is so very

tight around here these days, especially after the incident with the parent and the Geography paper. Soon after that they introduced the security locks. I never need them so I wouldn't know. Perhaps Mr Andrews would be the man to ask?'

'Yes, perhaps he is,' said Jefferson and headed off down the stairs.

The Lower Ground floor appeared to be exactly the same as all of the others. The only difference being that due to the lack of windows the atmosphere down there was altogether darker with a whiff of damp in the air. Jefferson turned right at the bottom of the stairs and passed rooms LG20, LG21 and LG22. At all of these doors he listened unsuccessfully for any signs of life within. Pulling back from the door to LG22 he reflected that he shouldn't place too much faith in this method, since he himself had been unable to hear Baywatch from outside his own office, (an activity he undertook as part of his possibility of disturbance checks prior to settling down to series two.)

As he walked past LG22 he thought he saw a flicker of movement at the other end of the corridor and instinctively he ducked into the toilet to his right. Once inside the toilet he wondered why he had done this. He reflected on the need to rid himself of the furtive manner that he had adopted so completely whilst working at Mycroft, Pigott and Welch. He told himself that it was now his job to make other people feel uncomfortable, and oddly guilty, just through his very presence. He also decided that he would be perfectly within his rights to ask Kenneth for the security code for every room in the building (he was after all the chief executive) and that he would do it the very next time he saw him.

Once these momentous decisions had been reached

Jefferson pulled *The Telegraph* out from his folder and turned flamboyantly to the sports pages. He began to read of England's pleasing progress in the second Test in Johannesburg when he heard the first sounds. He paused from his reading and held the paper very still as he listened for the sounds again. Back they came and it appeared that they were coming through the wall over his right shoulder. He leaned over to try to hear more. As he got closer to the wall he realised that he was hearing less and as he backed away he looked up to see a vent at the top of the wall. He settled himself back into his original position and listened carefully, but all was quiet. He briefly wondered if he had heard anything at all, then quite distinctly it came through the air vent, 'Moron, vermin, abortion, morpion, sewer rat, curate, cretin, crrritic, oh.'

Jefferson put *The Telegraph* carefully on the floor and pulled his trousers up. He then put the toilet seat down and clambering on to it he strained his ear towards the air vent. When it began again there were two voices.

'Now let's make up.'

'Gogo!'

'Didi!'

'Your hand.'

'Take it.'

'Come to my arms!'

'Your arms?'

'My breast!'

'Off we go.'

Then there was silence. Jefferson craned his ear towards the vent and waited there for a minute; the talking had stopped. He jumped down from the toilet seat, bolted out into the corridor and pressed his right ear to the door of LB23. He could hear nothing through the door and as he pulled his ear away Kenneth Andrews appeared at the top of the corridor. He called the length of the passage.

'Ah Mr Jefferson, the very man I have been looking for.'

'Oh hello Kenneth…'

Kenneth Andrews reached Jefferson with his usual haste.

'Is everything all right sir? You seem a little distracted.'

'Not at all, not at all.'

'I was just on my way to find you Mr Jefferson, I have some important papers for you to sign. Shall we head back to your office?'

'Kenneth I thought I heard something.'

Kenneth ushered Jefferson back towards the lift.

'Did you really sir? What brought you down to these murky depths Mr Jefferson?'

'Just taking a look around the building Kenneth, a little visible management.'

'Oh very good sir and was everything to your satisfaction?'

'Oh yes, all very satisfactory. Tell me Kenneth what are these rooms used for down here?'

'Oh these rooms are hardly used these days sir, only in the very busiest times of the year. It is so very dark down here, hardly the conditions we wish for, for our staff.'

'So are people working down here at the moment?'

'Oh no sir, there's no one down here at the moment sir, not at the moment. The lift sir.'

The two men got into the lift and Kenneth pressed the button for the ninth floor. Jefferson looked out as the lift doors shut. They ascended in silence and at the ninth floor they alighted to find Aggy pushing her trolley towards Jefferson's office. Kenneth Andrews positively bounced down the corridor.

'Ah Aggy, what excellent timing! Ensure Mr Jefferson gets the very finest tea and cakes this afternoon, he has had to endure the dark and dubious pleasures of the Lower Ground floor.'

Kenneth laughed and led the way into Jefferson's office. The papers were on the desk as Jefferson entered the office.

'What are they Kenneth?'

'Oh fairly routine stuff sir. They simply need your signature along with mine so we can authorise the buying of some equipment.'

'What sort of equipment Kenneth?'

'Oh computers and the like. It is getting so very hard for a pen and paper man like myself Mr Jefferson.'

'So how many computers are we buying Kenneth?'

'Oh the exact number escapes me for the moment but I shall check the invoice and report straight back to you if you so wish.'

'Very well.'

Jefferson signed the papers and Kenneth swept them away, thanking Mr Jefferson profusely. As he headed towards the door he passed Aggy, who was approaching Jefferson's desk. The two of them exchanged a brief nod before Aggy reached the desk.

'And how are we today sir?'

'Quite well Aggy,' replied Jefferson, 'quite well.'

'Will you be having your usual Chelsea Bun and a nice cup of tea?'

'No I don't think I shall today Aggy, not today. Just the tea for me today, thank you.'

'As you like sir.'

Jefferson stared briefly at the teapot before asking, 'And how are you Aggy?'

'Me? Oh I'm in the pink Mr Tweedy, in the pink.'

part three

chapter one

The staff at St George's Cross had been waiting in the school hall for nearly five minutes before Emma Carr and Valerie Bastic Styles arrived in a whirl of folders and overhead projectors. The women were late due to having to finalise the paperwork for an appeals panel hearing that evening, for a Year 8 boy who had been excluded the previous month for trying to force a Year 7 girl to have sex with him whilst he used an empty crisp packet as protection. The boy's mother was claiming that the girl had consented and that her son had been trying to do things responsibly.

Mrs Bastic Styles proceeded to set up the overhead projector whilst Emma Carr, inbetween turning round to check that the projector was being set up to her liking, addressed the staff.

'Predicted grades everyone, predicted grades.'

Any drop of interest that the staff may have held at the beginning of the meeting evaporated at the mention of the phrase 'predicted grades'. Emma Carr continued.

'I've had a close look at the way this has been done in previous years and in a word it was shambolic. And I think if you ask the majority of the staff I think they would agree with you.'

At the end of this sentence Bill Redgrave, the creator of the previous system for the collection of predicted grades, looked diplomatically towards the ceiling.

'As you all know I am passionate about teaching and learning in this school. I want us to discover ways together of enhancing the experience for every student we teach. And targets and benchmark data is a vital part of this vision. Every student should know exactly what they are expected to achieve – as a minimum, as a minimum …'

She paused to allow this point to sink in.

'We should be using this data to motivate our pupils to achieve their potential in their public examinations. As Andy Saville said, we want to clothe our pupils in the clothes of value added. I want them to see their benchmark data and then leap beyond it. This is my vision for this school.'

Emma Carr eyeballed her staff as she asked,

'Are we ready Mrs Bastic Styles?'

A voice from beneath the table behind her called, 'not quite head teacher.'

'Ah. Do we know how long we will be Mrs Bastic Styles?'

'A couple of minutes I would have thought head teacher.'

Those seated in the front rows of the assembly hall may have seen a moment of panic pass through Emma Carr's eyes. There followed ten seconds of silence as the head teacher consulted the cue cards that she held in her hand before in an act of desperation and against all of her principles for whole staff meetings, Emma Carr said,

'Well seeing as we have a couple of minutes, are there any questions?'

She glanced quickly around the room before adding, 'Good, well we'll just wait for Mrs Bastic Styles to...'

'Er head teacher.'

Emma looked to her left in poorly concealed horror to see Rosaline Osborne, the notoriously difficult teacher of Music, with her hand up.

Emma Carr pushed a smile on to her face and asked, 'Yes Rosaline?'

'Two things head teacher.'

Rosaline Osborne's questions always had 'two things'; the rest of the staff's interest perked up.

'For those of us teaching subjects where the data that the benchmarks are generated from is widely regarded to be next to useless, are we too expected to stick rigidly to this format for the predicted grades? And my second point is this. You talk about motivation; how do you suggest we motivate a pupil who at the start of a course is being told by all of the data that after two years of hard work he or she will get a grade E in my subject?'

Emma Carr paused a moment before beginning her answer. Her eyes flicked around the room at the eager faces of her staff.

'These are very valid points Rosaline and thank you for making them...'

From beneath the table came the voice, 'We're ready head teacher.'

'Ah thank you Mrs Bastic Styles. Rosaline we are very tight for time today, but please if you put your questions in an e-mail and send them to Janet I will answer them for you by the end of the week. Is that okay?'

'Well I would rather you answered them now.'

'I understand that but you can see that we are on a tight schedule for this meeting and with the work/life balance agreement in mind I don't want this meeting to go beyond four o'clock. So I'm afraid that's how we're going to have to do things today. Is that okay Rosaline?'

Rosaline chose not to respond.

'Thank you. Now Mrs Bastic Styles are we ready with the powerpoint presentation?'

'Yes head teacher.'

'Number one.'

Mrs Bastic Styles clicked the mouse in front of her.

'Thank you. Now if you look carefully, this bar chart shows you the data for the year 2006 cohort. Their benchmark data is in green, their predicted grades in blue, their CATS scores in yellow and their actual points score achieved in red. As you can see there is a clear disparity between the four colours and this is the area that I'm keen to address with this year's cohort. This is the data that you should consult before entering your grades on to the spreadsheet at QCommon, predicted grades, 2010/11. Number two please Mrs Bastic Styles...'

chapter two

Jacob Haliwell awoke from a fitful, post e taking sleep and saw that it was 12.15pm. It was Wednesday and he should have been in work at 10.00am. He weighed up his options. There was a message blinking on his answer phone that he decided to listen to later. He looked around at his room and saw the records and CDs scattered about the floor. He had spent the previous night and much of this morning listening in an e induced frenzy to every record in his collection – or at least that was the aim when he began. He had decided at around 7am that he hated every record that he owned and started to throw them into the bin outside the house. It was here that he encountered his neighbours dutifully setting off for work; he swallowed their pitying smiles before retreating to bed.

He lay on his bed and tried to conjure the image of Belle in his head. She would be teaching now or maybe on her lunch break. He knew this because she told him that she had her second teaching practice coming up and that she would be too busy to see anyone for a month or two. Her friend who was with her at the time had assured him that this was true since 'a PGCE course was one of the most stressful things anyone could do.' Jacob had mentioned war and chemotherapy but the friend said that he 'shouldn't belittle it with his own cynicism'.

He got up and picked his way through lots of records that he used to like and pressed the answer phone. The dulcet tones of Roy Downes shouted at him.

'Jacob Haliwell this is Roy Downes at *The Express* newspaper. It is 11.22am Wednesday the 17th December. If you're not in the office by 1pm today I will put your P45 in the post this afternoon and you can fuck off and try and get another job you lazy, drug head fuck. All the best, Roy.'

Jacob deleted the message and lay back down on the bed. He watched the ceiling for thirty seconds before reaching into the pocket of the shirt that he was still wearing from the night before. He walked into the kitchen and got a glass of water to help him swallow the ecstasy tablet. He then put on the nearest record to hand – a rare piece of German electronica, bought on a weekend trip to a Manchester – and settled in for the rest of the day.

chapter three

Jefferson was busy on the internet and phone. The e-mails from Ailsa were becoming increasingly fraught, fuelled by Jefferson's perceived lack of progress with the wedding arrangements. He fended her off with the successful completion of the wedding list, but she then insisted on some firm evidence of a booked church and a reception venue. He retaliated briefly, complaining that it was a huge job for one man to take on, but she saw him coming and reminded him in no uncertain terms that he volunteered for the job and had not as yet asked either her or her mother for any help, despite their continual offers of assistance. This spurred him into action and he secured the services of a printer just outside Penge who was happy to print the invitations and the order of service just as soon as Jefferson let him know where and when the event was taking place. With this logistical coup in the bag Jefferson turned his thoughts back to LG23.

He tried to return to LG23 the day before but found the lifts to be out of order and when he contemplated the lengthy walk down the ten flights of stairs, Aggy appeared, warning him that the stairs on the third, fourth and fifth floor were undergoing extensive repairs and so he would have to wait until the lifts were working again before venturing down there. The lifts returned to action just before five o'clock by which time Jefferson's curiosity had waned in favour of a quick pint in The Rose Bush, where he was joined by Ronald the driver who talked him through Arsenal's chances of winning the title that year. Jefferson waited for a chance to blame the referee for something but the occasion didn't arise.

Now with the wedding preparations completed for the day he was ready for a fresh reconnaissance of the Lower Ground floor.

Folder in hand, he looked both ways out the door before striding to the lift. The out of order signs had been removed from the day before and the lift arrived quickly. Stepping out on the Ground floor he greeted Lizzie with what he thought was just the right mixture of familiarity and purpose before taking the set of stairs down to the Lower Ground floor. At the bottom he turned right and walked to the door to LG23. Jefferson pushed at it and then tapped 321 in to the security pad but neither method opened the door. Unsurprised at his lack of success, he carefully looked around him before ducking into the same toilet as before. Once inside he locked the door and settled onto the seat expectantly. There was silence and after two or three minutes Jefferson wondered how long he was prepared to wait there. But then the voices came again.

'How long have you been here?'

'A good while sir.'

'You were afraid of the whip.'

'Yes sir.'

'The roars.'

'Yes sir.'

'The two big men.'

'Yes sir.'

'Do you know them?'

'No sir.'

'Are you native of these parts? Do you belong to these parts?'

'Yes sir.'

'That's all a pack of lies. Tell us the truth.'

The last word was followed by a scream and then a complete silence. Jefferson wondered if he should try to intervene. He tried to look through the vent by standing on tip toe on the toilet but to no avail. As he stood there the voices began again.

'You say we have to come back tomorrow?'

'Yes.'

'Then we can bring a good bit of rope.'

'Yes.'

'Didi.'

'Yes.'

'I can't go on like this.'

'That's what you think.'

'We'll hang ourselves tomorrow.'

'Well shall we go?'

'Pull on your trousers.'

'What?'

'Pull on your trousers.'

'You want me to pull off my trousers?'

'Pull on your trousers.'

'True.'

'Well? Shall we go?'

'Yes let's go.'

Jefferson listened at the vent with his mind struggling to register what he heard. He was torn between waiting to hear more and going to knock on the door. He waited but the voices appeared to have stopped so he clambered down from the toilet seat, unbolted the door and turned towards LG23. He got to the door and listened again before knocking on the door. Once he had knocked, he knocked again and waited. The third time he knocked as loudly as he could and shouted 'Hello. Hello this is Jefferson Tweedy could you open the door please? I am the Chief Executive of StanEd and I demand that you open the door.'

As he waited for a reply Liz the receptionist came down the stairs.

'Mr Tweedy is everything all right?'

'Oh hello Lizzie. Yes everything is fine but I need to get into this room. I don't want to alarm you but I've good reason to believe that somebody may be on the verge of harming themselves in there and I've no means of getting in. Where are the blasted security codes? This is simply ridiculous."

'Like I said Mr Tweedy, it's Mr Andrews that deals with that sort of thing after the business with the parent…'

'And the geography paper I know, I know.'

'Well I was only trying to be helpful Mr Tweedy.'

'I know you were Lizzie and I apologise for being short with you but this is just so frustrating. Where is Kenneth?'

'Well that's what I came down for sir. He called to see if I knew where you were. He says he's got some very important documents that he needs you to sign.'

'But I need him down here.'

'Well I presume he's waiting for you at your room sir, perhaps you can ask him up there.'

Jefferson exhaled a sigh befitting a chief executive under stress and followed Liz back up the stairs. He got into the lift and was greeted by Kenneth Andrews and Aggy outside his room on the ninth floor.

'Mr Jefferson there you are. You know sir it does make things very difficult if I have no means of knowing where you are. These documents are very important and an afternoon's delay could have terrible ramifications for the board's productivity.'

'Kenneth, who is in LG23?'

'I beg your pardon sir?'

'I said who is in LG23?'

'Well like I said only the other day sir, those rooms are very rarely used due to the damp conditions.'

'Someone is in there Kenneth and I want to know who it is. I am the chief executive of StanEd and I would like to know who is working in this building and what exactly they are doing.'

'Cup of tea sir?' interjected Aggy.

'Not now Aggy, thank you.'

'Now Mr Jefferson I'm sure there has been some mistake but I am as keen as you are to clear up any misunderstanding. Now why don't we go into your room, sign these documents, have a cup of tea and then you and I will go down to LG23 and resolve this issue once and for all. It is clearly causing you some vexation and as I said to Mr Roger – vexation is the enemy of a successful chief executive.'

'I've got those custard creams that you like sir,' said Aggy.

'Very well but straight after you will show me inside LG23. I have a feeling that something terrible may happen down there.'

'Really sir?'

'Yes, I do Kenneth.'

'Well we shall be as quick as possible in this task before going to investigate.'

Kenneth beckoned Jefferson into his office and Aggy followed straight behind them. By the time Jefferson sat in his chair, Aggy had placed a cup of tea with two custard creams in the saucer on his desk.

'There you are sir. I began to wonder when you weren't here for your afternoon tea and biscuits. I thought Mr Tweedy must be off ill, he never misses his afternoon tea and biscuits.'

'Look Aggy, with the greatest respect, it is not up to you what I do and don't do and if I don't want to be here for my afternoon tea and biscuits I won't be. Is that clear?'

'I'm sorry sir, I didn't mean to offend sir.'

'Now Kenneth where are these papers?'

'They are here sir. If you wouldn't mind putting a signature at the bottom, there are six items that need signing; a printing bill, a delivery of some anthologies and a few other bits and pieces. Now whilst you are doing these I must just pop outside for a moment and when I return we shall make our way down to LG23. Will that be satisfactory for sir?'

'Yes, yes and please make it quick Kenneth. I really would like to get to the bottom of this business as quickly as possible.'

As Kenneth Andrews left, Aggy turned around her trolley and headed for the door. Jefferson watched her go and swore that there would never be a repeat of such impertinence again.

It was five minutes later whilst waiting for the lift with

Kenneth Andrews that Jefferson first felt his stomach begin to move. It took on a shifting quality combining an uneasy stillness with heaving lurches. He breathed deeply a couple of times and exhaled noisily.

'Is everything all right Mr Jefferson?' inquired Kenneth.

'Yes, absolutely fine Kenneth.'

The lift arrived and both men stepped in. It was as he entered the lift that Jefferson knew he had lost the battle to control his bowels. He slammed the button to re-open the doors and hurtled out of the lift towards the nearest toilet. By the time he had covered the short distance from lift to toilet he was holding a supporting hand to the seat of his trousers to avoid any unseemly leakage. As he crashed into the toilet cubicle his trousers were already undone and his forehead was covered with sweat. He turned his face skywards with an overwhelming feeling of bliss as, secure on the toilet seat, he unclenched his sphincter muscles. Kenneth Andrews stepped out of the lift and asked quizzically through the toilet door,

'Is everything alright Mr Jefferson?'

When he received no reply he turned to his left and spoke to the on looking Aggy.

'Very odd Aggy, Mr Jefferson doesn't appear to be himself. I fear he becomes more like Mr Roger with every passing day.' And with that Kenneth Andrews about turned and bounced off down the corridor.

chapter four

Michael Harris, the head of English at St George's Cross School, had been on the phone for getting on for ten minutes. The two colleagues that were marking GCSE coursework in the English Office at the time heard him speak only intermittently over those ten minutes and never in full sentences.

'English.

Number three.

14245.

Michael Harris.

Option two.

1204/B.

Number one.'

He held the phone up to them at various intervals and they could hear *The Four Seasons* playing on the other end of the line.

'The last time I called them they had one of the Nolans singing songs from *Blood Brothers*, said Michael Harris, 'now it's the dreaded *Four Seasons*.'

'Well that's an improvement anyway.'

'Mmm…'

'Is it Nigel Kennedy?'

'Who cares?'

He waited again. He began to slowly shake his head and covering the mouthpiece spoke again to the two marking teachers.

'This is worthy of Kafka. Some unsuspecting fool calls up with an innocuous question that they want answered and before they know where they are they are dragged into some hellish parallel world of endless answer machines, Nigel Kennedy and redirected calls. Do you know I don't think I have ever spoken to the person I needed to speak to with this lot. In all my time spent hanging on this bloody phone – not once – just someone to answer one of my questions. In fact I know I haven't. Which does of course beg the question of why do I keep calling them? An excellent question and one that I would find almost impossible to answer.'

Towards the end of this speech Valerie Bastic Styles appeared at the door.

'Mr Harris.'

He pointed at the phone to show that he was busy.

'Have you got a minute? It is very important, the head teacher would like to see you.'

'Could you tell her I'll be along when I've succeeded in making contact with the undead at StanEd.'

A look of disbelieving joy came into Michael Harris' eyes and he held his hand up and spoke into the phone.

'Ah yes hello, I wonder if you can help me?'

Valerie Bastic Styles crossed from the door and proceeded to put her finger on the phone and disconnected the line. She then spoke very slowly and deliberately to the head of English.

'I'm afraid Mr Harris that the head teacher is very busy and the matter she wishes to talk to you about is very important. Now you can call the examinations board at any time but she needs to speak to you now. Now if you would like to come along.'

Michael Harris breathed deeply several times with his eyes fixed on the disconnected telephone. Valerie Bastic Styles had already made her way to the door and the head of English jerked out of his seat, smiled maniacally at his colleagues and followed the deputy head teacher out of the office.

He watched her bustling stride in front of him as they made their way through the school. They crossed a paved area where Mrs Bastic Styles barked at a pupil for not having his shirt tucked in and then entered the reception area for the school where the offices for the senior management team were situated. As they headed for the head teacher's office they passed a woman in a two piece suit sitting primly on a chair just to the left of the reception desk. Michael Harris looked fleetingly at her and surmised that she must be there for the head of Year 9 interviews. The post of head of Year 9 had recently been vacated by the departure of Harry Wells on health grounds. Harry Wells had been at the school for as long as anyone could remember and it was rumoured that he attended the school as a pupil before that. Over the past eighteen months the appearance and demeanour of Mr Wells had deteriorated to such a point that the pallor of Harry's face and the increasing bizarreness of his dress had been a source of wonder and speculation for the entire body of staff and pupils at St George's Cross. This had reached a climax six weeks before when Harry disappeared amid rumours of breakdowns and taking a hockey stick to Cornelius Evenett in Year 11.

Michael smiled winningly at the candidate and followed Mrs Bastic Styles towards the head teacher's office. She knocked briskly on the door and was answered with a call of 'enter'.

Michael thought that Mrs Carr looked as if she had been waiting for them.

'Ah Mr Harris, sit down.'

'Thank you.'

'I'd appreciate it Mrs Bastic Styles if you would stay and take some notes of the meeting for me.'

Michael's eyebrows furrowed whilst the deputy head teacher eagerly gathered the piece of A4 paper that the head teacher offered her.

'Now if you're ready Mrs Bastic Styles we'll begin. Mr Harris let me begin by telling you why I've asked you to come here today.'

'Okay.'

'I have reason to believe that you or a member of your department was exceptionally rude to both myself and the other members of the school's staff at our last Personal Development day.'

'Right. How was that exactly?'

'I quite distinctly heard – and Mrs Bastic Styles will second me on this won't you Mrs Bastic Styles…?'

'Indeed head teacher,' nodded Valerie Bastic Styles.

'A call of 'for fuck's sake' as I left the hall at the end of what had in every sense been a hugely successful and enjoyable PD day. I hope you agree with me on that point Mr Harris.'

'Do you want me to answer that now or are your questions purely rhetorical?'

'Please answer Mr Harris and I'd appreciate it if you answered honestly.'

'I thought it was hilarious head teacher but not in a good way.'

'And that I'm afraid Mr Harris is the root of your problem. This school has been wallowing in a culture of underachievement and bad results for too long and when someone comes in with a new way of doing things…'

'Like you,' said Michael Harris.

'Like me, with a new way of doing things to try and challenge that deep rooted apathy they are met with a wave of cynicism and negativity by the likes of you Mr Harris.'

'I don't think you could accuse my teaching of being apathetic Mrs Carr.'

'Well that's a matter of opinion as well Mr Harris. Yes your department gets satisfactory results…'

'Well above the school average.'

'But not above the borough average Mr Harris and that is what we are aiming for. Parts of your department's value added score were very questionable indeed and please don't forget that.'

Michael Harris looked away and shook his head.

'And so Mr Harris I ask, did you make the aformentioned comment at the last PD day as I left the assembly hall?'

There was a silence in the room before the head of English began his answer.

'It will pain you to hear Mrs Carr…'

'Head teacher,' interjected Valerie Bastic Styles.

Michael shot her a glance before continuing, '…that it was not me that made the blasphemous comment to which you refer. I may well have felt like saying that and indeed a few stronger words sprang into my mind during the course of the day, but I restrained myself, since in a position such as mine

I believe a man must set a suitable example for his young and impressionable colleagues.'

'But do you know who did say those words?'

'Of course I do head teacher, but if you think I am going to inform you of their name then you are sadly mistaken. Besides I wouldn't dream of stealing Mrs Bastic Styles' thunder; I'm sure it's only a matter of time before her renowned detecting skills finds you your man. After all she does have some past experience of this sort of thing. Isn't that the case Valerie?'

'May I remind you of your tone Mr Harris.'

'You may head teacher. Now have we finished?'

'You said 'your man' in your previous sentence. Are we to take it then that the perpetrator is male?'

'I don't believe this.'

'So it is?'

'Are we finished?'

'Yes I suppose we have finished and may I say that I have been deeply disappointed by your attitude in this meeting Mr Harris; disappointed but sadly unsurprised.'

'Good.'

As he left the office Michael Harris walked up to the smartly dressed candidate for the job of head of Year 9 and shook her hand.

'Do yourself a favour, go home.'

She had not formulated a reply by the time Michael Harris walked out of the door.

chapter five

Jefferson Tweedy had spent the past two days on a makeshift bed next to the toilet of his home in Balham. The experience of the rush to the ninth floor toilet was repeated at hourly intervals for the first day and a half before he dared to take some dry toast and a glass of lemonade just after what would have been lunchtime on the second day. This prompted something of a rush a couple of hours later but Jefferson felt that he had turned the corner. Ailsa called him three times a day, normally just as he sat down on the toilet, and offered commiserations and advice for her 'poor baby'. On the second day she wondered whether he might be able to arrange the food for the wedding between trips to the toilet and thought that it was about time they thought about flowers. She had seen a dress she liked on the internet and warned Jefferson not to try and look at it on any account. Jefferson promised to do his best to avoid the temptation before excusing himself and paying another of his increasingly painful trips to the toilet.

On the second day he also received a surprise call from

Lord McLeish of Dunblane. He recognised his steely Scottish tones immediately.

'How are you Geoffrey?'

'Oh you know Lord McLeish, been better.'

'I hear you've a stomach upset.'

'Yes, I'm afraid so.'

There was a pause in the conversation which Jefferson felt obliged to end.

'And how are things with you sir?'

'Very good. Listen Geoffrey I was calling to say well done on your work so far at StanEd. We're all very pleased with the way things have gone and we look forward to you continuing the good work. We're sure you'll keep it up. As you know we've got the examinations and results coming up in the not too distant future and that of course is where we all earn our corn. It is so vital in this first year that things run smoothly and of course I've no reason to believe that they wouldn't.'

'Absolutely.'

'There'll be speeches and the like but we'll talk about them nearer to the time.'

'Of course. As soon as I'm back on my feet I'll be straight to it.'

'How long do you think you'll be?'

'Oh a couple of days, you know how these things are.'

'Jolly good. And how are the arrangements for the wedding? Has Ailsa got you running around?'

'Oh yes. Between you and me I'm not sure we're going to get everything done in time for August, but don't tell her that.'

'Well if you need any help just ask her mother, she specialises in that sort of thing. She loves a project does my wife.'

'Thank you Lord McLeish, I might just do that.'

'Rest up Geoffrey and we'll see you soon.'

'Yes, see you soon.' Jefferson put the phone down just in time for another dash to the toilet.

chapter six

There was silence in room LG23. Kate Woodslit, in role as Meg in Pinter's 'The Birthday Party', sat alongside Laurence Chevalier as Stanley. He sat impassively as she whined into his ear.

'It's your birthday, Stan. I was going to keep it a secret until tonight.'

'No.'

'It is. I've bought you a present. (Meg gets up and picks up a parcel, bringing it over to Stanley.) Here. Go on. Open it.'

'What's this?'

'It's your present.'

'It isn't my birthday Meg.'

'Of course it is – open your present.'

(Stanley looks at the parcel dumbly and then opens it.)

'It's a drum, a boy's drum.'

'It's because you haven't got a piano. Aren't you going to give me a kiss?'

Kenneth Andrews opened the door. He was about to speak before being quietened by the frantic waving of the director Richard Curtain. Kenneth mimed an apology and sat down in the nearest available chair. The director stroked his lilac neckerchief and turned his attention back to the drama.

'There are some sticks in there.'

'Shall I put it around my neck?'

(Stanley looks dumbly at her before putting the drum around his neck. He then begins to walk around the table beating the drum regularly. On the second turn around the table his drumming becomes more erratic and Meg begins to look concerned. He finally stands above her and drums savagely. He then drops the drum, steps into it and begins to strangle her. Kate screams,

'Stanley!'

'No, no, no, cut, cut, cut,' cried Richard Curtain. 'For Christ's sake Larry what are you doing love? You're thinking the end of Act Two, we're in Act One here. It's just a savage beating of the drum and then lights out. No strangling.'

'Richard may I have a word?' interjected Kenneth Andrews.

'Kenneth please, I'll be with you in one minute. Look Larry if we don't get this straight now, we'll never get it straight.'

Behind the actors a phone rang once. As Richard Curtain explained the difference between the end of Act One and the end of Act Two 'The Birthday Party', the phone diverted onto a recited list of options. A pre-recorded female voice informed the caller: 'If you wish to discuss exam entries press or say one, if you wish to place an order press or say two'. Simultaneously a digital clock on the desk began to tick. As the message finally reached 'if you wish to speak to an operator please press seven,' the digital clock had clicked around to 45 seconds. The caller then made their choice and Vivaldi's The Four Seasons began to play. Intermittently over the music a woman's voice would repeat 'Thank you for calling StanEd. All our operators are busy at the moment. You can contact us on e-mail at enquiries@staned.org.uk. Thank you for holding.' As the digital clock clicked around to 4.32, Jean Plowstraight, who was idly manning the desk, began to look mildly disconcerted. She pressed another button and the pre-recorded voice began again. 'Thank you for holding, all our operators are busy at the moment. To help us to process your call please give your centre number after the tone...I'm sorry I did not hear your answer to the last question. Please say your name and position clearly...I'm sorry your answers have not been registered, please press the star button to begin the procedure again.'

'You're petrified Larry. You've been running from your terrible past and they've caught up with you. The pretence is over, the cosy little life in a south coast B and B is under attack. They're here for you.'

'Why does he stay Dickie? Why does he stay? He knows they're here and yet he stays with this dreadful old crone; no offence Katie love.'

'To move is to acknowledge his guilt Larry. Throughout the play he pleads ignorance. Once he does not act immediately he cannot act at all. It's a terrifying and all too human dilemma.'

'So no strangling at the end of Act One?'

'No strangling at the end of Act One. We save that terrible act of betrayal for the denouement of the party scene itself. The moment where he vents his helpless anger on the very woman who has offered him a bolt hole from his sinful past.'

'Jolly good Dickie.'

The digital clock beside the phone had clicked around to 9.53 and Jean Plowstraight straightened herself in her chair.

'Persistent bastard.'

As the clock ticked to 10.00 she picked up the hand piece and smiled.

'Good afternoon this is StanEd, thank you for holding, how can I help you?'

The line went dead and Jean Plowstraight said 'Suit yourself,' before turning to the other actors and smiling,

'Another satisfied customer.'

'He probably died on the line, poor bitch,' said Larry Chevalier.

Kenneth Andrews took this moment to take the floor. 'Now if we could all gather over here please since I do have some very important matters to discuss.'

'Well make it quick Ken we need all the rehearsing we can get. These plays don't put themselves on you know,' said Richard Curtain.

Kenneth Andrews waited for the company of actors to assemble in a circle of chairs before beginning. He spoke in measured tones.

'Well this is what we need to talk about. I'm afraid the rehearsing will have to take a back seat for a while.'

There were howls of consternation from the actors before Richard Curtain spoke for the troop.

'Ken, you wretched man. You said we had until April.'

'And you will have until April, Richard and time after April as well – that I can guarantee you.'

'Have the numbers come in then?' asked Jean Plowstraight.

'No the numbers aren't in yet Jean, although they will be

in soon and that's when we really need to get to work. No, this is a slightly different situation and one that will only last for a couple of days.'

There were murmurs from the company before Larry Chevalier stood up in a manner reminiscent of his well received Prince Hal and projected,

'What exactly are you are you asking of us Kenneth and how will it impact on my Stanley?'

He sat back down to have his shoulders rubbed in appreciation by Katie Woodslit and the actors listened intently to Kenneth Andrews' words.

'You are free to rehearse as usual for the rest of today...'

'Good, good.'

'...but tomorrow and possibly the day after I shall need you to carry out the jobs that you learnt when you first arrived.'

'But this is outrageous Kenneth,' barnstormed Richard Curtain. 'Our agreement, and I quote, was that on Friday mornings we respond to the week's e-mails and the rest of the week is free for our art. The only departure from this routine is for the entering of your numbers, which is estimated to take three weeks and is to be completed at any point between April and July.'

His voice quivered on the last syllable of July and those seated beneath him could clearly see the flare of indignation in his nostrils. Kenneth Andrews spoke over the cries of agreement from the rest of the company.

'Richard I understand your position but I come to ask you for a favour. I am not one to scaremonger as well you know, but suffice to say if these next couple of days are not negotiated safely then all of our futures may be in doubt.'

'Are you invoking the spectre of redundancy Kenneth?' said Richard Curtain.

'Absolutely not Richard. I am simply saying that the rehearsal space that you get paid to use for forty nine weeks of the year may no longer be available to you.'

The actors hushed and contemplated this dreadful fate.

Kenneth continued. 'Now that would be the very last thing that I would wish for as well you know. I am a keen devotee of your work and indeed thought your recent version of 'Macbeth' to be nothing short of a triumph.'

Murmurs of 'Many thanks' emitted from the company.

'And so I ask you to oblige me by putting your rehearsals on hold for two days and for those two days you will be required to perform the jobs we practised when you arrived back in September.'

Kenneth Andrews' words hung in the air and Richard Curtain looked first at him and then at the rest of the actors. He then waved them in to the centre of the room to form a huddle of decision. After a minute or so of murmured discussion and much earnest nodding and shaking Richard Curtain detached himself from the group and addressed Kenneth Andrews. He bowed deeply from the waist and then straightened up with a small adjustment of his neckerchief.

'In light of your kind words and in the spirit of the community of the Arts – we shall.'

chapter seven

The side doors had been thrown open to allow some wafts of spring night air to infiltrate the stifling heat of the St George's College school hall. The alphabetical rows of plastic blue seats were filled by 7.15pm and the audience members that had arrived later than this were now standing in the side aisles and at the back of the hall. The school jazz band and a singer were running through their repertoire of jazz standards at the front of the hall and the music was accompanied by the low hum of chatter from the waiting audience. The singer was a sixth former with shaggy brown curls who looked too old to be at school. He was hurtling through a rendition of 'The Lady is a Tramp' whilst the members of the audience who were clapping tried manfully to keep up with him.

The singer sat out the band's rendition of 'Take Five' and then at 7.35pm the hall lights dimmed and the crowd sent up a whoop of excited encouragement. Accompanied by a drum roll of epic proportions two slim figures mugged their way through the velvet stage curtains before standing, arms aloft, basking in the crowd's applause and whistles. On the left stood a handsome sixth form boy from St George's College and on the right stood an equally handsome sixth form girl from St Ignatius' Girls School. St Ignatius' was the local school for girls that lent girls with a dramatic disposition to the college for most of their school shows. The comperes gestured for their audience to be quiet and the crowd briefly settled down before erupting in response to their hosts cries of 'Good Evening.' Over the top of the response the hosts called out,

'Good Evening I'm Rory Jackson.'

'And I'm Jenny Alexander.'

'And together we are your hosts.'

The crowd roared their approval, whilst backstage wigs and suspenders were being adjusted amidst pulled faces and predictable jokes.

'So without further ado let's get on with the show.'

'To begin our show we are lucky enough to have some very foxy ladies.'

'Oooohhhhh'

'That's right Rory. The strapping lads from 12DG are here to give you a treat.

Please put your hands together and give it up for Britney, Christina, Madonna and Scary Spice, ladies and gentlemen I give you – The Divas.'

The curtains opened to a wall of screams and wolf whistles. The boys stood with their backs to the audience striking a variety of exotic poses. The crowd stood up as the music began.

In her office at St George's Cross School the figures on the spreadsheet were swimming in front of Emma Carr's eyes. She had been trying to 'get a handle' on the latest figures showing a comparison between the value added attainment of Afro/Caribbean students on free school dinners with their equivalent white Caucasian students. She knew there was something useful in the data but at this time of night she was struggling to pick out the pertinent information.

On Wednesday nights Luke stayed at her mother's house to give Emma the chance to catch up on her paper work. In preparation for these nights she had bought herself a futon bed that was kept in a cupboard in Janet's office; she had also brought a few sets of work clothes from home which were also kept in there.

At 7pm every Wednesday she called her mother's house and spoke to Luke. Tonight he told her how grandma had made him a cake and then asked if they could get a dog like grandma's. She'd heard the voice call out 'your mother's not in enough to look after a dog,' and she'd said that grandma was right, it wouldn't be fair on the dog. Luke had replied, 'okay' and then informed her that he was off to bed because grandma had promised to read him a story with monsters in it. She'd said that sounded lovely and told him she loved him.

Emma pushed back on her chair and then got up to stretch her legs. She walked to the window and watched as the caretaker headed down the path and towards the school gates. As he pulled the gates together she could see the graffiti that scarred the metal and made a mental note to remind the caretaker to get rid of it in the morning. Once the gates were pulled together the caretaker reached for the enormous set of keys that he carried around on his belt and locked the gates for the night. As they clanged shut, Emma's attention was drawn to the sound of laughter which carried into her office.

She looked to her right and realised that it must be coming from the college.

In St George's College the audience were enjoying the last few moments of a sketch entitled 'Staff Room' which featured a cast of sixth formers imitating an array of teachers from the two schools. Howls of delight went up as the sketch finished with the students playing Mrs Williams and Mr Castle engaged in a steamy clinch that ended with both of them falling onto the sofa with legs akimbo.

The curtains shut and Rory and Jenny rushed back on to the stage.

Rory shouted,

'Who'd have thought it eh?'

Whilst Jenny held up a card that prompted the audience to bellow,

'Everyone!'

'Right then, next is for many the highlight of the evening. In a night of stars this is the biggest star of all. Each year he honours us with a performance and this year we are as delighted as ever to welcome him back to the Sixth Form Show. Ladies and gentlemen I give you the head master of St George's College – Mr J.P.P. Montgomery!'

The crowd roared and stamped their feet as the doors at the back of the hall swung open. There stood J.P.P. Montgomery, resplendent in blond pig tail wig, shimmering red dress and tottering red heels. The crowd roared their approval at his entrance and then hushed as the band struck up. J.P.P. Montgomery sashayed down the aisle through the introduction and then began in a Rex Harrison style sing/talk.

'I'm a just a girl who can't say no,
I'm in a terrible fix.
I always say come on let's go,
Just when I oughta say nix.'

By the time he had reached the stage, a screen with the words to the song had dropped into position and the head teacher picked up a huge stick from the side of the stage and vaguely pointed behind him as he continued to sing. Legs that betrayed a rugby playing past and a stomach that confirmed a lifelong passion for good living, stuck out of the satin red dress and bobbed and wobbled along with the song. His preferred action to accompany the singing was a theatrical opening of his heavily made up eyes followed by a heavy wink to prompt a cheer from his adoring audience and this was a trick that he drew upon freely. As the song moved towards its climax, he turned and wiggled his backside extravagantly towards the audience before throwing down the stick and hitching his skirt up a notch. He then threw his left hand high to the ceiling and then followed it with his right and this was the pose in which he finished his routine. The crowd whistled and roared their tributes and after removing his pig tail wig Montgomery took their applause, bowing deeply and waved lavishly as he departed the stage.

Rory Jackson ran back on stage and threw his hands towards the door where Montgomery had departed and shouted,

'Our head master,' before joining the rest of the audience in their applause.

chapter eight

When Jefferson's stomach could be relied upon to make it
through a whole day without numerous frantic dashes to the
nearest toilet, he returned to work. Kenneth Andrews greeted
him with zealous bonhomie and was 'delighted to see our
leader back and looking in such fine fettle'.

Jefferson also accepted a warm welcome back from Aggy,
before settling into his office and checking his e-mails. There
were two from Ailsa and three from his mother-in-law to be.
In a moment of weakness – which in hindsight he put down
to his recent feverish condition – he had asked Patricia
McLeish to help him with the wedding arrangements. Within
an hour of the request she faxed him a double sided sheet of
instructions. Each task had a detailed summary of its
contents and beside it a set of initials signifying who was to
carry out that particular task and a date for when it was
expected to be completed by. After a close inspection
Jefferson surmised that he had only two tasks. The first was
to decide upon his choice of best man and ushers and the
second was to arrange the suits for them, Lord McLeish and
himself. On reflection this seemed to Jefferson to be an

excellent outcome and he printed off the list and tucked it safely into a drawer.

The e-mails from Ailsa conveyed her delight that he had finally chosen to involve her mummy in the arrangements and thanked him for all the hard work he had done so far on the wedding. He noted that she made no mention of his recent illness and briefly wondered if she was having an affair.

He also took the opportunity to check the progress of his bid of £65 for a genuine World War II German helmet on eBay. He had lodged the bid on the morning of his dash to the ninth floor toilet and now found to his dismay that the helmet had been sold the previous day for £80; he wondered if he would have been prepared to bid that high for it.

Midway through this contemplation Kenneth Andrews arrived at his door. Jefferson noted that Kenneth's hair appeared to be sporting a touch more hair product than was normal for him and this made his parting appear more severe then usual.

'I thought I'd give you time to settle in Mr Jefferson. Is everything satisfactory sir?'

'Yes thank you Kenneth.'

'And how are you feeling sir?'

'Very chipper Kenneth, very chipper.'

'Delighted to hear it sir. You'll be delighted to know that things have run wonderfully smoothly here sir. It really is a tribute to the systems you have put in place that even without your presence the great machine can still function.'

'Kenneth I was wondering...'

'Yes sir?'

'About LG23?'

'You took the words out of my mouth sir, of course LG23. Unfinished business so to speak sir.'

'If you like. Not that I wish to seem pushy.'

'Not at all sir. Would sir like to accompany me now?'

'Well it's as good a time as any isn't it.'

'Absolutely Mr Jefferson.'

Kenneth motioned extravagantly towards the lift and Jefferson thanked him. As they got into the lift Kenneth asked,

'Are you feeling quite well sir?'

'Yes thank you Kenneth, I don't know what came over me the last time.'

'Perhaps something you ate sir?'

'Possibly, possibly.'

They got out on the ground floor and both greeted Liz on the reception desk. She smiled and said,

'Nice to see you looking better Mr Tweedy.'

'Thank you Liz, I've never felt better.'

They descended the stairs to the Lower Ground floor and turned right towards room LG23.

'Here we are sir,' said Kenneth and knocked on the door. They waited for a moment before Larry Chevalier opened the door.

'Ah good morning Laurence I was wondering if we might have a look around. Mr Tweedy has expressed a strong desire to see the troops in action so to speak. Is now a convenient time?'

'Well we are very busy as you know Mr Andrews, but we're always pleased to oblige the likes of yourself and Mr Tweedy.'

'Very kind of you.'

Kenneth Andrews walked into the room and Larry Chevalier sidled up beside Jefferson.

'If I may say what an honour it is to have you look around our work station sir.'

'Oh not at all, not at all.'

'I can't tell you how much me we appreciate the improvements you've made here at StanEd. We're proud to work for you sir.'

Jefferson felt his hand being grasped in a vice like grip and the odd man in front of him looked him dead in the eyes.

'A privilege sir, a privilege.'

As Jefferson freed his hand from the clammy grasp of the staring eyed employee he walked into the centre of the room and looked around. To his right the phone rang and he listened as Jean Plowstraight brightly answered the caller's enquiries. Kate Woodslit sat with glasses on the end of her nose and pored over a computer screen. She rocked back on her chair and asked,

'Richard, just remind me the un-annotated anthologies come in for 2011 don't they?'

'That's right, but only for the 2024/A syllabus. 2024/B comes in the following year.'

'Thanks.' And she tapped the response into the computer.

Richard Curtain himself was leafing through a pile of papers. He looked up at Jefferson,

'Order forms and more order forms. The syllabus has never been more popular Mr Tweedy.'

Jefferson turned to Kenneth.

'But I thought you said this room wasn't being used.'

'Well it wasn't Mr Jefferson, but we are coming up to our busiest time of the year and the English enquiries unit which you see in action here have had to utilise an extra room due to sheer demand.'

'Can we handle the extra demand?'

'What do you think?'

He looked at Jean Plowstraight as she spoke into the phone, 'That's alright sir it was a pleasure. Is there anything else I can help you with now? Many thanks for your call.'

'But what about the voices I heard in the room?'

'Where did you hear these voices sir?'

'Well in the toilet?'

'Really sir?'

'Yes through an air vent.'

'Oh yes sir? And this was a couple of days before your funny turn in the lift wasn't it sir?'

'Well yes, but I don't think the two things are linked.'

'Absolutely not sir. Well, have you seen enough sir or would you like to stay a little longer?'

'No that was all very impressive. Many thanks everyone and keep up the good work.'

'We will,' chorused the conscientious actors and by the time Jefferson and Kenneth had made their way back to the ninth floor Larry Chevalier had already placed his hands around Kate Woodslit's neck and placed his foot firmly inside the children's drum.

Meanwhile in the English office at St George's Cross, his hand still on the receiver, Michael Harris announced to no one in particular, 'I don't believe it; I've just made contact with the undead!'

chapter nine

Jacob Haliwell had been indoors for the best part of a month. His only contact with the outside world was leaving a couple of messages on Belle's answer phone which she had not responded to.

He never returned to the offices of *The Express* and duly received his P45 through the post the day after Roy Downes left the message on his answer phone. On a couple of occasions since, he had bought a copy of the paper and noted that the temp girl from the foreign desk was now doubling up as entertainment correspondent. The celebrity photographs had changed slightly in recent weeks, focussing on the participants of a recent reality television show as they cashed in on their new found, soon to be lost, fame, but other than that everything remained the same. Jacob spent a few minutes thinking of headlines for the pictures and was slightly disconcerted to find that his efforts were no better than the temp girl's.

After a month inside Jacob wandered out and sat in the park, then walked down the high street and discovered a world he had never known before. A world of people who spent their day in the local Wetherspoon's pub nursing a pint of shandy and staring out of the window at the passing people. A world where the cared for and the caring filled their days with walks to the shops and around the park. A world where men of a certain age longed for the routine of a working day and stood and listened while their wives chatted to their friends.

Jacob went home and went to bed.

The day after, Belle called.

'Jacob?'

'Hello Belle.'

'How are you?'

'Great, yourself?'

'Really busy. I've got my final assessment next week.'

'Is that the one that decides whether or not you've passed?'

'Pretty much yeah.' She paused. 'So I called *The Express* and they told me that you'd left.'

'Sacked actually.'

'Yeah they did say that. The words 'useless cunt' were mentioned as well which I thought I'd tell you just to lift your spirits.'

'Much obliged; who did you speak to?'

'Roy Downes.'

'Charming isn't he?'

'Every girl's dream. So what have you been doing?'

'Er, nothing,'

'Well you must have done something.'

'No quite literally, nothing.'

'Good then. It's important to make the most of these little time outs.'

'I did call up for a couple of quizzes on a daytime show

but didn't get through. I knew the answer as well. Which of the following is a former Prime Minister of Great Britain a. Tony Blair or b. Lionel Blair.'

'Shame.'

'Isn't it. He's not so good on the politics but boy can he dance.'

'So what are you going to do?'

'Belle, I have no idea.'

'Oh.'

'Can we go out soon?'

'Soon yes but I've got to get these next few weeks out of the way. You can't believe how much work there is to do.'

'I bet.'

There was a pause.

'Look why don't you pick me up from school on Thursday. I've got a quiet day on a Friday and I'd rather have an early one and then get home.'

'Great, where is it? Forest Hill?'

'No that was the first placement at St Stephen's, I finished there at Christmas. This place is in Dulwich, St George's Cross School. We finish at 3.00pm.'

'Long day then.'

'Don't start, you have no idea.'

'I know, I know. Will it be in the A to Z?'

'Yeah, it's on St George's Road.'

'That figures. What's it like there then?'

'Hard. You've met the head teacher at that syllabus launch, Emma Carr.'

'Oh yeah I remember her, she was impressed that I worked on the Entertainment desk.'

'Perhaps you can further impress her with the fact that

you've now been sacked and replaced by a girl called Cydney who spells Nigeria with two gs.'

'I'm sure Ms Carr would understand very keenly that it was an act of principle that caused me to throw myself on my journalistic sword.'

'Your ecstasy laced sword.'

'I'm off it.'

'Oh bully for you. What was it about looking at yourself in the mirror and seeing a sad mid-thirties man lost to a drug from his far ago youth that made you give up?'

'Thank you.'

'Besides if you asked Mike Harris about Emma Carr and principles he'd laugh out loud.'

'Who's Mike Harris?'

'The head of English at St George's Cross.'

'Is he not a fan then?'

'You could say that. He says that she doesn't like teachers.'

'Isn't that a case of self loathing?'

'He says that she doesn't consider herself to be a teacher, she sees herself as a manager.'

'What do you think?'

'Oh I don't know yet but I have observed a lot of other lessons as part of my course and there are some spectacularly bad teachers, so I suppose she's got to do something.'

'What's this Mike Harris like?'

'Oh he's brilliant. Don't get me wrong there are a lot of brilliant teachers but there's a lot of rubbish here as well.'

'Well tell me who they are and I'll get round and tell them when I come over there on Friday. If I've learnt one thing from King Dick Gittens' regime it's how to tell people they're shit.'

'I'm sure they'll be delighted but you're not allowed to include me in that. I'm only just starting, I'm allowed to be bad at it.'

'I'm sure you're not.'

'No I'm not actually but it wouldn't do to blow one's own trumpet would it?'

'Heaven forbid.'

'Heaven forbid. See you there then.'

'See you there. 3.00?'

'3.00.'

chapter ten

The Guinness hospitality tent at Cheltenham races was packed with noisy race goers. Some, like J.P.P. Montgomery, were fresh from St George's Blue's triumph in the two o'clock race, whilst others despite the very best of intentions had not yet managed to see any of the actual racing. These people chose rather to hear tell of the races in the safety of the Guinness tent, lest an expedition to track side should result in either a loss of drinking time, no re-admittance to the hospitality tent or a return to find the Guinness had run dry. None of these calamitous outcomes could be risked and so they settled for second hand tales of photo finishes and torn up betting slips before solemnly promising to make it down for the next race.

As J.P.P. Montgomery spilled the champagne over the top of his glass he looked up with mock wide eyes and said,

'I must be losing my touch!'

The assembled group of St George's College governors broke into gales of laughter and lifted their glasses as Montgomery proposed the toast.

'To St George's Blue …' he paused for dramatic effect and looked around the group, 'and the St Leger.'

'To St George's Blue and the St Leger,' they echoed before drinking fully from their flutes.

As they savoured the moment, a grey haired man with a florid face asked, 'Is she really ready for the St Leger, Philip?'

Montgomery sipped well from his champagne before answering,

'My dear boy, did she look as if she wasn't ready for it today?'

Montgomery went on. 'I'd go as far as to say that if she runs like he did today she'll win the damn thing.'

'It was a good field she beat.'

'Indeed it was and she simply pulled away from them.' Montgomery paused to top up his glass of champagne. 'Listen let's not get carried away but I speak regularly to dear old Buffy down at the stables and she tells me that worse horses than St George's Blue have won Classics. Her plan was for her to show well today, which I think we all agree she did…'

'Hear hear!' chimed the group.

'…and then have her on the gallops in the run up to the big one.'

Behind them a pack of athletic young men entered the tent on a wave of loud laughter and shouts. Montgomery looked disapprovingly over his shoulder before turning back to the group of governors.

'This used to be the sport of kings you know.'

The governors looked towards the laughing pack and watched as a gaggle of blonde women selling cigarettes converged on the group of young men. One blonde was picked up by the tallest of the men and thrown over his shoulder to a great shout of 'aye ayes' and 'go on big fella.'

A slightly built governor with steel rimmed glasses drew the group's attention away from the rowdiness by asking,

'How are things at the school Philip?'

'Oh pretty good really Paul. We battle on in the face of outside interference and mindless administration. You wouldn't believe the sort of things we're required to do but then that seems to be the way it's all going.'

'And what do you make of this new board – StanEd is it?'

'Not a lot. I had the pleasure of hearing the great Jefferson Tweedy speak at the launch.'

'He's the guy in charge isn't he?'

'Yes the new wunderkind of British education.'

'And?'

'He never speaks for more than a minute. He stands up, delivers few bon mots and then he's off. It's a classic piece of New Labour smoke 'n' mirrors.'

'He's not good news for us though is he?'

'If I thought he'd have any impact Paul I'd have a view on that, but how many of his like have we seen before?'

'Quite right but there is this new syllabus isn't there?'

'Oh yes and our boys will do very well in it. If you're bright, you're bright. The point that these people miss with such unerring accuracy is that the type of exam that you choose to give these kids is a complete irrelevance; it is the means to the end, not the end in itself.'

'I notice Miss Carr from over the road is never out of the local paper. There doesn't seem to be a week goes by without her announcing some innovation or other. How do you find her Philip?'

'Not enough syllables.'

'Pardon?'

'She doesn't have enough syllables in her name. And that may be metaphorically true as well.'

'No doubt she's all in favour of these latest developments.'

'Oh the divine Miss Carr could barely hold her water after the Reverend Tweedy had preached. If she had mentioned 'level playing fields' once more I don't know what I should have done. Oh yes the zealous Miss Carr can see her future bright and clear before her.'

A huge Neanderthal roar went up from behind them and they turned to see the athletic boys pouring Guinness all over one of the blonde cigarette girls. She feigned horror and squealed whilst the boys screamed their encouragement.

J.P.P. Montgomery turned back to the group of governors, 'Time for the 3.30 I think gentlemen.'

chapter   eleven

Jacob arrived at St George's Cross School at three o'clock on the Thursday afternoon. He caught a train and a bus to get there and spent the journey hoping that Belle had taken her car to school. He had shaved for the first time in a couple of weeks and looked carefully at himself in the windows of shops and cars as he walked past. He found that he preferred the look of himself in the windows of smaller cars; he thought it was something to do with the angle, the commanding under shot of the Mussolini propaganda pictures. He also found that the shops with tinted windows were more flattering than those that reflected him in the stark and pallid reality. He asked the bus driver where he needed to get off for St George's Cross School to which the driver replied,

'You'll know – they'll all be getting on.'

And sure enough they arrived. The uniform consisted of a black jumper and a grey blazer with a red and black striped tie. Most of the boys seemed to favour a shortened version of the traditional tie, worn loosely in a fat knot three quarters of the way up the shirt. The jumper was often hidden by a hooded top and baseball caps and trainers seemed to be compulsory. As the pupils surged on to the bus, waving their passes in the general direction of the driver, Jacob felt a distinct sense of relief that he was getting off. His mind went back to his own school days and school assemblies where his teachers warned him and his peers that their presence in large numbers may be perceived as being threatening by members of the public, especially the elderly. He wondered if he was becoming elderly.

As he got off the bus he found himself amidst a hoard of school children. The noise level was extraordinary. None of them appeared to talk below the level of a shout and their preferred form of conversation was a bellowed exchange with a friend who had to be standing at least ten feet away from them. When he set out on his journey he envisaged a quiet period of observation outside the school before meeting a smiling Belle at the gates. At no point did he imagine encountering any children and now he he wasn't sure that he liked it.

What would he be mistaken for here? A parent? A paedophile? An ice cream man? Or the older boyfriend waiting for his school age girlfriend? By his recollection these were the only people that hung around outside school gates. He feared that to the casual on looker his age and conspicuous lack of a van probably placed him in the paedophile category.

Would Belle meet him out here or was he supposed to go in and meet her?

He contemplated having a walk round the block but then chose bravery and entered through the school gates. He figured that he could wait in the reception if Belle wasn't ready.

The grounds of the school were fairly empty except for a

few pockets of children standing around, waiting. As he followed the signs to reception he walked across a paved area surrounded by tired looking buildings and a series of conspicuous yellow bins with huge signs urging students to 'Take a Pride in Your Environment'. Behind him another long distance conversation was taking place between one of the group of loiterers and a girl thirty yards in front of him.

'How long does she say you're gonna be?

'I've got a Level.'

'Ah, long mate.'

'Wait for me yeah.'

'You're long mate.'

'No wait for me yeah.'

The girl turned back and headed into one of the buildings whilst Jacob looked around for the reception. The signs led him into a building that seemed older than the others. The other buildings were painted in garish shades of blue and purple which reminded him of some bastard hybrid of a swimming pool and a playground, but the reception building was made of red brick and obviously represented the 'traditional' heart of the school. Inside the building Jacob was greeted by a middle aged woman behind a desk. She had dyed blonde hair and an open smile.

'Can I help?'

'Yes, I'm here to meet my friend, Belle Jones.'

'Is she a teacher?'

'Yes. Well she's a student, you know a trainee.'

'Oh right, which subject?'

'English.'

'Right you take a seat and I'll give the English department a call.'

Jacob looked around the walls. They were covered with a mixture of students' art work and laminated photocopies of inspirational mottos such as 'You only start to achieve when you start to believe' and 'What have you done today to make you feel proud?' Jacob felt as if he had been called to see the head master. The woman called over to him.

'Do you want to go over? She's busy at the moment but she won't be long.'

'Thanks. Which way is it?'

'Out of the door and it's the first building on the right. You want room CGN.'

'Many thanks.'

Jacob walked back out into the paved area. He looked around him and contemplated the fact that people actually worked in places like this for a living. He had not thought of school since the day he left Greenford Boys and had certainly never associated them with adult life. When he met people that said they were teachers he wheeled out the usual lines, 'it must be great to be doing something worthwhile,' and 'that must be very rewarding,' but he had never actually thought about what it meant to be a teacher. To work in a place like this all day and to actually try to teach the kids that he'd seen getting on the bus. The thought made him shudder. He tried to envisage Belle as a teacher, actually in the classroom. He couldn't imagine her telling anyone off and certainly not those boys with the hooded tops on the bus, but then he couldn't imagine anyone telling off those boys with the hooded tops. He felt very middle class.

He reached the building on the right and went in through the double doors. He turned left down a corridor and looked into the classrooms as he passed them. Children's work was displayed on all of the walls and teachers sat hunched over desks. Music came from one room and the sound of a hoover from another. As he neared the end of the corridor he peered into another classroom and saw Belle standing over a small looking boy who was sitting at a desk. Not wanting to be seen, Jacob edged away from the window and leant against the wall on the other side of the corridor. Belle then moved away from where she was and he could no longer see her. He edged forward and looked through the classroom window; she was sitting next to the boy. He watched as she pushed her hair back where it had fallen over her face and he could see that her cheek was slightly flushed. Now he was next to the door he could hear the muffled voice of the boy reading from the book in front of him. After a minute or so the boy stopped reading and turned to Belle who appeared to be answering his question. He watched attentively and then turned back to the book. The boy read for another minute or so during which time Jacob realised the noise of the hoover had stopped. The boy's head raised and then he began to outline with his hands a vast shape of some kind in front of him, he started to waggle his fingers rapidly as if he were representing fire with his hands and then he stood up and grabbed his blazer from behind a chair and put it over his head before acting out a tableau of hopping and jumping in front of Belle. Jacob looked both ways down the corridor to check that it was empty and then looked back into the room. The boy was back at his desk and Belle now had the book and was reading aloud. She read for a minute more before closing the book and turning to the boy. Jacob moved away from the window and returned to his original position. Soon the door opened and the boy, now complete with hood and trainers, looked briefly at him before turning left and heading down the corridor.

A moment later Belle came out of the room and stopped when she saw Jacob.

'You're here.'

'I'm here.'

'Do you normally skulk round school corridors?'

'Only on Thursdays.'

'Well you my friend have just missed a moment to treasure. Now it will mean nothing whatsoever to you but Raymond Baxter has just asked me, and I repeat asked me, if he could stay behind and read some more of the book with me.'

'Who's Raymond Baxter?'

'Raymond Baxter is a little sod who is not allowed out at break time, for fear of what he will do to the rest of the school community.'

'Which book?'

'*The Outsiders* by S.E. Hinton.'

'I've read it, it's a good book.'

'I know, it's a very good book, but the extraordinary thing is, Raymond Baxter thinks it's a very good book. Now he didn't say that exactly but he asked to stay behind and read some more of it in his own time. He was hanging around outside and I thought he was waiting for a mate and then when everybody had left he came in and asked. Now we only did ten minutes but my God, my God, this is something wonderful. I've got to tell Mike.'

Belle headed off to Jacob's left and he followed her into an office where a man in his early fifties was sitting at a computer screen. Belle began talking as soon as she saw him.

'Mike, Raymond Baxter has just voluntarily stayed behind to read *The Outsiders*.'

The man turned from the computer with a theatrically quizzical expression, 'Are we talking about THE Raymond Baxter?'

'The very same.'

The man got up from the computer screen and shook Belle by the hand – Jacob noticed that he was wearing a wedding ring.

'My dear girl, if I may just take the liberty of congratulating you on a remarkable feat. Savour the moment – for these are the very things that we are here for. Well done indeed.'

Releasing his hand the man turned to Jacob and offered him the same hand.

'I don't believe we've been introduced. I'm Mike Harris, pleased to meet you.'

'Jacob Haliwell, I've heard a lot about you.'

'You must excuse our joy but we tend to get over excited by little things like that around here. Are you the journalist that Belle's always talking about?'

'Sort of, I used to be.'

'Well take a seat Jacob and just bear with me while I borrow Belle for a little longer. We have the pleasure of entering predicted grades for the GCSE class that we share and we need to have completed them by close of play tonight.'

He turned to Belle as she sat in the chair next to him and said, 'This my friend is the very epitome of the sublime to the ridiculous.'

Jacob watched as the pair of them looked towards the screen. Mike continued, 'Now I doubt you're familiar with the charms of predicted grades Jacob seeing as you brave the murky depths of the outside world but they are a constant source of pain and heartache for us teacher types. In essence the examination boards – or should I say board now we are in the brave new world of StanEd – ask us every year to do their job for them and tell them what we think our pupils will achieve. Presumably it's so they can have a quick look down them at some point after they've marked the exams and check that they haven't made a complete bollocks of the whole business. So in this age of precision, data on every child, the humble teacher sits down in around March of each year and uses their professional judgement, a hunch, a gut feeling, their wealth of experience or a toss of a coin to tell our friends at StanEd what we think er…'

Mike Harris looked closer towards the screen,

'…Leonard Baxter in this case, who is incidentally the illustrious brother of that well known bibliophile Raymond Baxter, will get in his English GCSE examination in June. So Belle, what do you think?'

'What for Leonard?'

'For Leonard.'

'But I haven't seen him since I've been here.'

'Precisely. And I know you've only been here three months Belle but don't think that it's anything personal because I've taught him for eighteen months now and I have seen him twice.'

'Why has he come in twice?' asked Belle.

'Ah, Leonard turns up regular as clockwork on 'Own Clothes Day'. Don't ask me how he knows about it since he's never in school to get the information but sure as eggs are eggs Leonard Baxter will be here once a year, resplendent in cap, gaudy tracksuit and with gold chain a swingin'.

'Have you ever met his parents?' asked Belle.

'No I can't say I have. I don't know if dad's about but I did once call mum who assured me that she despaired of Leonard just as much as I did and that she had no idea what to do with him. Apparently she works in the civil service or something of the sort and the upshot of all this is, she's never at home enough to make sure that Leonard is here.

So with all this information to weigh up and process in our most professional manner what grade do you think we can predict for our Leonard?'

'Well he's not going to pass is he.'

'If he should pass Belle, I shall personally walk into Frau Carr's office, get down on one knee and ask her to make an honest man of me.'

'I'll hold you to that. So we're looking from U to D grade.'

'Now I do ask you at this stage to take into account another element in this delicate process. Will Leonard Baxter even grace the examination hall? He is after all a busy man and may decide that spending two hours sitting in a sweltering hall trying to complete an English paper that he is utterly unprepared for, is not the best use of his time. On the other hand if he does turn up I have it on good authority from those that saw him in the lower years, that he is not altogether stupid and does actually possess fairly solid English skills.'

'But we have to presume he will turn up don't we?'

'I would say so, we must be optimistic.'

'He hasn't got any coursework has he? So that will lose him 40% to start with so if he does turn up and has a good day using all those skills he picked up on the 'Own Clothes Days' over the years, I would say an E.'

'So would I; an excellent choice Miss Jones. Now just bear with us Jacob whilst we decide the future of the next twenty nine of our darlings and once they are completed I insist on taking you both out for a drink.'

chapter twelve

J.P.P. Montgomery sat poring over the UCAS reference form for one Julian Fisher. Montgomery always taught a class of A Level Politics and this had continued after the College introduced the Baccalaureate four years before. Fisher was a member of his present Year 12 class and a very able member at that. He had got his Oxbridge application in early but Montgomery noted with interest that Fisher had not applied to study Politics, Philosophy and Economics and made a mental note to discuss the matter with him in the next lesson. He then decided that perhaps the reference should wait until after that discussion and putting aside the form he pulled *The Racing Post* from the top drawer of his desk. St George's Blue was beginning to get some very favourable press, even being tipped as a contender for some of the big races later in the season and nothing gave Montgomery greater pleasure than to read about his beloved Blue in the press. As he scanned the pages for references to her, there was a knock at the door and after a shouted 'come in', Nigel Rose popped his head around the door.

'Ah Nigel, do come in, so nice to see a friendly face these days.'

The silver bearded deputy head settled into the chair in front of Montgomery's desk.

'How goes it? Read anything decent lately?'

'Mmmm, I've told you about Mankell haven't I? Swedish crime. Wallander's the detective, good I think. Sort of procedural crime novels, you follow him as he works it out, none of your blinding flashes of inspiration it's bloody hard work for him you know. I rather like it. Lots of depressing Swedish weather.'

'I've read one – 'Sidetracked', loved it. The killer dresses up as Geronimo, bloody good.'

'Yes, that's him. A lot of people think that's the best one, I don't, but a lot of people do.'

The two old friends paused.

'What news from the staff Nigel? What are they saying about me in the corridors?'

'Oh they seem pretty bobbish. A bit of spring wouldn't hurt of course.'

'What about that wretch Castle?'

'Oh Bryn wouldn't dream of speaking his mind in front of me. They all know that what I hear goes to you.'

'Are you saying I need some new spies Nigel?'

'Probably Philip, but are you going to bother getting any?'

'Probably not old boy. I feel the sands of time slipping away; besides I rather like having spies that only report the positive to me.'

'Not much use though are they?'

'Oh rest assured the likes of Castle will get me in the end. The tide's with them and all of us dinosaurs will be swept away by the brave new world of Bryn Castle and his spreadsheets. I wouldn't mind so much but he is such a cheerless wretch don't you think? One always hopes that the man to finally overthrow you will be someone worthy of the job but how rarely that happens.' Montgomery paused for a moment's reflection.

'Any other news from the front? Oh before you go on. Do you know why Fisher hasn't applied to do PPE?'

'No idea.'

'He's not thinking of doing a 'new' subject is he? I must speak to that boy.'

'There is one other thing Philip, it is time for predicted grades again.'

'Oh and I haven't done them again have I?'

'I'm afraid not; it's just the Baccalaureate group.'

'So tell me, just for old time's sake, why do we do these again?'

'You really want me go through this again?'

'Go on, persuade me.'

'We do it for the examination boards...'

'Exam board Nigel, singular. Yes, the estimable StanEd and our leader Herr Tweedy.'

'So that if a pupil is absent for the exam they can then award a discretionary grade based on teacher assessment. That's it.'

'So in case one boy misses the exam, every teacher in the country has to send off a predicted grade for every single pupil entering GCSE, AS level, A2 level or the Baccalaureate examinations. It's a masterpiece isn't it, a masterpiece of unnecessary form filling. Their genius knows no ends. Well I suppose I shan't need to do it for much longer once the wretched Castle gets his claws into me. Have you got the form?'

'Naturally.' Nigel Rose produced the sheet of paper from the folder he was carrying.

'When do you need these for, Nigel?'

'Now,'

'Jolly good, just give me a minute.'

chapter thirteen

The pub that Mike Harris took them to was called The George and Dragon and sat in the middle of St George's Road. As Jacob followed Mike and Belle into the pub he looked around and to his unschooled eye it appeared the entire clientele was made up of teachers. He was somewhat guided down that train of thought by Mike telling him in a stage whisper as they entered the doors, 'watch yourself in here the place is crawling with bloody teachers,' but nonetheless he could just feel it. As they stood at the bar he tuned his ear into snatches of the numerous pockets of conversation filling the air and his ears were filled with cries of 'bloody Josh Jackson' and 'so busy, just not enough time,' from every bar stool and table.

Mike clutched the drinks and directed them to a table in the corner.

'Don't catch anybody's eye; otherwise you'll be cornered by a scientist, foaming at the mouth and spitting, as he rants about this, that and the other in his Year 8 class. Beware Belle, these people will infect you but always remember that it doesn't have to be like that.'

He smiled and then raised his glass,

'Well anyway, cheers and it's lovely to have a drink with you both and here's to Belle's moment of triumph this afternoon with our new convert Raymond Baxter.'

They chorused 'Raymond Baxter,' and drank. Then Jacob asked,

'Why do you come here if you don't like it?'

'An excellent question. One, because it is local and on the way home and two, because of the crippling nature of habit and the abject paucity of my imagination.'

'I'll drink to that.' Jacob flicked his eyes towards Belle and asked, 'So how's she doing at this teaching game?'

Belle crumpled her face at him as Mike answered.

'She is doing exceptionally well. I'm a firm believer that teachers are born not made and she is one of those people who are born to it. Of course you need to learn the tricks as you go along but the essence must already be there. Plus of course she has come to it a little later and from a different world which I always think is a good thing. Yes, she's a class act. Now I just need to persuade our head to stump up the money to keep her.'

'Will she?'

'Oh, who knows.'

'And what's she like, the new head? Did you know we met her at the launch of StanEd?'

'Did you really? You lucky things. Well she is better than the previous head if only for the fact that she is always here and as far as I'm aware has not as yet run naked around the playground; but she is incredibly heavy handed and can be unbelievably crass. I don't actually think she's that bright but I'll say this for her, she is monstrously tenacious. She's also a shameless careerist and no doubt once we've been put through the ringer of her initiatives, she'll be off probably to some job in the educational establishment where she can further lash unsuspecting members of the teaching profession.'

'How long have you worked here Mike?'

'This is my tenth year.'

'And do you enjoy it?'

The head of English's eyes twinkled. 'Do you know, it's a bugger of a job. It's appalling on so many levels: the pay is distinctly average, the days are arduous, the working conditions are frightful, the clients are frequently rude, uninterested and occasionally aggressive and there's an increasing mound of paperwork that never seems to have anything very much to do with the job in hand: and yet, and yet there are moments – like the one our Belle has experienced today – when all that is utterly unimportant and you get this wonderful thrill; and do you know Jacob, I still get them. Not everyday but I get enough. And that of course is why the likes of Frau Carr are so dangerous, because we teachers don't actually care two hoots about what she gets up to. And the reason for this is because ultimately she is irrelevant because she is not who we are working for, she is not why we are here. We are here for the children, they are who we work for and that's why we do the job. Ah, it is the most terrible and glorious of bonds.'

Mike Harris' attention was drawn by an incident over Jacob's shoulder.

Jacob turned around to see two women and two men pouring lager over each other.

'Before you are representatives of the maths, history and P.E. departments of St George's Cross school. Impressive eh?'

He paused to take in the performance before him before continuing.

'I saw one of our esteemed colleagues there in the staff room at lunchtime and he was reading *The Express*. Now call me old fashioned but I do rather wonder what a man whose sole brain food for the day is a piece of sub pornographic tosh can possibly be teaching the country's youth.'

'I couldn't agree more,' said Jacob

'We both used to work for *The Express*,' said Belle.

'I know dear girl and neither of you work for them now which is to your eternal credit.'

Mike Harris looked again at the teachers as they began to clap hands to encourage a colleague who was striving to drink a pint of lager in one gulp. When he achieved it, the colleagues around him burst into applause and whoops of approval. The head of English turned back to Jacob and Belle and sighed, 'Perhaps Frau Carr has a point.'

chapter fourteen

Emma Carr spoke into the phone.

'No tell her that she can't. We cannot set that sort of precedent. If I give it to her what will I say to the next one who asks?' She listened briefly before continuing. 'What she chooses to do in her spare time is of no consequence to me and I certainly will not be swayed but such talk in these sort of negotiations.'

Valerie Bastic Styles poked her head around the door and Emma motioned for her come in.

'Well you tell her that and then get back to me with what she says.'

She put the phone down and shook her head.

'Honestly. Hello Valerie what can I do for you?'

'There are two things Emma. The first is excellent news – we have been awarded the Investors in People certificate. The notification came through in the post this morning and it comes in with immediate effect.'

'Oh Valerie that is wonderful news.'

'Isn't it?'

'And many thanks for all your hard work on this. I know

how much time and effort you put into this and we have been rewarded.'

'Thank you.'

'Let Janet know immediately. I want this announced to staff at Monday's briefing and see if we can't get an article in the local paper. What's the name of that man you know there?'

'Ray.'

'Yes call Ray and see if he'll do an article. Also tell Janet that I want it put on all the letterheads as quickly as possible. Oh this is terrific news, well done Valerie.'

She looked at her deputy head as if she was wondering why she hadn't already dashed off to complete the tasks.

'There was one other piece of news that I wanted to share with you head teacher.'

'Oh of course there was, go on.'

'Well this is of a more personal nature.'

'Oh.' Emma Carr leaned forward to reflect the more intimate turn of events.

Valerie looked at both floor and ceiling before speaking,

'Barry moved out last week.'

Emma Carr's face creased into a show of heartfelt sympathy.

'Oh Valerie I am so sorry.'

'Yes – well it has been coming. We've not got on terribly well for a while now and he thought it might be a good idea if we had some time apart.'

'And what do you think?'

'Oh I don't know really. I think it's probably for the best.'

'Do you know where he's gone?'

'To his mother's he said.'

'Oh Valerie that is terrible. Is there anything I can do?'

'Well that was what I was hoping to ask.'

'Go on.'

'What with Barry leaving and all I haven't really slept very much in the last few days.'

'Would you like some time off?'

'Oh no I wouldn't dream of it, we're far too busy. No what I was thinking was I know you've got a bed here, I was wondering if I could use your office to sleep – perhaps at lunchtimes. Just so I can catch up a bit.'

Emma Carr tried to keep sympathetic eye contact with her deputy head teacher whilst she thought. Valerie went on.

'Obviously it wouldn't be a long-term thing, it's just that there isn't anywhere else in the school that's suitable. What with sharing my office with Vikram and I just don't think I can face letting anybody else know just yet.'

'I understand. Of course you can.'

Emma Carr maintained eye contact whilst Valerie thanked her.

'Oh you don't know how much I appreciate this head teacher. It's just that if I didn't have school I think I'd fall apart. Obviously if anyone knocks on the door you must wake me up and we'll pretend that we've been having a meeting.'

'Quite.'

'Oh I can't tell you what a weight off my mind this is.'

'Don't mention it.'

Valerie headed towards the door. Emma watched her as she lingered at the exit.

'Is there anything else Valerie?'

The deputy head turned back towards her head teacher. The head teacher asked, 'Would you like to sleep now?'

'Would you mind? I am so tired.'

'The bed's in Janet's office – pop in and get it.'

She soon returned and laid the bed parallel with the desk.

'I'll just have twenty minutes. Do wake me at the end of lunch. Thank you so much for this head teacher.'

'It's no problem, Valerie.'

Within five minutes the deputy head teacher was snoring gently.

chapter fifteen

Jefferson sat contentedly in the toilet nearest his office. He unfurled *The Telegraph* from inside the obligatory folder and settled down to the sports pages.

Jefferson began with the horse racing pages which he found he was increasingly drawn to. This rise in interest had coincided with his discovery of the online betting services available on the internet. Since his future mother-in-law had relieved him of the wedding arrangement duties, he was delighted to find that he had even more time free to devote himself to the joys of the worldwide web. Only the other day he initiated himself in the art of spread betting after which he spent the day following the innings of Rahul Dravid for India against Pakistan at Kandahar on the internet. He hadn't won but by the end he felt sure that he could make the system work for him.

His betting on horses was generally of a more straight forward nature, although in recent times he had experimented with an accumulator at Doncaster that very nearly came in for him. He had also won twice on St George's Blue; firstly at Newmarket and then most recently at

Cheltenham. He loved any horse, team or player that won his loyalty through winning him money and this was how he was beginning to feel about St George's Blue. As he turned to the racing pages he found a large picture of St George's Blue in the middle of the page, with a smaller picture to its left featuring a well turned out older gentleman raising a champagne flute in celebration of a recent victory. There was a fairly lengthy article alongside the article which Jefferson scanned to find out when St George's Blue would run again. He was disappointed to see that it would not be until the St Leger in September. Also in the piece were quotations from the horse's trainer, one Buffy Shirley Beavan, saying what 'a special horse Blue was,' and also from his owner (evidently the man in the picture) one J.P.P. Montgomery. Montgomery spoke of 'the sport of kings,' and horses 'being born to greatness,' whilst the article also spoke of his role as the head master of St George's College in South London. Jefferson began to read the article more carefully. He knew St George's College from his school days. Their pupils used to get on the same train as Jefferson and had filled him with a mixture of envy and revulsion with their confident superiority. They always seemed to talk louder and laugh harder than anyone else on the train before they departed en masse and swaggered towards the imposing gothic building that Jefferson watched from the train window.

He had made a conscious decision at fifteen to hate all public schoolboys for the rest of his life and then found himself spending his entire career at Mycroft, Pigott and Welch pretending to be one. His colleagues there regarded 'local comp boys' as a species just below tea ladies and poofs in the evolutionary scale. Jefferson was never suspected of being one of these comp boys due to possessing the accent that he had been bullied so relentlessly for when attending Greenford Boys.

Whilst pondering the picture of St George's head master he got up from the toilet, flushed the chain and closed the paper. Preparing to leave he glanced at the front page and saw the headline,

SCHOOL QUIZZED IN SEX TAPE SCANDAL

He raised an eyebrow and sat back down to read the gory details.

chapter sixteen

J.P.P. Montgomery laid his copy of *The Times* flat out on his desk and adjusted his glasses.

'Bloody hell is he pissing on her?'

Nigel Rose left his copy of *The Guardian* and walked around the desk and examined the photograph over Montgomery's shoulder.

'Well it's blacked out in my paper but yes from what I can make out that is indeed what he is doing.'

'Dirty bugger. Where was this?'

'In the gymnasium apparently.'

'Christ, how wonderful.'

Nigel Rose walked back to the other side of the desk and ran his finger down the print.

'And I quote, 'Mr Clarke and Mrs Kelly would tie each other to the wall bars before carrying out various acts of sexual degradation upon each other.'

'Pissing on each other.'

'Yes.'

'And it says in mine that they had 'an agreement with the caretaker'.'

'He wasn't the one filming them was he?'

'No apparently he opened the school for them during the holidays. He says that they told him that they had a lot of work to catch up with.'

'I'll bet they did – bloody hell.'

'They're both married you know.'

'Who took the photographs then?'

'It's film isn't it?'

'Well whatever it is – would they have needed somebody to do this or could they do it themselves?'

'I suppose they could probably set it up themselves couldn't they? On a tripod or something?'

Montgomery looked up thoughtfully from his paper. 'I'm always intrigued by how these things begin. When do you tell a girl that you wouldn't mind tying her up in the gym and giving her a golden shower whilst she's there?'

'These types know each other don't they.'

'Do they? Lucky buggers.'

Montgomery paused.

'Hey, you don't think there's any way we can set young Castle up with one of these do you? Catch him abusing himself on film, pleasuring himself over a piece of data.'

Nigel Rose stifled a laugh. 'Philip really.'

'It's worth a thought. Stranger things have happened old boy; you never know who they are. What were this pair? Physics teacher and what?'

'She taught R.E.'

'Oh, she didn't. Oh it's absolutely priceless isn't it.'

J.P.P. Montgomery exhaled quickly and smiled.

'Poor old Ms Carr. So now we know what all those initiatives were about.'

He leant against his desk and crossed his arms.

'Should I send Ms Carr some flowers do you think? What's the done thing in these circumstances?'

'I'm not entirely sure; it's not something I've had experience of before.' Nigel thought for a moment before continuing. 'I suppose the question is what exactly would you be sending the flowers for? On reflection I think my answer is no to the flowers.'

'I suspect you're right; I shall settle for keeping a supportive silence. Well at least our boys will be able to get home in peace tonight without running the gauntlet of the George Cross welcoming party.'

'Oh there's always a few hanging around though regardless of whether they're at school or not.'

'I know it's extraordinary isn't it and they always look to be the sort that least want to be at school yet they're always here. Nothing else to do I suppose.'

'Perhaps not.'

'Still, away with such small talk, what are you reading at the moment?'

'I've gone back to a bit of P.G. Wodehouse actually, bloody good.'

'Oh yes, which one?'

'Aunts aren't Gentlemen.'

'Very nice.'

'What about yourself?'

'I've gone back to the great man Chandler.'

'Oh lovely.'

'*The Big Sleep*. I'm increasingly of the mind that it's his best.'

'Not a particularly unusual view it has to be said Philip.'

'No I know but not one that I have always shared. By Christ he can write can't he?'

'Oh yes, they are things of beauty.'

Montgomery looked at the painting on the far wall of his office and said,

'Have you ever had a go at any of that stuff?'

'What stuff?'

'You know, bondage and all that.'

'No, why, have you?'

'There was one girl out in the Far East that suggested something along those lines but do you know, I came over quite prudish; blushed like a school girl and told her not to be so silly.'

'And how did she take it?'

'Not very well actually. She screamed 'We shall never see each other again'. She may or may not have called me an English pig for good measure but that was the drift of it.'

'That was the end of that then.'

'It certainly was. No doubt she found someone more inclined to go along with her wishes.'

'Marjorie's never shown any inclination towards it. I don't think we've ever even spoken about it.'

'Are you saying that you wouldn't be averse to the idea Nigel?'

'Do you know I don't really know. It's not something I've spent a great deal of time thinking about.'

'No, my only reflection after this girl in the Far East was perhaps I'm more English than I thought I was. I was genuinely shocked. She came out of the bathroom dangling these bloody great handcuffs and some spiked thing and I just thought Christ, this is a bit rich for my blood.'

'What about Lib?'

'Oh God no, I just can't imagine it.'

'I'd imagine that's what they said about that girl in the paper, the head of RE.'

'Yes probably. Christ do you think these women are desperate to sling on the old leather and do unspeakable things to us?'

'Maybe so.'

'Maybe Lib and Marjorie are being held back by the likes of us. Us squeamish types that faint at the thought of anything other than the military two step.'

'Speak for yourself old boy.'

'Oh I see, you're one of them as well are you, committing depraved acts behind the privet hedge. Sodomy in the suburbs and all that.'

'No, although the chap three doors down was rumoured to be a naturist.'

'What mowing the lawn in the all together was he?'

'Well we never saw him if he was.'

'And tell me, did you detect a satanic glint in Marjorie's eye when said neighbour was mentioned in conversation? I tell you my boy they're all at it. We're being left behind old boy, last year's stock. There'll be no call for the likes of us soon you know, obsolescent, taken over by a bunch of fetishist, data munching rogerers. Ah well there's nothing we can do about it Nigel, just lie back and think of England old boy; dear old Blighty.'

chapter seventeen

Emma Carr burst into her office almost tripping over the prone form of her deputy head.

'Oh good morning head teacher.'

'No it isn't Valerie, no it isn't; look at this.'

She tossed a copy of *The Daily Mail* down to her still sleepy deputy head. 'Page five Valerie, page five.'

She waited as Valerie focused her eyes on page five and then turned the page on its side to see if she could make more sense of it from that angle.

'But isn't that Chris Clarke?'

'Yes Valerie it is and if you look closely you'll notice that the woman on the floor is Rachel Kelly, our head of Religious Education.'

'But what on earth is she doing there?'

'A question you could just as well ask Mr Clarke. What you are looking at are pictures taken from a video film sent to the press by the parents of one of our pupils.'

'But how? I don't understand.'

'Neither did I until this morning when a man from *The Mail* called me to explain.'

With her hair slightly askew, Valerie got up from her bed and sat down opposite Emma. 'And what did he say?'

'It might be quicker if you read the article it's all in there.'

Valerie Bastic Styles settled over the paper and began to read. Before long she looked up at Emma.

'They were shown it in a cover lesson?'

'Yes. The teacher didn't arrive and they picked a video to watch. It was apparently entitled 'Velocity and Impact''.

'Well what on earth was it doing in the classroom?'

'This is something that nobody knows but rest assured I shall be quizzing Mr Clarke on that very matter as soon as I can get hold of him.'

The deputy head teacher continued to read.

'So how did the press get the video?'

'Josh Jackson took the video home and showed it to his parents.'

'Oh no.'

'And the Jacksons in a state of high outrage chose to contact *The Evening Standard* and here we are.'

She looked again at the newspaper.

'Isn't that the gymnasium?'

'Yes Valerie and if you look closely, that is the school blazer that Mrs Kelly is wearing; apparently they got it out of lost property.'

'But if they're both in the picture how did they film it?'

'Well, who knows, but you can't help but wonder about that equipment that was stolen from the Media Studies department at the start of the year can you?'

'And Mr Clarke had this in his classroom?'

'Not only was it in his classroom Valerie but it was on display in his classroom. Of course if he'd have set his cover work properly this would never have happened.'

Valerie sat shaking her head.

'So what do we do now?'

'Well I've closed the school for the day for starters. Now we've just got to get rid of the press – you'd better brush your hair. And I've spoken to Mr and Mrs Jackson and told them that we didn't approve of their actions and that we thought they should have come to us first.'

'And what did they say?'

'They said that they didn't approve of their son being shown a pornographic film starring his Physics teacher during school time.'

'And what did you say to that?'

'Well there wasn't much I could say.'

The two women walked towards the office door.

'Oh this is the last thing we need Valerie, we'll be a laughing stock.'

'What'll we say to the press?'

'I don't know Valerie, I really don't know. That's what we need to talk about.'

chapter eighteen

When Jefferson finally departed the toilet with the newspaper under his arm he found Kenneth Andrews peering into his office.

'Ah there you are Mr Jefferson.'

'Morning Kenneth, how are you?'

'Never better, never better.'

'Did you read about this business at St George's Cross school?'

'Not in detail Mr Jefferson, not in detail. It is such a busy time of the year. What is the nature of the business?'

'Sexual depravity in the gymnasium Kenneth. Not something you know about I'm sure.'

Jefferson's bantering tone was greeted with an almost imperceptible scowl. Very briefly Jefferson could see Kenneth's teeth and then Kenneth returned to his usual self.

'Oh no sir, not my cup of tea at all.'

Jefferson decided to shift the conversation.

'I know St George's Cross, it was on the train route I used to take to school.'

'And is it a good school sir?'

'No it was awful in my day – rough. I don't know what it's like now but I can't imagine it's changed much.'

'It doesn't sound like it with the students getting up to those sort of tricks.'

'Oh no Kenneth it was the staff. It was the teachers that were caught.'

'Oh how unfortunate.'

There was a pause whilst Kenneth's thoughts seemed to drift away before he bounced into Jefferson's office.

'Well sir the predicted grades are all in from the schools and we're hard at work. Will you be hoping to see any of the teams at work?'

'No, no I don't want to burden them at this busy time of the year,' said Jefferson with his thoughts turning to a possible Yankee bet at Epsom that he had spied whilst on the toilet.

'Absolutely Mr Jefferson. Well I'll let you get on since I'm sure you've plenty to do.'

'Barely enough hours in the day are there Kenneth?'

He escorted Kenneth out of the door and pushed the 'meeting in progress' sign across the door before shutting it and returning to his desk. He toyed with the idea of a brief episode of *Baywatch* before settling to the race card at Epsom, but decided to get straight on with it. He wondered whether Ronald the driver would be interested in a drink after work and thought he might call him. He found the driver to be a fount of knowledge on both football and racing bets and Jefferson would happily stand him a few drinks to try and glean a little knowledge for the next day's tips. He picked up the phone as he cast his eye over the runners and riders in the 2.30 at Epsom and as he was about to dial Ronald's number he realised that there was a voice on the line. He listened carefully and recognised it as Lizzie from reception. He took his hand off the mouse and covered the receiver with his hand. Lizzie spoke again,

'I'm sorry about the wait Lord McLeish, he's there now. Would you like me to put you through?'

'What do you think?'

'Very good sir.'

Jefferson quietly got himself into a more comfortable position and waited. After a moment Kenneth Andrews' voice came on the line.

'Lord McLeish?'

'Kenneth.'

'Hello sir.'

'I spoke to Gordon last night and he wanted me to confirm that you are absolutely clear about our expectations.'

'Yes sir.'

'A clean run is imperative and standards are vital. They must be seen to improve; a visible and discernible improvement. Is that clear?'

'Absolutely sir.'

And how is Mr Tweedy recently?'

Very good sir.'

'Excellent.'

And the line went dead.

Jefferson could hear Kenneth's voice saying,

'Sir? Sir?' before putting the phone down.

Jefferson too put the phone down and reflected on the conversation. He felt a boyish guilt at listening in on the conversation but was pleased to hear himself praised. He thought about Lord McLeish's words on standards and made a note to use the word in his next conversation with Kenneth.

chapter nineteen

Jefferson got the chance to raise the issue of 'standards' the very next day but he forgot to mention it in his conversation with Kenneth.

He had been browsing through *BetFair* when there was a knock at his door. After closing the site and restoring the e-mail page Jefferson called,

'Come in.'

He then went through his usual pretence of being immersed in his work for a full thirty seconds after the knocker had entered the office. He would fix his eyes on the computer screen before raising his head with a murmured 'sorry,' to see who had entered his office. In truth it was always either Kenneth or Aggy but Jefferson felt that it was important to maintain this routine since Mr Pigott had used it every time that Jefferson entered his office whilst at Mycroft, Pigott and Welch.

As Jefferson dragged his eyes away from the imaginary work on the screen, their focus fell on a pair of bright red heels. An image of Kenneth and Aggy in scarlet stilettos briefly flickered through his mind whilst his eyes continued to work their way up the figure. By the time Jefferson reached the lustrous raven coloured hair he was of the opinion that he had never seen a more beautiful woman. He smiled sheepishly and his search for something suitable to say was interrupted by Kenneth's perky voice.

'Mr Jefferson, may I introduce Samantha.'

The vision in a red business suit stepped forward and held out her hand.

'Pleased to meet you sir.'

Jefferson rubbed his palm down his trouser leg before offering it to Samantha's.

'Very pleased to meet you.'

There was a moment's pause before Jefferson asked,

'Will you take a seat?'

Both Kenneth and Samantha took their seats at Jefferson's desk and Jefferson watched out of the corner of his eye as Samantha crossed her legs and pushed her hair behind her ear.

'Now Mr Jefferson,' Kenneth began, 'I have taken a bit of a liberty and I wonder if you can forgive me?'

'Really Kenneth what is it?'

'Well sir I was thinking about what you were saying earlier this month, about how busy you were and the pressures of work that you faced; and of course with your being the chief executive the pressures are far greater for you than any of us.'

'That's what I'm paid for Kenneth.'

'Up to a point Mr Jefferson but a man like you can end up taking too much upon himself for the good of the examination board.'

Jefferson laughed in a self-deprecating manner.

'No really sir, it's true and now what with all of the estimated grades from the schools having arrived and the examination season nearly upon us, well I've made an 'executive' decision that I hope you'll agree with. What I've decided is to employ Samantha here to help you with your administrative burden, to lighten the load of the humdrum and so free you up for the sort of 'blue sky thinking' at which you are so adept.'

Kenneth looked at Jefferson whilst Jefferson looked at Samantha.

'Well sir?'

'I don't deny that the work load can be a lot for one man to carry and an extra pair of hands always comes in handy doesn't it?'

'Absolutely Mr Jefferson. So what I was proposing Mr Jefferson was that Samantha take the office next door which I don't know if you are aware is linked to this office by those double doors.'

'Is it really? Well it sounds perfect.'

'And Samantha is happy to begin straight away aren't you Samantha?'

'Oh yes Mr Andrews.'

'Jolly good. Well I'll leave you two to get acquainted and I'll pop up a little later to see how you're settling in Samantha.'

Kenneth bounced up from his chair and smiled at both Jefferson and Samantha. He walked backwards away from them still smiling before sliding out of the door.

Jefferson looked after him for a moment before turning to Samantha and asking, 'Cup of tea?'

As she answered 'No thank you,' the double doors to

their right swung open to reveal a beaming Kenneth Andrews.

'There we are, all ship shape and Bristol fashion.' He gestured extravagantly towards the room and then he was gone.

From where he was sitting Jefferson could see a large wooden desk placed in the centre of the room whilst the rest of the room appeared to be empty.

Samantha raised herself fluidly from the chair and smiled,

'Well I better get started. Is there anything you would like me to do straight away?'

And as she said this she removed her red suit jacket and Jefferson coughed slightly at the sight of her fulsome bosom. He eventually realised that it was his turn to speak in the conversation and gathered himself to say,

'No, no, just make yourself comfortable and we'll see how we get along.'

'Well just let me know; I'll be through here waiting for instructions.'

'Jolly good, jolly good.' Jefferson watched her depart and then purposefully opened up an e-mail from his future mother-in-law and tried to train his mind on to the issue of table displays.

chapter twenty

The two women watched as the caretaker shut the school gates. They then walked swiftly back to the head's office and shut the door. Emma slumped over her desk and Valerie lay down on the futon bed.

'Oh what a day Valerie.'

'Wasn't it head teacher.'

'They were so aggressive weren't they? Did you see that one from *The Express*? He was practically shouting at me at one point and the photographers were even worse.'

'They're like animals aren't they. How could you do that for a living?'

'I know, still I thought it went okay didn't you?'

'Yes, there's not much we can say really is there? Terrible thing, they will be duly punished so sorry that the pupils were exposed to this etc etc.'

'I know. God, what do you think they'll be like with Chris and Rachel?'

'Oh it doesn't bear thinking about. Hasn't Chris got children as well? His poor wife.'

'I know. Mind you I have little or no sympathy for the pair of them.'

'No. Oh I bet Mr and Mrs Jackson are loving this. I mean fancy going straight to the papers, what sort of people would do that?'

'Money I suppose.'

'Oh of course it is, how naïve of me; of course it's money.'

The women stopped talking and reflected on the day. Valerie looked at Emma.

'I quite enjoyed it really.'

Emma looked back at her.

'So did I.'

Both the women started to laugh and Emma looked in mock horror at Valerie.

'He was pissing on her!'

The women shrieked with laughter.

chapter twenty one

Kenneth Andrews knocked three times on the door, then paused and added a further two short knocks. After a brief pause Kate Woodslit opened the door and put her finger to her lips. She whispered to Kenneth,

'Richard is giving us his Pozzo.'

'Oh lovely,' whispered Kenneth.

Kenneth followed Kate into the room and sat down to watch the rehearsal. In the centre of the room Richard Curtain stood erect with a bowler hat on his head. In his hand he held a lead that was tied around the head of Jean Plowstraight. She was on all fours, apparently in the pose of a dog with her head hanging down. Richard Curtain pulled viciously on the lead and Jean Plowstraight jerked head upwards. Richard began:

'Good. Is everybody ready? Is everybody looking at me? Will you look at me pig? Good. I am ready. Is everybody listening? Is everybody listening? I don't like talking in a vacuum. Good let me see.'

Larry Chevalier who was sitting in the seat next to Kenneth called out,

'I'm going.'

Richard continued.

'Don't interrupt me. If we all speak at once we'll never get anywhere.

What was I saying? What was I saying?'

Larry again, 'Bags. Why? Always hold, never put down. Why?'

'Ah why couldn't you say so before? Why he doesn't make himself comfortable. Gentlemen the reason is this. He wants to impress me so that I'll keep him. He wants to mollify me, so that I'll give up the idea of parting with him. He wants to cod me but he won't. In reality he carries on like a pig. It's not his job. He imagines that when I see him indefatigable I'll regret my decision. Such is his miserable scheme. As though I were short of slaves!'

Richard appeared to be finished but there was silence in the room as the audience sat in deference to Richard's towering performance. Richard himself had bowed his head and stood in silence. His eyes were shut and he breathed deeply. After a full twenty seconds and with his eyes still closed Richard raised both of his index fingers and his eyebrows before exhaling loudly and opening his eyes. As he opened his eyes the onlooking actors and Kenneth broke into awed applause at their leader's performance.

Kate Woodslit shook her head and turned towards Kenneth and whispered,

'So brave, so brave.'

Richard himself wiped his brow with a silk hanky that he had been offered by Kenneth. He slowly came to take a seat and as he settled into the chair Larry Chevalier leant over and patted him on the back murmuring 'Wonderful,' before turning to shake his head in wonder at Jean Plowstraight. Richard Curtain raised his arm and pointed it towards his fellow actress and called, 'Jean, Jean, Jean,' before leading a new round of applause for Jean and her stunning Lucky.

As this final round of applause died down Kenneth got to his feet and gushed,

'Just wonderful. Richard you never cease to amaze me and little Jean so realistic. I was simply spellbound. Well done everyone.'

This was the cue for another round of applause before Kenneth gestured for silence and changed his voice to a more serious tone.

'I must implore your patience as I change to a very different but equally important subject. As an examination Board, we must prepare for what is our 'Hamlet'. All of the predicted grades are in and we must set about the arduous but absolutely vital business of entering the grades on to the GCSE and A Level spreadsheets.'

There was a collective groan from the actors.

'Now as you are aware you will be joined in this task by all the other actors in the building as well the musicians, artists and the circus troupe.'

'Work shy bastards.'

'Ah come come Larry, I have spoken to River the Ring Master and he assures me that after the regrettable events of last year's dry run he will ensure that they put their noses to the grindstone this time.'

'I'll believe that when I see it. Those dwarves were nothing short of a menace.'

'I have it on good authority that they are no longer with the troupe and have found gainful employment elsewhere.

Now listen very carefully everyone about the task in hand. I cannot over-estimate the importance of completing this task with absolute precision, since all of our livelihoods depend entirely upon the successful completion of the next two weeks.

As a group, room LG23 have been allotted the schools beginning with the letters P right through to and including S. You have three weeks from today to complete the work. To re-iterate about the task; all of the predicted grades from those schools are in my office and I shall bring them to you forthwith. Your task is then to transfer the grades for each pupil in each subject in each school onto the corresponding spreadsheet on your computer. So you will find a spreadsheet for each pupil in each school listing the GCSE examinations that they are sitting. You then transfer the data exactly; except for, and this is very important, the students that you are allowed to increase or decrease.

'Is it four or five pupils per school that we change?' asked Jean Plowstraight.

'That will depend upon the number of pupils in the cohort. You will see the number at the top right hand corner of each sheet. Just to re-cap it is five pupils per fifty in each subect. So in a school with one hundred candidates you will change ten pupils per subject. Now the important thing to remember is that these changes must be shared equally with half going up and half going down. Is that clear?'

'Yes Kenneth.'

'And the rest stay as they are in the predicted grades sheets from the schools.'

Kenneth Andrews looked intently around the room daring the information not to be assimilated.

'The other vital detail that you may need reminding of is

at that at the top of each sheet, next to the number of pupils in the school, you will find a large letter O or D. Now the O means that that school has recently been visited by OFSTED. Where schools have a letter O on their sheet then that cohort of students have an additional ten grades moved up out of every fifty. Remember, five D grades are turned into C grades and five A grades are turned into A* grades. Is that clear?'

'Yes Kenneth,' chorused the company of actors.

'Now those schools with a D on their sheet are DUE a visit by OFSTED. These schools have eight grades out of each fifty downgraded. Once again A*s to As and C grades to D grades. Is that clear?'

'Yes Kenneth.'

'Now all that information is laid out very clearly on the e-mail that I sent you at the start of the year and I'll send it again just in case anybody has mislaid the last one.'

Richard Curtain raised his hand.

'Sorry to go over this again Ken but just to clarify, no pupil goes up or down more than a grade do they? In other words I can't use two of my allotted changes on one pupil.'

'No, you must not deviate from the predicted grade by more than one grade either way.'

'Yes I thought so, thanks for that Ken.'

'Now are there any other questions at this stage?'

'Are there any guidelines as to the pupils that we choose to move up or down?'

'No that is at your discretion just so long as you abide by the figures and quotas that I have just reminded you of. Any other questions?'

Kenneth looked around the room and was greeted by shakes of the head.

'Right. I'll bring the grades in now and you can get on straight away. And remember everyone, this is our 'Hamlet.''

He skipped out of the door and Larry Chevalier grumbled, 'How dare he invoke The Sweet Prince in such tawdry context.'

'I know love, I know,' consoled Richard Curtain, 'but the sooner we get this done, the sooner we'll be back to your Stanley. And let's not forget that much as we may moan about our Ken, without this place we'd all be back in the church hall in Orpington.'

'Heaven forefend,' cried Larry Chevalier and crossed himself to ward off such evil spirits.

Kenneth Andrews popped back into the room,

'Mustn't forget my keys.'

As he departed again Jean Plowstraight called,

'Oh Kenneth, what about la Tweedy, will he be bothering us during these next few weeks?'

'Oh no,' replied Kenneth, 'I don't think you'll be seeing any more of the great Jefferson Tweedy.'

chapter twenty two

Jefferson had started dreaming about Samantha. During Monday night's sleep she appeared as an ice cream seller in a van with 'Crushed Nuts' written on the side. When Jefferson asked for a 'ninety nine' she had asked him if he 'wanted a flake in that' and he had then been unable to get his change out of his pocket despite repeated attempts. The boys at the back of the queue then started laughing at him and he had ran off without his ice cream.

The following night she appeared only in body since when the woman who appeared to be her turned around she revealed herself to be Patricia McLeish wearing the bright red dress and rather more make-up than was usual for her.

Samantha then disappeared from his dreams for a couple of nights before returning again the previous night in a dream that Jefferson could only describe as 'steamy'. It was to his very great consternation when he awoke needing a wee at a most inopportune moment in proceedings and despite his best efforts to recapture the magic on his return to bed, Samantha was not to be seen again.

And so it was these thoughts that preoccupied Jefferson

Tweedy as he peered over his computer at Samantha. She was shuffling some papers in the adjacent office and Jefferson fiddled with his mouse as he leant closer to his computer. His attempts at intimacy had been somewhat stymied by the complete lack of work that he had to give her. He had tried to conjure some paperwork from thin air but without success and so was reduced to the occasional call of 'everything all right Samantha?' and a couple of enquiries about bogus papers. She said that she hadn't seen them but assured him that she would keep her eye out for them. After that she went back to tapping away at her computer.

Jefferson thought that he could occasionally sense her looking at him but by the time he turned to look at her she was back to her computer screen. He assured himself that he didn't actually want a re-creation of last night's dream, just a bit of attention; after all they were sharing an office. In addition to this, her presence made it very difficult for him to watch any of his, by now fairly extensive collection of, DVDs and videos and so after a few hours trawling through his favoured websites he was beginning to get slightly bored. The answer to this boredom he decided was to call Ronald the driver. He might be willing to be coaxed out for a lunchtime drink if he was in the area and then he could invite Samantha to join them and it could all be quite pleasant. He waited until the ringing tone ended before accepting that Ronald wasn't answering his phone and then had another look around the office.

In frustration he decided that he would have a walk around the building and see how things were getting on; it had been a while since he had seen the workers and a Mycroftian aloofness must be tempered with the occasional guest appearance from the boss.

It was as he was about to open the door that he heard the scream from Samantha's office. He shot through the double doors and found her bent over her chair.

'Samantha whatever is the matter?'

'It's my eye.'

'What wrong with your eye?'

'I think something flew into it.'

'Oh dear.' Jefferson paused. 'Well shall I have a look at it?'

Samantha nodded, sat up straight and then threw her head back, all the time blinking her eyes frantically.

'Now sit still Samantha and I'll soon sort this out.'

'Oh be careful Mr Tweedy, go gently.'

Jefferson had a quick look around the office to check that Ailsa hadn't that moment arrived back from America and then moved towards the heaving chest of the stricken Samantha. He cleared his throat and asked,

'Now which eye is it Samantha?'

'The right one Mr Tweedy, oh please be careful.'

He leant over and moved towards her face. He readjusted his position two or three times and finally found a position of excruciating discomfort that required his legs to be set as far apart as they could possibly be with his left leg slightly bent so that his crotch could be kept at least six inches away from any possibility of physical contact. As he approached Samantha's face he noticed that her cherry red lips were slightly parted (due to the pain he presumed) and her eyes gazed directly at him.

'Now easy does it, I'll just have a little look. The right one you say?'

'Yes Mr Tweedy.'

He bent over and felt her breath on his cheek. His mind cast back to the last time he had been this close to a woman and shuddered. He hoped that his contorted position would save him any such embarrassments this time. As he brought his hand up towards her eye he felt Samantha's hands press against his chest.

'Oh Mr Tweedy. Is there anything there?'

'Yes, I think there is Samanatha.'

He looked closely into the invaded eye and could only see himself in its reflection.

'Can you get it Mr Tweedy?'

Jefferson could see nothing untoward in the eye but felt that now he was in this position he ought to show willing and finish the job. The poor girl was clearly in some distress and if in the name of calming her fears he had to stay bent over her for a little longer, then so be it. He moved his finger very tenderly towards the eye.

'Now steady on, I can see the problem. Just hold tight.'

Jefferson had meant it as a figure of speech but on the command Samantha threw her arms around him pulling his body on to her. Valiantly trying to keep his mind on the job Jefferson moved his finger towards the eye. He brushed it into the corner of the eye before carefully drawing it away.

'Got it.' He disengaged himself from Samantha and held out his finger.

'See it? It was an eyelash.'

Samantha looked closely at his finger, holding it in place as she did so.

'Oh yes, I see it.' She looked up dreamily at him. 'Thank you Mr Tweedy.'

In his office Kenneth Andrews squealed with delight at the television screen on his wall, clapping his hands together repeatedly.

'Oh excellent work my dear, excellent work. You just keep that silly boy there.'

chapter twenty three

Down in room LG23, the waiting actors sat in a circle of chairs talking of past triumphs. Larry Chevalier was in full flow,

'I don't think I've seen anybody who can deliver the bard as mellifluously as dear Johnny Gielgud. I was telling you, wasn't I Jeanie, how I saw his Prospero at the Old Vic; we were simply enchanted. And do you know, and Dickie will vouch for me on this, I swear he made eyes at me as he delivered 'Our revels now are ended.' I looked up at him and he looked down at me; it was simply magical. It was only some officious stage door Johnny that insisted 'Mr Gielgud did not wish to be disturbed post-performance,' that prevented us discussing it in the green room. But we knew what had happened, we knew.'

Larry drifted away in a sea of what 'might have beens' and the actors mused on his tale before Jean Plowstraight began to talk.

'I'll never forget 'Oh What a Lovely War' with Joan Littlewood. She was simply extraordinary.'

'You were in that weren't you Jeanie?'

'A mere spear carrier Katie, but as Joan constantly reminded us 'there are no small parts, only small actors.'

'How true,' murmured Richard Curtain.

'But to be around her and to watch her at work; such energy, such drive and we all felt as if we were a part of her dream, that together we could achieve something wonderful. Change the way the world saw itself through theatre. I'd love to have gone to America with them but my Henry came along and it's no life for a baby. His father went though. He wrote and told me it had been an enormous success. I was pleased for them.'

The door opened and a beaming Kenneth Andrews entered pushing a trolley full of papers.

'Now then, take your seats everyone and I shall distribute your allotted batches of results. Remember I shall collect these sheets at the end of each day so they can be safely stored in my office. Now Kate you will have schools starting with P, Richard you will have Q, Jean R and Laurence S. Now it may be that some of you will have more schools than others; simply work carefully through your batch and if you finish, offer to help a fellow member of your company with theirs. I shall be here at least three times a day to carry out spot checks on your work and may I remind you that you have three weeks to complete this hugely important task. Now are there any final questions? No? Excellent.'

And with that he disappeared through the door.

The actors looked around at each other for a moment and sighed. Nobody was in any particular hurry to get started and so to lift collective spirits, Larry Chevalier asked,

'So how shall we be dispensing our favours today? By which criteria shall we be choosing our lucky risers and less fortunate fallers? Where will our gift of the rising grade go? Will it be the numbers game? Every tenth pupil miraculously finding that their Chemistry skills were better than they'd ever dreamed. Will it be by subject? Will the arts be blessed with a generation of unwitting Branaghs and Brittens? Will it be for a name that reminds us of a favourite aunt or a love we once lost? Or will it be the faithful pin just like your grandma likes to pick her horse for The National? Ah, it is all in our gift everybody; the children of Britain await.'

Kate Woodslit picked up the predicted grades sheets for Pabstow High School. It crossed her mind that she had no idea where that was and a glance over the sheets gave her no further clue as to its whereabouts. She clicked the screen in front of her and Pabstow High came up. Both the screen and the sheet displayed a large O next to the school's name and Kate glanced at the sheet of paper, blu tacked above her computer, to check what this meant.

'OFSTED have been in recently, good good; that will have done a power of good.'

Below the school's name were displayed the surnames and first names of the school's entire GCSE cohort. Next to the pupils' names were a series of boxes with various subject names above them. Kate adjusted herself in her seat and laid the sheets down next to the computer. She manoeuvred the computer's mouse and then began to type.

'Right, Jennifer Abbott. Art B (type), Business C (type), English A (well done Jennifer, (type), English Literature B (type), French D (type), Geography A (type), Maths C (type) and Science DD (type, type). Well they're not a bad a set of results Jennifer – if a little disappointing in the sciences. I do of course have the power to turn you into a very respectable

Biologist but I am choosing not to on this occasion. One mustn't cast one's gifts away too quickly, we have a long day ahead of us.'

'Katie love, must you verbalise every single thought that passes through your mind?'

'Sorry Larry, I just find it all quite exciting.'

'You wait until you've been doing this for a couple of weeks, you'll find the sparkle soon goes out of Christmas.'

'Right who's next? Ooh Katie Ash, I've got a Kate, I've got a Kate. Right. Drama B, no I think your performance deserves better than that Katie love, A (type), English I think you're an A* Katie well done (type), Literature A (type), German C (type), Maths D, no, no Katie believe me it's not easy without Maths GCSE, C (type), Music A, lovely(type), Sciences CC (type, type). Well done Katie, you have done very well. The fruits of a clear and rigorous revision programme no doubt.'

'So you are blessing those of like name are you young Kate? We shall be burdened with a whole raft of geniuses with the name. It is all well and good for you to bestow your favours on your namesakes but I find Laurence is such an over looked name these days.'

'Then you shall have to bestow your favours elsewhere, Larry,' said Richard Curtain.

'I have the same problem Larry, Jean is so very yesteryear,' said Jean Plowstraight.

'Good grief,' exclaimed Richard Curtain.

'What's the matter Dickie?'

'Well I've got one here called Anandarajadan, Chibi.'

'I beg your pardon.'

'Now where is one to start with that? Is it a boy, is it a

girl? I am presuming from the layout of the other names that Chibi is its first name but how would one know otherwise? Poor thing, fancy blighting a child with a name like that.'

Richard Curtain looked down the rest of Queenstown School's cohort.

'Good Lord and there's one here called…' he tiptoed through the pronunciation, 'Sivananathanadan, Printhiga. Where are these people from?'

'I fear my chances of finding a Laurence diminish by the moment,' interjected Larry.

Richard Curtain read on,

'Grzacko, Zbigniew, Mendra Datot, Zopoditic, Looch.'

The rest of the actors began to scroll down their screens and call out names.

'Pandiangandan, Lahagus.'

'Ravin, Niyazi.'

'Hamdallahan, Mustafa.'

'Okara, Sunshine Jesus.'

'Arafa, Yudisia.'

Jean shook her head in bemusement.

'Even some of the names that smack of being recognisable are unintelligible. Joshena, Sheneena, Thaleen, Nodden. It's just extraordinary. Who are these people?'

Baffled, the actors murmured amongst themselves before continuing with the job of awarding the nation's children their GCSE grades.

After ten minutes Richard Curtain was the first of the actors to complete a school's whole set of GCSE results when he completed Queenstown School.

Once the set of results were entered he clicked print on the computer screen and picked up one of the A4 envelopes from the pile beside him. The printer spewed out the print outs and each pupils' results were surrounded by a perforated edge ready for the school to separate. At the end came the master sheet with all the results for all the school's pupils on it followed by a sticker with the school's name and address. Richard folded all of these sheets and placed them in the envelope. He then planted the sticker on the outside of the envelope, sealed it and then placed it in the tray next to his computer.

chapter twenty four

'I feel a bit guilty being out on a school night.' Belle poured herself another glass of mineral water and pushed aside the plate where her starter had been.

'Well I promise to have you home and tucked up by 10.30pm.'

'You wish love.'

'And anyway you used to be out every night of the week,' said Jacob who was also drinking mineral water.

'There's just something different about teaching. It's weird because it's really hard to say exactly where it comes from but there is just this sense that you don't go out during the week.'

'Sounds awful.'

'I know and if you have been out the night before, everybody else seems to be talking about their lesson planning and their marking and you just feel like you're letting people down. It's terrible.'

'It sounds positively Catholic.'

'Well quite and it's not easy for a lapsed Convent girl like me to handle.' She laughed and sipped from her water. 'And the other thing is that they're all so painfully conscientious. You know there is still something of the journalist left in me and now I'm hanging around with these uber disciplined teaching machines.'

'Do I detect a falling out of love with your new calling?'

'No, I'm being a bit unfair but then we did go out together a couple of Fridays ago and some of them just talked about the kids all night. It's like they're obsessed.'

'Mike didn't seem like that.'

'No he isn't and neither are most of the people; maybe I'm being unfair.'

'And of course the members of the journalism profession were charming and likeable to a man.'

'Quite. I'll shut up now. There is a difference though. It is almost impossible to teach with a hangover or not enough sleep.'

'How many are there in your classes?'

'Thirty odd. So there's just no respite.'

'So you can't play every journalist's favourite, the 'going to research a story' card then?'

'No absolutely and you can't just sit in front of a computer for a couple of hours until your head clears. It's always full on, regardless of how you're feeling and that just puts people off; the night out is rarely good enough to justify the hell of the following day.'

'Sounds ghastly, sounds like parenthood.'

'Only with one hundred and fifty kids a day.'

'Mmmm, not good.'

'Oh I suppose I'm just sorting out how I want to do this. Not everyone's a machine; some of them have managed to retain some normality.'

'Then that's what you've got to aim to do then, isn't it?'

'You're right.'

'Am I? Great, I haven't been right in years.'

'And one thing that I really struggle with is the whole ma'am thing.'

'Is that what they call you?'

'Yes, it's awful isn't it? It's like a term of address from a 1930s butler and all the boys are supposed to use it for female teachers. I feel like saying to them 'please my name is Belle, I don't want to be called ma'am by anyone ever.'

'Could you tell them not to use it?'

'Mike was telling me that a teacher in the English department a few years ago told one boy that when they were in a one to one situation like a detention or something he could call her Julie.'

'That doesn't sound like a particularly good idea.'

'It wasn't because sure enough he told the rest of the class and in the end the head teacher had to go into the class because the whole lot of them were chanting 'Julie, Julie' at the top of their voices.'

'So ma'am it is then.'

'I suppose so but there must be a way round it.'

'My sister went to school with a girl that changed her name so many times that when she went in to do her O levels she couldn't remember what name she'd registered under. They had to send a teacher out to check the records.'

'What names did she use?'

'I can't remember them all but I do know that one of the changes was from Sharon to Crystal.'

'Crystal?'

'I know. Frying pans and fires spring to mind.'

'Crystal's still better than Tyson, we've got a load of Tysons at our school.'

'God, I don't trust people that call their dog Tyson, no matter their kids.'

The waiter brought their main courses and placed them in front of them. Both of them had chosen the fish and murmured their thanks to the waiter as he offered them the black pepper. As the waiter departed Belle continued,

'Look, you know my contact at *The Independent*?'

'Matilda, was it?'

'Yeah. Have you spoken to her yet?'

'I tried to call her a couple of weeks ago and she was busy.'

'Of course she was busy; she was covering all the business at St George's.'

'I know. That's why I didn't really want to get too involved because I don't see there's much of a step up from covering Jordan's puppies to school sex scandals. I might as well go back to King Dick if I'm going to work on that.'

'Fair enough but it won't all be that will it. You should still call her.'

'I will, I will.'

'Did I tell you that a woman in my department reckons she went out with that bloke in the video?'

'Go on. Was he the RE teacher?'

'No that was the woman. She reckons there wasn't a whiff of that sort of thing, all very straight up and down; she couldn't believe her eyes.'

'Hidden depths of depravity you see. Do they know who filmed it yet?'

'No not yet, although the possibilities are endless. Listen, are you really going to call Matilda?'

'Yes.'

Belle paused.

'I think I might call her now.'

'Belle you really don't need to...'

By the end of the main course Jacob was booked in for the next day to cover the return of a British heavyweight boxer to Heathrow Airport, following a painful defeat in the States. Jacob promised Belle, that if all went well he would name his first born, regardless of sex, after the man.

chapter twenty five

Jefferson could have sworn that Samantha's tops were becoming slightly more revealing with every day that passed. He remembered a boy in the school cricket second XI once proclaiming that his girlfriend had 'tits like torpedoes'. Jefferson had laughed along with the other boys but could remember thinking that it was an ugly phrase and that it probably wasn't very nice to be talking about your girlfriend like that in front of other boys. Nonetheless that was the phrase that kept popping into his mind each morning as Samantha arrived in progressively lower cut tops. The weather had not become noticeably hotter and Jefferson also noted that Samantha would remove her jacket or cardigan much earlier in the day than had previously been her wont.

Jefferson watched these proceedings with a keen eye from behind his computer during breaks from the ball by ball internet coverage of India versus Pakistan in Madras. His particular interest this week lay in the progress of VVS Laxman whom he had provisionally backed to score between 60 and 75 runs. Laxman was presently on 34 and all seemed well but the match had broken for tea and this seemed an opportune moment to keep tabs on developments in the adjacent office.

As Jefferson looked up Samantha was midway through a luxurious stretch that thrust her breasts forwards in a quite spectacular fashion. Jefferson leaned slightly closer to his computer screen wondering how long he could dare to keep watching before the risk of discovery became too strong. The white top that Samantha had chosen for today afforded Jefferson an unimpeded view of her cleavage and it was this that he was studying as she came to the top of her stretch. Jefferson knew that from this point on, his time was limited since the downward turn of the stretch would also bring an opening of the eyes and a look around the office. He snatched a final lingering look before turning his attention back to VSS Laxman in Madras. Unsurprisingly since it was not even a minute since he had last checked, the cricketers were still at tea and Jefferson started to wonder if he could risk another glance at Samantha. He tapped two or three letters on the keyboard in the name of appearances before poking his head over the top of the computer. Samantha was looking straight at him and Jefferson ducked back down beneath the screen. He regretted his retreat instantly and wracked his brains for a work based topic of conversation with which to save the situation. None was forth coming and so he returned to an industrious tapping of the keyboard.

Whilst considering his next move the phone on his desk rang and he grabbed it with a force he rarely displayed in the workplace.

'Jefferson Tweedy.'

The voice of Liz the receptionist came on the line.

'Oh hello Mr Tweedy, Ailsa's on the line.'

Jefferson paused as he took a moment to register who exactly Ailsa was before replying,

'Ah yes, jolly good, put her through.'

Jefferson waited for an instant before hearing Ailsa's voice on the line.

'Hello? Hello Jefferson, it's me.'

'Hello darling how are you? I was just thinking about you.'

'Oh were you? Aren't you nice.'

'How are you?'

'Oh, busy but really well. Yourself?'

'Oh the same, it's a busy time of year this end what with the exams coming up and all of that.'

'Oh I can imagine. Listen, have you spoken to mumsy recently?'

'Not really why?'

'Well she was speaking to the vicar at the church that she's booked and they need to decide upon a date for…'

Ailsa's voice drifted away as Jefferson peered over the top of the computer and found Samantha smiling over at him. He smiled sheepishly back at her and gave a coquettish little wave. In the background he could hear Ailsa talking about confetti but in his head Jefferson was wondering whether or not he had looked stupid waving at Samantha. Had the wave made him look immature? He told himself to pull himself together and dragged his thoughts back to his fiancée.

'Ailsa darling.'

'What?'

'I miss you, when are you coming home?'

'You know when I'm coming home Jefferson don't be so silly.'

'Well it feels like a long time doesn't it?'

'I know but we've both got a lot to do and it'll soon be August.'

'I suppose so.'

'So anyway the photographer says that we have to choose whether we want him to take shots inside the church or…'

Jefferson strived to listen to the rest of the conversation and agreed that yes the question of filming the ceremony was a tricky one after which Ailsa got called back to her work and Jefferson was left alone with the ample temptations of Samantha.

chapter   twenty   six

On a sweltering day in the middle of May, Jefferson got stuck
in the lift with Samantha. Having read *The Telegraph* from
cover to cover and with nothing better to do he had
announced rather grandly that was going to undertake a tour
of the building. He was mildly surprised by the speed of her
reaction, but she swore that she had to come and see Liz on
reception and would he mind if she came down with him? He
nobly replied that it would be a pleasure and turned towards
the door, thus missing Samantha's furtive pressing of the
button under her desk.

When the bell rang and the light flashed in Kenneth
Andrew's office he was looking through a magnifying glass at
the screen in front of him, poring over the predicted grades that
the actors in room LG23 had entered. He had spent the previous
few days checking the work of the circus troupe in room LG7
and now he applied the same methodical approach to the work
of the actors. He left the screen on schools starting with S, put
his magnifying glass down and looked at the flashing light.

'On your travels again are we Mr Jefferson? Well we'll
have to see about that.'

He turned to the screen on his wall and watched the CCTV footage of Jefferson and Samantha leaving room 9/11. She was bending down as if searching for something on the floor and he turned around to help her. Kenneth murmured 'well done,' and lifted the phone nearest to him. He began to talk almost immediately.

'Are you watching them mother? Good. The lift I think; could you do the honours? Excellent.'

He put the phone down and continued to watch the screen. After a moment's more scrabbling around on the floor the two figures moved towards the lift and pressed the button.

Jefferson was pleased that Samantha had found her earring and as they waited for the lift he wracked his brains for some interesting conversation.

'Warm today isn't it?'

'I hardly know what to do with myself.'

'Really?'

'I don't seem to be able to get comfortable in any position.'

The lift arrived.

'Ah good here it is. Please after you.'

He ushered her into the lift and after a quick look over his shoulder followed her in.

It was between the sixth and fifth floor that the lift got stuck. It shuddered noisily and then ground to a halt. Jefferson looked closely at the doors before realising that they had not stopped at a floor and they were not going to open.

Samantha's face was frozen in a look of melodramatic horror,

'But what's happened sir?'

Sensing that as the chief executive of StanEd he ought to

take control of situations such as these Jefferson spoke in his most authoritative tones.

'Now there seems to be some problem with the lift; there's absolutely no need to panic and I'm sure it will all be sorted out very quickly. I'll just press this emergency button and I'm sure we'll be out of here in a jiffy.'

As Jefferson pressed the emergency button with increasing frequency and fixed what he hoped was a reassuring smile on his face, Kenneth Andrews was on the phone again.

'Well done mother, yes I can see that he's safe and sound now. How long? Oh what do you think? Is three hours enough? Long enough to get him a little hot under the collar and to give us a chance to get done what we need to do for the day. Excellent; listen I've got to go, there's somebody on the other line.

Ah Lord McLeish what an honour to hear from you...'

Within minutes of the lift stopping Samantha had unbuttoned a pair of buttons on her blouse and insisted that Jefferson fan her with his jacket to try and fend off what she was sure was imminent heat exhaustion. She insisted that she needed to have her hand held to help her through the next few critical minutes. Jefferson found it difficult to do both this and fan his jacket and so settled for simply holding her hand whilst wobbling the tail of his jacket in her general direction.

It was as he was doing this that he decided that if the emergency services had not responded to his first series of presses of the emergency button then it was hardly likely that they would respond to a second series and so he and Samantha would simply have to tough it out together, handing their destiny over to the powers that be.

She was now sitting in the corner of the lift, breathing deeply to try and 'control her racing heart,' and was spending quite long periods of time with her eyes closed, only occasionally opening them with a flutter to gaze with a mixture of distress and adoration at Jefferson. She would mutter 'thank you, thank you for being so kind,' before returning to her deep breathing routine. The jacketless Tweedy looked on with a similar mixture of wonder and distress whilst hunting for a topic of conversation appropriate for such a moment. As if reading his mind Samantha opened her eyes and looked up at him; breathlessly she gasped 'talk to me sir.' Grasping for the first topic to come to mind, Jefferson sat down next to her, made himself comfortable and asked,

'Are you familiar with the business of spread betting?'

In his office Kenneth Andrews was still listening to Lord McLeish on the phone.

'I cannot overstate the need for absolute precision in this year's set of results Kenneth. We simply cannot afford the horror of recent years, the sheer unpredictability of the thing. How can a government reassure the public that the nation's education is in good hands if they have no control over the outcome? There were simply too many element Xs: all those examination boards, the markers, the teachers, the pupils. How can a government trust a system with so many fallible human links in its chain? The public don't want fallibility, they want results and they want improvement. They want to know that their Johnny is getting what he deserves and that is what this system will give them.'

'Absolutely, Lord McLeish.'

'And don't think that your role is being underestimated in

delivering this Kenneth. There are a lot of people, even more senior than me, who have admired the way that you have managed the situation so far and they are very keen to see that you can deliver the desired outcome. And rest assured that if you do, you will be handsomely rewarded; suffice it to say that you would need to keep a close eye on The New Year's Honours List – for services to education and all that.'

'Oh really Lord McLeish, you do flatter me.'

'It's not flattery Kenneth it's just reward. Now remember what I say.'

'I do sir, every day.'

'Jolly good, now back to work.'

When the phone went dead Kenneth sighed and envisaged his name with letters after it. He glanced at the screen above him and saw Samantha and Jefferson huddled together in what appeared to be a pleasingly compromising clinch, before with renewed zeal he pressed the return key on his computer and put his magnifying glass to the next page of results.

When Jefferson finished his fastidious description of the complicated science of spread betting, Samantha was still rapt in thoughtful concentration. He had noticed that she let his hand slip from hers midway through his re-telling of his enormous stroke of fortune during Pietersen's century for England at The Oval and listened opened mouthed for the rest of the account. Her heavy breathing had stopped and she absent-mindedly fastened one of the buttons on her blouse. When he finished she asked,

'Can you make a lot of money from this then?'

'Well it's like all betting, you need some knowledge and plenty of luck, but it does seem slightly less fortuitous than other forms of gambling.'

'Only we need some money.'

As she said this she gasped slightly and flicked her eyes to the lift door.

'Who's we?'

Samantha paused briefly.

'Me and Barry.'

'And Barry's your…'

'My boyfriend and we're having to stay at my mum's at the moment but we saw this place in Sidcup that would be just perfect and Barry's very handy so once we were in we wouldn't need to pay out for builders or anything, but we just haven't got enough saved to do it at the moment and we've been looking around for ways to make some money; that's why I took the job here. I do this and then I work in the evenings and Saturdays; honestly it's killing me.'

'I bet it is.'

'And Barry's working all the hours that God sends but it doesn't feel like we'll ever do it.'

'Well look I don't think spread betting is the way to solve your problems; I'm sure something will turn up. I said that to Ailsa the other day – Ailsa's my fiancée and we're getting married in August – and she's terribly worried about the wedding preparations and all of that but I told her there's really nothing to worry about.'

'Ah bless, are you getting married in a church?'

'We are.'

'Oh I'd love to get married in a church. Is your Ailsa going to wear white? What colouring is she…'

By the time the lift doors finally opened just over two hours of wide ranging discussion later, Samantha had given Jefferson no end of useful advice on the outfits that he and his best man should wear for the wedding, whilst he had told her that she and Barry sounded like the perfect couple and that talking about all of this had made him realise how much he missed Ailsa and how he couldn't wait for August to arrive. He made her promise that she and Barry would come to the wedding and she promised that she would have saved enough money to be living in that place in Sidcup by then. As they stepped out of the doors he placed a fraternal kiss on her cheek and they walked arm in arm back to the office.

chapter twenty seven

At St George's Cross, Emma Carr had instigated the most comprehensive series of revision sessions the school had ever seen.

'We must target those students performing below their benchmark, Valerie.'

'Quite right Emma.'

'I think the borough is absolutely right to do away with study leave, it gives us the chance to really keep the students focused on what is after all the reason why they have been in school for these past eleven years.'

'Or not in school in the case of Leonard Baxter.'

'No sign of him?'

'I'm afraid I spoke to Mr Harris and he said that attendance in general had been rather disappointing and Leonard and a few others had not been seen at all.'

'I'm afraid Valerie we cannot make our policies around the likes of Leonard Baxter; for every one like him we must think of the five that are gaining so much through this revision programme. And what was Mr Harris's opinion on the programme? Sceptical I dare say.'

'He wasn't overtly negative so I think we should take that as a small victory.'

'Good, I'm sure he sees the sense in it; I do think that ultimately Mr Harris and I are striving for the same thing even if we do approach it from different angles. Now I must be away to my R.E. revision session. Honestly I do curse that woman Kelly at times, did you see her in the paper again at the weekend?'

'Was that *The Express*?'

'Yes, she's absolutely shameless. If I have to read one more detail about what she and Chris Clarke got up to in school time I shall scream.'

'And did you see the pictures?'

'I rather wish I hadn't Valerie. What must the parents think when they see the school uniform used for such purposes? It turns my stomach it really does.'

'And I've had the woman on from the union again saying that they are going to contest her dismissal. Apparently we are persecuting her for her sexual preferences.'

'Oh honestly these people. And I suppose they'll be pressing for compensation despite the fact that she was boasting in the paper last week that she has earned more in the past month than she did in her entire teaching career.'

'I think I was reading that she's due to be on one of those reality TV shows soon, so I'll suppose she'll make more money from that as well.'

'No doubt. I can't begin to tell you how depressing I find it all but there you are. Now I'm going to get on with this revision.'

As the head teacher left the office she almost walked into Jonas Kirwan, a ponytailed young man from New Zealand who had been brought in to cover the Physics revision lessons left uncovered by the departure of Chris Clarke.

'Oh hello Mr Kirwan, how are you today?'

'Not too bad Ms Carr but I've found something that I think you ought to look at.'

'Is it important Mr Kirwan since I do have a class to take?'

'I think you need to see it; have you got a DVD player in your office?'

They went back into the head teacher's office and surprised Valerie Bastic Styles who was brushing her hair.

'Could you set the DVD player up please Mrs Bastic Styles.'

'Certainly head teacher.'

As they waited Jonas Kirwan explained.

'I found it when I was looking for the DVD on Reflection and Refraction.'

The deputy head teacher pressed play and the now familiar setting of the school gymnasium flickered up in grainy images.

'Oh no,' said the head teacher.

The figure of Chris Clarke was standing boldly in front of the camera and next to him stood a woman wearing a cricket helmet and nothing else. Clarke asked 'are we rolling?' and with that the woman turned towards him and removed her helmet. The head teacher reached for the stop button and announced,

'I think we've seen enough don't you?'

'It does go on for nearly half an hour,' said Mr Kirwan.

'Yes well I'm sure it does but I think the best place for this is in the bin. Now can I please ask for your assurance that news of this will go no further than this office?'

The two others nodded their heads.

'Good. Now if you could go back to your lesson Mr Kirwan and I thank you for your diligence and honesty in this matter.'

The physics teacher left and the two women were left looking at each other. It was the deputy head who spoke first.

'Rachel Kelly never had her hair as light as that did she?'

'No Valerie she didn't.'

chapter twenty eight

J.P.P. Montgomery smiled down upon the assembly of upper sixth formers in front of him. Everyone in the room knew what was coming but this only added to the air of warm anticipation in the room. Each year the head master saw the leavers from St George's College off in the same style and it had become a moment to be treasured by each successive year.

He paused, savouring the moment, before asking,

'Shall we go and say goodbye to the old place then?'

The hall erupted in a cacophonous cheer and Montgomery descended the stairs and threw open the side doors. He walked on and the one hundred and fifty or so sixth formers followed behind him. They came out into glorious sunshine and followed as the head led the way to the centre of the immaculately kept school grounds. Along the way there was a hubbub of laughter and chat and various students signed each others books and shirts. Some gave piggy backs to others and photographs were posed for in wilfully wacky style. As they looked up to see that Montgomery had stopped, the noise subsided and the students gathered around him on all sides. He turned the full circle of the group before he began.

'Look carefully at your surroundings everyone. Look here to the bell tower that you have heard ring every day for the past seven, or more, years of your life. Look at the imposing gothic architecture of the old building and think of the times spent in there. Look at these magnificent playing fields which all of you have graced at some point and think of your time here. Think of the people that have given their lives to imparting knowledge to you and think of the knowledge that you take away with you. Think of the beauty of learning and the insatiable wonder that is the human mind and use your learning for good. Never forget how privileged you have been to attend a school such as this and never despise those that have not had your good fortune. Your time here draws to a close and you must embrace that change. Spare a thought for those that you leave behind and then stride forward and take your place in this glorious world we live in. You go with all of our very best wishes.'

The group applauded and members of the first XV rugby team cried luxuriously. Boys took the opportunity to hug the girls that had arrived in the lower sixth and whom they had looked at longingly for the past two years' worth of lessons. The girls, aware of their motives, indulged them for the sake of the occasion and J.P.P. Montgomery slipped away unnoticed by the group to go back to his office and reflect on the terrible sense of time ebbing away that he felt at this time every year.

Nigel Rose would be there waiting for him and they would share a glass of whisky and wonder where the time had gone.

part three

chapter one

In late May the public examinations season arrived and tested the examination aged pupils from around the country on the knowledge and skills that they had learnt in their eleven, twelve or thirteen years of school life.

At St George's Cross School, Valerie Bastic Styles still shattered after a sleepless night on the head teacher's futon bed, went temporarily word blind as she dismissed a GCSE Maths exam and after searching painfully and fruitlessly for the word 'playground' finally instructed the pupils to depart for 'the er, the er….. sunshine area' which prompted howls of delight and an unseemly rush for the back doors.

At St George's College, Nigel Rose watched on as the College Chaplain led the pupils in prayer before every exam and silently prayed for his wife Marjorie and for her full recovery from the recently diagnosed cancer.

Belle Jones looked anxiously at the exam questions on the English Literature GCSE paper and assured herself that she had covered the theme of law and justice in *A View from the Bridge* in sufficient detail. Michael Harris thought that it was a very reasonable paper and quietly congratulated himself on the fact that he had covered the mutual benefits of George and Lennie's relationship in *Of Mice and Men* during the final revision session the day before. They then shared a moment of delighted surprise at the fact that Leonard Baxter managed to attend all three of the English exams, before going down to the pub to talk about the summer holidays.

All around the country, hundreds of thousands of examinations were sat and the papers were dutifully collected in silence before being delivered to the school's examinations officer. He or she then tied the papers up and carefully stored them before sending the whole enormous bundle off to StanEd to be delivered to the appropriate marker, a specialist in their respective field, whom it was presumed would then pore over it carefully, mark scheme by their side, and bring all their hard won knowledge to bear on each answer before awarding the final mark and grade – in the process helping to decide the academic fate of that particular child.

And then pupils fly away on holiday and forget about their studies before returning to receive their grades through the post or at school. And the teachers also go away on holiday and forget about their classes before returning and hoping that most of their pupils get what they deserve and a few get a little more than they deserve.

chapter two

In June when the endless bundles of actual examination papers started to arrive at StanEd's headquarters from the country's schools, Kenneth Andrews got to work quickly. He had noticed a distinct thawing in relations between Jefferson and Samantha after his idea of trapping them in the lift seemed to backfire somewhat.

'What are you playing at Sammy?'

'What do you mean Ken?'

'The lift. You go in there a smouldering sexpot and come out like a maiden aunt.'

'We were chatting.'

'Chatting? The government's not paying you to chat, they're paying you to tantalise him and keep him out of mischief through sexual distraction.'

'But Ken it's not easy to keep it up for hours on end; sometimes I'm not in the mood, and he's a really nice bloke.'

'May I remind you, darling sister, of the precise nature of your duties here at StanEd. One, to remain absolutely silent about everything that you see and do whilst in this building. Which I presume the Government Secrets Act which you have signed is sufficient to guarantee and two (and your only other role as far as I'm aware) to sexually distract Jefferson Tweedy; a task that you are clearly failing to do at present.

We cannot afford to have that buffoon wandering around this building, poking his nose in wherever he may choose.'

'I know all that Ken.'

'Then why don't you do it you stupid little bitch? And if a government contract is not enough to concentrate your pitiful little brain then think about the outrageous wages we are paying you to sit around all day and distract an idiot. Think about being able to afford a nice semi-detached with Barry, because believe me sweetheart this money is the only way you'll ever be able to afford it. Have I made myself clear?'

Samantha did not reply.

'Well?'

She nodded a muted assent.

'Good. Now sort yourself out.'

After he sent her out Kenneth called Aggy into his office and ordered her to stock up on laxatives and told her that if necessary she should be prepared to give Tweedy a large enough dose to keep him out of action until next year's exams, never mind this year's. Aggy took it with her usual calmness and told her son to simply give her the word.

Kenneth took the lift to the basement and tapped in a number on the security lock. The door opened stiffly and Kenneth took a while to adjust his eyes to the blue darkness of the room. The blue light was coming from a small television screen in the far corner of the room. In front of the screen sat two men of feral appearance. As they heard the approach of

Kenneth Andrews they turned and acknowledged him with a gesture that could be placed somewhere between a grin and a sneer. Both men were unnaturally hirsute and the little skin on their faces that remained uncovered by hair, shone blue from the light of the screen. Kenneth Andrews held his hand over his mouth and gagged slightly on the smell of the room as he approached the two men.

'Ah good afternoon Sherwood, good afternoon Sidney how are we this fine day?'

The two men made no vocal response but nodded quickly at Kenneth Andrews. Kenneth shuddered at the monstrous and inhuman sounds that emitted from the television screen and echoed around the dripping black walls of the basement; he decided that he would rather not know what the two men were watching.

Without taking his eyes off the two men, Kenneth side stepped over to the nearest wall and found a light switch which he turned on. The light cast a weak glow over the room. As his eyes adjusted, Kenneth could see the vastness of the basement room. All around the room sat mountains of anthologies and exam papers. Some of these papers were boxed up whilst others sat slippery from the damp of the room. Kenneth risked a fuller intake of breath before signalling for both of the men to stand up and follow him. When he thought that they had understood his signal Kenneth set off for the far corner of the room before turning around to check that they were following. He clicked his fingers twice to hurry them along and then watched their progress. When the hairier of the two men – Sidney he thought – walked, his back was practically horizontal, almost at a perfect right angle; the other – presumably Sherwood –

walked upright but with a distinct drag of his right foot. Kenneth opened his eyes slightly in horror before turning and continuing to weave his way between the vast containers and piles towards the far right hand corner of the room. At one point he thought he had lost the men but then heard an enormous and fluid sneeze from just behind him and walked on with a slight shudder.

Kenneth stopped when he came to an enormous skip like container in the right hand corner of the room. Over the top of the container was a vast cover, in the middle of which was a hole the size of a large round television. Out of this hole came a chute which led down to the floor by Kenneth's feet.

Kenneth waited for the men to catch up with him and once he thought he had what could be described as their attention he began to talk very slowly.

'Now Sidney, Sherwood you have got a very important job to do in the next few weeks. Are you listening carefully?'

The men nodded and Kenneth thought he had better get on with it before he lost their attention completely.

'Each morning you will start a fire in this container, like we did the day you arrived here.'

This news prompted visible delight in the two men and they began to jump up and down and slap each other heavily on the back. The one on the left began to make flame like noises and wave his arms in the air and Jefferson had to call them to order again.

'Now listen carefully. You will start the fire at eight o'clock…'

The mention of the word fire provoked some more arm waving but Kenneth pretended he hadn't seen it and continued stoically.

'…I shall then arrive at nine o'clock with a bundle of papers. Now there are lots and lots of bundles of papers so you will be very busy and it may take two weeks to burn all of the papers.'

The thought of two weeks of fire was evidently beyond Sherwood and Sidney's wildest dreams and they both began to slap each other heavily on the back again. For one moment Kenneth thought the hairiest one was going to slap him on the back but Kenneth took a swift step backwards and barked 'No,' in an authoritative tone and the hairy one went back to slapping his friend. As the slapping quietened down Kenneth continued.

'Now when the papers arrive, you are to bring them over to this container which will have the fire in it…'

Kenneth dared them with his eyes to start slapping each other again,

'…and then you place them carefully in this chute. The chute is then lifted up and the papers will fall into the fire and burn.'

Kenneth allowed them a moment's slapping before concluding,

'It is very important Sherwood, Sidney that all of the papers are burnt.

Nothing must be left over. Do you understand?'

Sherwood and Sidney nodded solemnly and Kenneth said, 'Good. Now go back.'

The men right angled and dragged their way back to the light of the television screen and sat themselves no more than a foot away from the screen. Kenneth briefly caught sight of the source of their entertainment and felt his stomach turn. He put his scented handkerchief to his mouth and hurried to the door.

chapter three

J.P.P. Montgomery hummed into the phone as he waited for it to be picked up. The far back tones of Buffy Shirley Beavan came on the other end of the line.

'Buffy Shirley Beavan.'

'Buffy you darling girl how the devil are you?'

'Philip what a lovely surprise.'

'Isn't it always?'

'Oh of course you lovely thing, what else is a girl to look forward to?'

'Ah you say the sweetest things Buffy, you make an old man very happy.'

'Oh you don't know the half of it Philip. Now how can I help you darling?'

'Well I thought I'd just call to check how those gallops are going old thing. By the way I know I said it before but I thought she looked in tremendous shape at Newmarket.'

'Yes she wasn't bad was she.'

'The press have been very complimentary haven't they?'

'Ah now let's not get carried away by the press Philip; we know how notoriously unreliable they are.'

'I know, I know but it does my old heart good to read some nice clippings. As you know I don't get out much these days and must take my small pleasures where I can.'

'Nice to hear you're still working the same old routine Philip. I shall never tire of it of course, although you should have done so years ago.'

'Ah the famous BSB tongue, acerbic and dangerous; I like a sharp tongue on a woman. You've always reminded me of a young Lauren Bacall, circe *The Big Sleep*.'

'Oh please. Now if we could get back to business. Your St George's Blue is going very nicely thank you. The gallops are good for her and young Sean is taking good care of her. If ever you want to come down and have a look at her in training you know you're more than welcome.'

'And what about the St Leger?'

'What about the St Leger?'

'Can she win it?'

'Yes she can win it but so can five or six other horses so let's not get carried away shall we.'

'No, no you're absolutely right, one step at a time and all that.'

'And how is Lib?'

'Lib is in particularly rude health at present. She is heavily involved in some scheme for helping Zimbabweans who are trying to or have escaped the Mugabe regime. Terrifying stuff some of it, it really is.'

'I imagine so.'

'Yes Lib is in good form and we're all okay this end.'

'Well, like I say, if ever you want to come up and watch Blue train you're more than welcome.'

'That's very kind and I may well take you up on your

offer. We're off soon and I could come down during some of my copious free time.'

'You lucky thing, how long have you got?'

'Just the eight weeks for the summer break, Buffy.'

'Oh Philip, how will you manage?'

'I know. Look take care Buffy, nice to speak to you and I'll see you soon.'

'You too Philip, bye.'

J.P.P. Montgomery put the phone down and went to deliver his end of year assembly to the whole school.

chapter four

The summer passed in a burst of unusually hot weather. J.P.P. Montgomery and Lib spent most of July in France at their house in Provence. Lib painted and retained e-mail contact with her friends at the Zimbabwean embassy, whilst Philip read crime fiction and wandered around the locale challenging elderly men in cafés to games of chess. He remained unbeaten for eight days of the holiday until the ninth night when the wrong side of a bottle and a half of excellent local red wine he was comfortably beaten by a man wearing an eye patch, whom he suspected of drinking absinth.

Emma and Luke Carr went away with Emma's parents for ten days to a hotel in Spain that had promised on the brochure to offer entertainment and activities for children. On arrival it became clear that the entertainment for children comprised of the hotel having a swimming pool which they were forced to sit around for most of their stay being splashed by 'bombing' children. Emma grew accustomed to the noise after a couple of days but her father decided to frequent a café in the town centre and read the English papers. Luke was then sick ('something in the water,' said her mother) and was confined to his room for three days, during which time Emma found herself enjoying re runs of *Cheers* and *Mash* on Sky television whilst comforting Luke when he woke. The three books that she had so looked forward to reading remained untouched in her bag and by the end of the ten days she had rowed with her mother and was looking forward to getting home.

Both head teachers arrived home in good time for the arrival of the exam results. The A Level results arrived on Thursday 19th August and St George's College was delighted with the performance of their students. All achieved their required grades and duly accepted the places at their chosen universities. Montgomery held his usual champagne celebration in his office for staff and noted with no great surprise that Bryn Castle chose not to join them.

St George's Cross was unaffected by the arrival of A level results since it had no sixth form but Emma Carr sat at home and read the press articles about the continuing fall in educational standards and how A grades were easier to achieve with every passing year. Valerie Bastic Styles called from her sister's house in Hornchurch where she was spending the summer and asked what time Emma would be getting in to school the following Thursday for the arrival of the GCSE results. They agreed that they ought to be in for eight o'clock so that they could be the first to look at the results and get to work on producing the data analysis for the teachers to look at.

The following Thursday morning arrived and it was a beautiful August day. All around the country head teachers, teachers, parents and pupils made their way into schools.

J.P.P. Montgomery and Emma Carr both drove to work and enjoyed the lack of traffic the school holidays brought. At the lights on the main road, Montgomery saw Emma in his rear view mirror and gave her a little wave and crossed his fingers theatrically before pulling away from the traffic lights and into St George's Road.

Both head teachers arrived to find their closest allies at the school already there. Nigel Rose mock saluted Montgomery as he drove into the car park and Valerie Bastic Styles waved enthusiastically as Emma got out of her car.

'They're all here,' called Valerie Bastic Styles 'I put them on your desk and I promise I didn't have a peek at them!'

The two pairs of teachers walked into their respective head teacher's office at the same time and Montgomery sighed, 'Here we go again,' as he picked up the large envelope on his desk and began to open it with the knife that he kept in his drawer.

Emma Carr breathed deeply over the package and looked at Valerie Bastic Styles. Valerie crossed her fingers and Emma set about opening the package.

As Nigel Rose and J.P.P. Montgomery cast their eye over the paperwork the first few results caused a furrowing of brows. They said nothing and continued to look down the sheet before Montgomery looked up at Nigel Rose and said,

'Something's badly wrong here. Get on the phone to the board.'

Meanwhile in the head teacher's office at St George's Cross an early optimism at the first few results quickly grew into a state of impossible ecstasy. The accompanying shrieks of joy as pupil after pupil spectacularly surpassed their predictions didn't quite carry into the office of J.P.P. Montgomery at St George's College but they very nearly did.

Emma Carr looked at Valerie Bastic Styles and said,

'There's been a mistake hasn't there?'

'How can there have been? These are our pupils and the paper work has got St George's Cross written all over it.'

'I know but Leonard Baxter has got seven As and two Bs. Is that possible?'

'Perhaps he was revising from the resources we set up on the Virtual Learning Environment. We all knew he wasn't a stupid boy.'

'Do you really think so?'

'Well how else can they be explained? It's all here. I just think all the things you have tried to do this year have paid off and as a result we have a simply outstanding set of results head teacher.'

The phone on the desk rang and Emma Carr pointed for Valerie to answer it; as Valerie began to talk Emma looked out of the window.

Valerie Bastic Styles put her hand over the mouthpiece and called for Emma's attention.

'It's Ray from the *Advertiser* he wants to know if we want him to do an article on the school's results this year.'

Emma looked out of the window and watched the weather vane at the top of St George's College chapel spin around in a rare gust of August wind. She turned around slowly to face Valerie and said,

'Yes, tell him to come down here and tell him we've got a bit of a story for him.'

chapter five

Ray Gains, reporter for the *South London Advertiser*, was not in a hurry to get to St George's Cross. He had been stuck for twenty five minutes at a temporary traffic lights tail back on the South Circular and this suited him rather well since the thought of covering yet another year's exam results did not fill him with any sense of joy or uplift. As a young man he dreamed of being a sports writer on one of the national newspapers, a highly respected yet humorous sage of sport; but as he would tell anyone who cared to listen, the opportunities never arrived for Ray Gains and now he plied his trade covering whichever small fry stories his sub editor chose to send him to.

As he stepped out of the car at just gone 10 o'clock Valerie Bastic Styles began to run towards him.

'Good morning Mrs Bastic Styles.'

'Oh Ray, something extraordinary has happened, please come inside.'

Ray Gains followed her into the building and into an office where Emma Carr was sitting at the desk.

'Ray, this is Emma Carr the head teacher.'

'We've met, how are you Mrs Carr?'

'Outstandingly well, thank you Ray.'

'So how are the results this year?'

Ray asked the question with a good idea what the answer would be. In the last couple of years the school had not been interested in the press knowing their results and Ray had treated the news of OFSTED's special measures with great sensitivity, choosing instead to run a feature on the arrival of Mrs Carr and accentuating the wind of change that was blowing through the school.

'Extraordinary Ray.'

'How pleasing. An improvement on last year?'

'Yes an improvement on last year.'

'Do you have the figures available yet?'

'We do.'

Ray sensed that Mrs Carr was holding something back but went on with his well versed line of sensitive questioning.

'Would you be prepared to divulge the figures at this stage?'

The head teacher paused and looked out of the window; both Valerie Bastic Styles and Ray Gains looked on and waited.

'We would.'

'Excellent – so last year's 5 A*-C grade passes were?'

'18%'

'Righty ho and this year's?'

Emma Carr paused again before answering.

'100%'

Ray Gains looked up from his piece of paper and held his pen in mid air. The head teacher continued to look out of the window whilst Valerie Bastic Styles beamed down at him.

'I'm sorry Mrs Carr, did you say 100%?'

'100%'

'Are we are talking 5 A* to C grades?'

'Isn't it extraordinary?' cried Valerie Bastic Styles. 'And it's all down to Emma and her wonderful energy; she has quite simply turned this school around in spectacular style.'

'100%?' repeated Ray Gains.

'100%,' confirmed Emma Carr.

'Here are the results if you want to see them.' Valerie Bastic Styles thrust a sheaf of papers into Ray's hand and urged him to look at them. As he did so he saw pages of A*s and As and as he turned the pages the smile of Valerie Bastic Styles grew ever larger.

'Isn't this a story Ray? Isn't she wonderful? One woman has single handedly turned a failing school into the most astounding success.'

As she talked, the headlines began to form in Ray Gains' mind. He could see them with his name beneath the copy. This was a story to sell on; Ray Gains could make the nationals with this one. He looked at his watch.

'Right ladies, if we get a move on I can have this one ready for *The Standard's* final edition.' Ray opened his notebook with a vigour that it hadn't seen for years and asked,

'Just remind me Mrs Carr, when exactly did you arrive at the school?'

chapter six

Nigel Rose was having trouble getting through to speak to anyone at StanEd. He turned to Montgomery and mused;

'It does strike me that in this age of increased communication it is becoming harder and harder to actually speak to anyone.'

Montgomery was looking over the GCSE results and shaking his head.

'These are miles out, these are bloody miles out. Look at this; Leo Rafferty E grade in English and an E grade in Literature. Now you could sit Leo Rafferty down blindfolded, with a hot poker up his arse and he still couldn't write you an E grade essay. And they're trying to tell us that he has done that in all of his exams except for Art where he had a good day and managed to get a D. This is Tweedy and his pals up to their usual tricks. Incompetent bunch of tossers. Get him on the line Nigel.'

'I can't get any answer at the moment, Philip.'

'Well stay there until you do and then tell them that I want to speak to Herr Tweedy and that he'd better have some answers for me, the miserable little prick.'

At StanEd headquarters, Liz the receptionist – following the instructions of Kenneth Andrews – finally took the answer phone off at one o'clock in the afternoon. She had learnt from bitter experience that phone calls on results day rarely brought good news and so when Mr Andrews had assured that there would be no deluge of calls this year and that she should keep it on answer phone, she had been surprised but highly delighted. It was only when Kenneth Andrews walked past and asked if there had been any calls, that she took the answer phone off and prepared to answer the phone. She was quickly disappointed when it rung immediately.

'Good afternoon, StanEd.'

'Ah yes good afternoon this is Nigel Rose from St George's College centre number 69421. I have been trying to get through to you all morning because we have some serious misgivings about our school's GCSE results and I was hoping to speak to somebody about what we think is a mistake of the grossest proportions.'

'I'm sorry about that sir, but as you can imagine our operators have been very busy today. If you'll just hold the line I'll try to put you through.'

Nigel Rose rolled his eyes at the head master and waited. Montgomery continued to scoff over the results and regularly shouted out the names of their most able boys followed by an array of shocking exam results.

'Unbelievable,' he repeated. 'Have you actually spoken to anyone yet Nigel? Have you reached a human voice, have you breached Tweedy's fortress?'

'I'm on hold.'

'There's a surprise. You know I shouldn't get upset about

something like this because I know through years of bitter experience what an incompetent bunch of arses they are up there and yet every year they manage to surprise me with the levels of incompetence they sink to. This is all quite clearly a mistake and it'll all get sorted out but we're the ones that will have to spend the time chasing the cretins and we're the ones that will have to tell the boys that their results aren't ready and pacify the parents, whilst this rabble stick another dagger into the credibility of our education system.'

Nigel Rose held his hand up and Montgomery stopped talking. The voice on the end of the phone almost purred,

'Kenneth Andrews speaking.'

'Ah hello, this is Nigel Rose from St George's College, centre number 69421.'

'Good afternoon Mr Rose.'

'Good afternoon. We have received our GCSE results this morning and there has quite clearly been a terrible mistake. Last year we achieved a 100% pass rate for 5 A*–C grades and we believed that this year's cohort were if anything brighter than last year's and although we haven't done the figures as yet it would appear that we'd be lucky to have achieved 25% 5 A*–C grades. So we are certain there has been some kind of an error in the sorting of the results and wondered if you could look into it for us.'

'I'd be happy to do that for you Mr Rose. As I'm sure you are aware I'll need a little time to that, so if I could just take your details and if you could fax the master copy of your results through for the attention of Kenneth Andrews then I'll call you back when I've investigated your case.'

'What do you suggest we tell the boys when they come into the school for their results?'

'Oh I'll leave that to you Mr Rose, I'm sure you know the best way to deal with your school's particular needs. Good bye.'

Nigel Rose put the phone down.

'What did he say?' said Montgomery.

'He'll look into it and call us back.'

'So we just wait do we? What do we tell the boys?'

'He wasn't terribly helpful on that point.'

chapter seven

Kenneth Andrews received the fax from Nigel Rose at St George's College and was now looking through the thin pieces of paper holding the results the school had been awarded. He sipped at his cup of latte coffee and looked over the half moon spectacles he wore for close work. He tapped into his system and checked to see which room had entered the grades for schools beginning with S – the file told him that it was LG23.

'The actors,' he muttered to himself and pulled his seat slightly closer to the screen. He tapped a series of keys on the computer and waited. The results that St George's College had been given for this year equated to a 26% 5 A*–C grade pass rate and he wanted to find their results for the previous year. The list of schools came up and Kenneth scrolled down until he came to S. He found St George's College and next to it – 99%. He placed both his elbows on the desk and exhaled loudly. With a sinking heart he went back to the keyboard and called up the predicted grades for this year's results. The computer quickly told him what he already knew – St George's College 100%. He leant back on his chair and put his hands behind his head.

This was not good.

As he looked back at the screen he looked again at the results for St George's and his heart jumped with relief. He had misread it, their predicted grades were 24%; there was no mistake here. He re-adjusted his spectacles with relief and checked again. On this additional check his stomach dropped again and the root of the problem became clear. The figures for St George's College and St George's Cross sat side by side on the computer screen and intermingled before his eyes. He placed his hand across the screen to draw a line under St George's College and then pressed the return button to separate the two schools; the man at St George's College was right, his school had been given the wrong results. Kenneth presumed that the other school, St George's Cross, must have received the 100% pass rate belonging to their near namesakes and must therefore also be informed of the mistake.

Once this mess was sorted out Kenneth Andrews swore that the actors in LG23 would feel the full force of his fury and wrath but for now it was simply a case of calling the two schools and informing them of the administrative error, apologising profusely, before informing them that their examination results would be rectified with immediate effect. These were not easy conversations to have but experience told Kenneth Andrews that they were best done quickly and he set off to inform Liz of what he needed doing. As he got to the door the phone in his office rang; he returned to his desk and picked it up swiftly.

'Kenneth Andrews.'

'What the fucking hell is going on there?'

There was no mistaking the distinctive Scottish tones.

'Lord McLeish?'

'Do you know what I've got in my hand Andrews?'

'I've no idea sir.'

'Well let me tell you. I have the late edition of today's *Standard* and do you know what is plastered all over the front page of said *Standard*?'

'I've no idea sir.'

'Well I'll tell you. Some woman from a shithole school in South London crowing about the fact that her bunch of monkeys have achieved perfect GCSE results. Now I'll ask you again Andrews, what the fucking hell is going on there?'

'Did you happen to catch the name of the school in the aforementioned article sir?'

'What?'

'The school sir.'

'St George's something...'

'Would that be St George's Cross sir?'

'Yes, I think so. Why?'

'Ah well that is all in hand sir. There was, I admit, an administrative error that resulted in two schools having their results mixed up but it is easily rectified and rest assured the culprits will be punished immediately.'

There was a moment's quiet on the other end of the line as Lord McLeish digested what Kenneth had said. When he spoke again it was in a threatening whisper.

'I think you are rather missing the point Andrews. The fact that you have identified the cretin or cretins who have caused this embarrassment is neither here nor there. The important matter that you seem to have missed with such ease is the fact that the embarrassment has been caused and more importantly the embarrassment is in the papers. And as you well know Andrews, once the story is in the newspapers then you can never get it back. Once the good people of

London have perused *The Standard* on their way home from work – on the tube, on the bus, in their cars – it is too late for you, me or God Almighty himself to stop the story. It takes on a life of its own, it feeds and it grows and so the results are as they are. Do you really think that you calling *The Standard* and telling them 'I'm awfully sorry but there's been some terrible mistake, so the story that you led with yesterday is really not a story at all but it's all right because I've called the schools concerned and they've all been very understanding,' is going to change anything?

'But sir.'

'Don't but sir me. The whole idea of this project, and your entire reason for existing for the past year, was to avoid precisely this sort of shambolic press. To avoid the sort of press that made a laughing stock out of the previous examination regimes and ensured that they sunk without trace. Am I to go to the hugely powerful people that employed me, to employ you, and tell them that thanks to your brilliance half the people in the country think that Piss Stain High has got the best grades in the country? But don't worry Kenneth's gone to *The Standard* and they've promised to put a one line apology on Page 16 of tomorrow's paper and lead instead with StanEd cock up headlines.

So no Andrews, you will not be calling the schools to explain to them that there has been a small mistake.'

'But what about the other school?'

'What other school?'

'The school that should have got the brilliant results.'

There was silence on the other end of the line. Kenneth waited nearly thirty seconds before the response came.

'Fuck 'em.'

'I beg your pardon sir?'

'Fuck 'em.'

'Really?'

'Now listen carefully Andrews and I mean more carefully than when I told you to listen to me the last time when I was telling you not to make a badger's arse of this entire system. This is what has happened and this is what will have happened whenever anyone asks you about this whole sorry affair. This other school, whoever they are, are a victim of the new level playing field. We promised that all schools would be judged on their merits and this lot have failed to keep pace with the changes in education. Their methods have been shown to be hopelessly out of date; they are a dinosaur from a bygone age. As opposed to your other lot – Piss Stain High – who are in contrast a beacon school, an example to all the other failing schools in how to turn yourself around. And do you know how they have done it Andrews?'

'Government initiatives sir.'

'Exactly Andrews, government initiatives. And if all the other schools were good little schools and did exactly what we told them to do they too could be a beacon school with the best results in the country and make the front page of *The Evening Standard*. Is that clear Andrews?'

'Absolutely Lord McLeish.'

'Good, now get on with it and I would suggest that your first phone call be to *The Standard*, so we can place ourselves firmly on the crest of this publicity.'

As Kenneth went to put the phone down he heard Lord McLeish's voice bellowing, 'And Andrews.'

'Yes sir.'

'Make sure Tweedy stays well out of this.'

chapter eight

J.P.P. Montgomery and Nigel Rose sat by the phone in the office. All day, parents had called demanding to know when their children would be getting their GCSE results and Nigel's heart sank as it rang again.

'Shall I?' he asked.

'Be my guest.' replied Montgomery.

Nigel Rose pressed the button for speaker phone and then picked up the receiver.

'St George's College, Nigel Rose speaking.'

'Ah Mr Rose, it's Kenneth Andrews from StanEd here. Sorry I took so long to get back to you.'

Nigel Rose signalled urgently to J.P.P. Montgomery.

'Ah Mr Andrews, we've been waiting for your call, the parents are getting rather impatient down here.'

'I can imagine.'

'So have we sorted this out?'

'Well Mr Rose I have investigated your claim of a mistake and I can confirm after meticulous checks that there has been no error; your school was sent the correct results.'

'But this is impossible.'

J.P.P. Montgomery looked up from his desk. Nigel Rose went on, 'Are you telling me that our school has dropped from 100% pass rate last year…'

'As I understand sir it was 99%,' corrected Kenneth Andrews.

'….well 99% then to 20% or whatever it is this year.'

'It is 26% this year sir.'

'26% then. Are you telling me that this is the case?'

'Yes sir, that is the case.'

'Well this is preposterous, and I don't actually believe you, so naturally we will be asking for our entire set of papers to be re-marked immediately, in order to rectify this grave error.'

'May I take the opportunity to remind you sir that at the launch of StanEd, we stated quite clearly that there would be no re-mark facility available to schools, since the reliability of one professional examinations board would eradicate the need for such a procedure.'

As Nigel Rose began to formulate an answer J.P.P. Montgomery snatched the receiver from his hand and barked into the phone.

'Who is this?'

'I am Kenneth Andrews sir, can I help you?'

'Yes you can help me. I am J.P.P. Montgomery the head master of St George's College and it is quite clear that you and your people have made a cock up of the most enormous proportions and I'd like to try and get to the bottom of it. I have parents here wanting to know what exactly they have spent their £60 000 in school fees on, and frankly I think they are entitled to a few answers. Now my colleague and I have spent more than enough time speaking to monkeys such as yourself and it's about time we had a few words with the organ grinder, so if you could put me through to your fuhrer Tweedy, I'd like to hear what he has to say on the matter.'

'I'm afraid, sir, Mr Tweedy is not available at present but I could get him to call you back.'

'Why does that not surprise me? Well you do that my man and tell him J.P.P. Montgomery, the head master of St George's College, is awaiting his call and is rather eager to speak to him.'

Kenneth Andrews heard the phone slam down and took a moment to compose himself before replacing the receiver. After running a finger across first his left eyebrow and then his right he went off to find Jefferson Tweedy.

chapter nine

Kenneth found Jefferson sitting alongside Samantha in front of his computer screen. When he knocked on the door, Samantha was showing Jefferson the wedding dress that she knew she wanted, should Barry ever get around to popping the question. During this discussion she confessed that she was beginning to despair of him ever asking but it was best that a girl be prepared. She said that she thought he might have proposed on their recent tenth anniversary but her heart had sunk when he turned up wearing white jeans; she knew that Barry would never wear white jeans if he intended getting down on one knee and proposing.

Jefferson loosened his tie and briefly found himself genuinely interested in the wedding dress discussion; indeed it prompted him to spend a few animated minutes describing Ailsa's colouring to Samantha so that they could try to guess what sort of dress she would choose.

Kenneth walked part of the way into the room before saying,

'Samantha do you think you could give Mr Jefferson and myself a little time please?'

Kenneth watched her disappear into the adjoining office before pulling the chair up in front of Jefferson's desk.

'And how are we today Mr Jefferson?'

'Oh busy, busy, but we mustn't complain must we Kenneth.'

'Absolutely Mr Jefferson.' Kenneth pulled his chair a touch closer to Jefferson. 'Now the reason for my visit is this; as I am sure you are aware today was the day that the nation's schools received their GCSE examination results.'

Jefferson nodded, pleased that he was aware of that.

'And all appears to have gone very well.'

'Excellent, excellent.'

'Due in no small part may I say sir to your outstanding leadership.'

Jefferson bowed his head slowly.

'Now the reason I come to you is this. In a system as vast as the one we operate, there are bound to be those that feel aggrieved by the outcome, those that have an issue with their results and one such case has been on the telephone to me this morning. I'm sorry to say that he became quite agitated at points and finally insisted quite vehemently that he be allowed to speak to you.'

Jefferson felt a mixture of panic and pride at the thought that people were requesting him by name.

'Now I did try to placate him but with only limited success. The situation is as follows; he is the head master of a prestigious public boys' school in London and his school's results this year have been something of a disappointment to him and I fear he is looking to vent his anger. The truth of the matter is Mr Tweedy that he is fully aware that there is only one man responsible for his school's disappointing performance and that is him. I am afraid that since we have given all the schools a level playing field, some schools have been shown to be rather behind the times in their methods and the results have born this out.'

'I see. Sort of old fashioned if you like.'

'Absolutely Mr Jefferson. Now he has asked to speak to you personally and I'm sure he'll say much the same thing to you that he said to me. Now rest assured, I have checked the results with extreme care and there is no error or mistake here. I'm afraid our man's school has simply been proven to be not quite as successful as he would have liked us all to believe.'

'I see.'

'So many of these public schools are living in a bygone era Mr Jefferson and the triumph of the level playing field that we have established for our education system is that we can finally see which schools are genuinely achieving and which schools need to pull their socks up.'

'I see and which school is this Kenneth?'

'It's a school called St George's College, Mr Jefferson.'

Jefferson's mind flicked to schoolboy train journeys and the pages of *The Sporting Life*. 'Is it really Kenneth? I know that one. Is the head master a J.P.P. Montgomery?'

'It is sir. Sir your knowledge is simply outstanding. Don't tell me you're familiar with the names of the country's head masters.'

'One or two Kenneth, one or two. I find these little snippets come in so handy at moments like this, don't you?'

'Remarkable sir.'

'Now have you got a number for Mr Montgomery? I shall call him immediately; he is after all still a valued customer is he not?'

'Indeed sir. Would you like me to write a few ideas down for you sir? Should the conversation become difficult?'

'No no Kenneth, I think I'll be all right with this one.'

chapter ten

Kenneth Andrews picked up the phone in his office at precisely the same time that J.P.P. Montgomery picked up the phone in his office. They both were in time to hear the tones of Jefferson Tweedy employ a technique that he had heard Mr Welch use to great effect under similarly taxing circumstances.

'How's her training going?

'I beg your pardon?' blustered J.P.P. Montgomery.

'How's the training going? Is she going to be ready for the St Leger?'

'Who is this?'

'Am I speaking to J.P.P. Montgomery?'

'Yes.'

'J.P.P. Montgomery, head master of St George's College and owner of the country's most promising race horse?'

'Yes.'

'Jefferson Tweedy, chief executive of StanEd and number one fan of St George's Blue, delighted to speak to you. She's a lovely filly Mr Montgomery, you must be very proud of her.'

'Indeed I am Mr Tweedy.' Montgomery took a moment to gather himself and it briefly crossed his mind that this Tweedy may be better than he had given him credit for. Once recovered, Montgomery took the conversation on to safer territory.

'Listen here Tweedy, don't think that I am not delighted to hear that you have at least some taste but this is not the issue at hand old boy. Your lot up there have made the most monumental error and I want to know what you're going to do about it? I presume you are familiar with the details of the case?'

Jefferson began to answer but Montgomery continued,

'Now I've spoken to one of your lickspittles earlier today and he was what he is paid to be, vague and elusive, so I ask you the same question. How can it be that a school that achieved a 99% pass rate last year and has done since the beginning of time somehow drops to 26% this year. Are you going to deny that there isn't something just the slightest bit fishy about all of this?'

'Well Mr Montgomery as you are well aware we have introduced this year a change to the system where all schools regardless of status are required to be judged by the same standards...'

'Nonsense man and you know it. What system do you think we've been working in? Some kids do well and some kids don't and ours are kids that do well. Money, brains and opportunity has something to do with it.'

'With the greatest of respect Mr Montgomery, for too long pupils like yours have worked in a separate system, a system that may have led them to believe that they were academically superior. Now that all pupils sit the same examination, these results suggest that we may now have to address the idea that that was not the case.'

'I've heard all this from your mandarins and grey men Tweedy and you know full well it's a mendacious piece of guff. Now there's either been a colossal administrative faux pas, in which case I suggest you address it immediately, or else I'm being royally screwed by a New Labour conspiracy. Now which is it?'

'We have made meticulous checks Mr Montgomery and the results are correct.'

'Of course you need a scapegoat. Your New Labour pals don't want schools like ours, so what better way to get rid of us than to doctor a few of the results.'

'I assure you sir that no corporation that I was involved with would ever be involved with such bad practice and I would remind you that these are very serious allegations that you are making.'

'Indeed they are Mr Tweedy. Would you like me to speak a little slower so that you can write them down?'

'I shall put your comments down to the heightened state of agitation that you are in sir.'

'I am indeed in a state of some agitation due solely to the devious machinations of charlatans like you.'

'Now is there anything else that I can help you with today?'

'Are you going to address this issue Tweedy or will you happily stand by and watch as two hundred boys and their staff, myself included, are hung out to dry for the sake of some political master plan?'

'Thank you for your enquiry Mr Montgomery and the very best of luck to St George's Blue in the St Leger, I shall be place a bet on her. Goodbye now.'

As Jefferson Tweedy put the phone down on the swearing J.P.P. Montgomery, so did Kenneth Andrews. Kenneth smiled to himself and said,

'Excellent work Mr Tweedy, excellent work.'

chapter   eleven

Jacob Haliwell received an excited and hurried phone call from Belle telling him about the extraordinary turn around at St George's Cross.

'The school have done amazingly well in their results. Michael has just called me and says it's almost beyond belief. He's convinced there has been some enormous mistake but *The Standard* have already run with a front page and I can get you interviews with Emma Carr and the rest. And Leonard Baxter got two As in English. You should get down there and get some interviews. The nationals'll lap it up – failing comprehensive in miracle turnaround and all that and an attractive young head to boot; it's the story of the summer.'

Jacob wasn't so sure about the last bit but here he stood in Emma Carr's office.

He recognised the woman in the chair as the head teacher but not the woman standing bolt upright next to her. It was this woman that came forward first.

'Hello there, I'm Valerie Bastic Styles you must be the gentleman from the press.'

'How do you do? I'm Jacob Haliwell.' He shook her hand and then approached the desk.

'Hello Mrs Carr, I don't know if you remember me but we've met before.'

'Remind me.'

'At the syllabus launch at the Grosvenor.'

'Oh of course you were there with Belle Jones weren't you?'

'That's right.'

'She's done terrifically well here you know.'

'She'll be pleased to hear you say so. So the first thing to say seems to be congratulations.'

'Thank you.'

'An extraordinary set of results. Have you got the precise numbers?'

The deputy head teacher produced a printed sheet of the results broken down in detail.

'Many thanks,' Jacob glanced over the results, 'these are wonderful.'

'Thank you,' the two women murmured in unison.

Jacob continued. 'Now what I had in mind was a profile piece on you Emma. That'll include stuff on your background, your private life if you wish to include that, some stuff on your educational ethos and what exactly it is you did to turn St George's Cross into the success story it is today. Does that sound okay?'

'That sounds fine.'

'We need to strike that balance between educational integrity and the human interest element.'

'Quite. Which paper are you writing for Mr Haliwell?'

'Well I'm a freelance journalist so essentially we can sell

it to whichever paper we choose. I did though take the liberty of calling a friend of mine at *The Observer* before I came over here and they are very interested in taking it for Sunday's edition.'

'Lovely.'

Emma Carr took a moment to push her hair behind her ear before beginning.

'Well central to my ethos is the importance of a school's staff. The school was recently awarded the Investors in People award and I can't tell you what an important step that was on the path to success...'

Jacob Haliwell took shorthand notes as well as taping the interview whilst Valerie Bastic Styles nodded enthusiastically at thirty second intervals during the first telling of the story of how St George's Cross School rose to greatness.

chapter twelve

Pleased by the way the interview with J.P.P. Montgomery had gone, Jefferson Tweedy felt every inch the chief executive of StanEd. He leaned back in his chair and crossed his legs. Samantha came through the doors and asked,

'Is everything all right Jefferson?'

'Yes, I just had to deal with a disgruntled head. He was pretty irate actually claiming we'd made a cock up with his school's results, but we've checked it all with a fine tooth comb and there's absolutely problem.'

'Oh that's alright then. It sounded like you dealt with it very well.'

'Really? That's very kind of you.'

Jefferson spun around on his chair and then said,

'I think I might go for a little walk; just to stretch the legs so to speak.'

'Do you want me to come with you?'

'No no you're okay, I just want to see how the troops are getting on.'

'Are you sure?' she asked thrusting her breasts towards Jefferson.

'No really I'm absolutely positive. There comes a time when a chief executive must walk these corridors alone.'

He laughed before walking out of the door and calling the lift. Samantha hesitated for a moment then went back to her desk and reached for the button that Ken had told her to press in such a situation. She hovered over it for a moment before she pulled her finger away; she then buttoned up her blouse and called up the bride's tiaras web site she'd found.

Jefferson was heading towards the workers in LG23. He knew they had been hard at it recently and thought they would welcome a morale boosting visit from their leader. He got out of the lift on the ground floor and greeted Lizzie with a breezy 'afternoon,' before skipping lightly down the stairs to the lower ground floor.

As he disappeared down the stairs she pressed the button for such occasions but her light flashed unnoticed in Kenneth Andrews' office as Jefferson Tweedy's tour of the building continued uninterrupted.

Jefferson turned right at the bottom of the stairs and approached the door to LG23. He restrained from knocking and looked up and down the corridor. All was silent as he leant up against the door. At first he heard nothing and resigned himself to having to ask Kenneth to let him into the room, but as he started to back away from the door he heard the muffled noise sound of raised voices. He leant closer but couldn't hear any more clearly and so stepped back from the door. He looked up and down the corridor before turning quickly to his right and walking into the nearby toilet. He locked the door and sat down.

The voice raised in anger could now be heard quite clearly and as Jefferson listened it dawned on him that it was the voice of Kenneth Andrews. He adjusted himself on the toilet seat and listened.

'I do not care about 'your Stanley', Laurence, all I care about is the fact that someone in this room has put all of our livelihoods in jeopardy due to their stupidity and I am intent upon finding out exactly who it was.'

There was a silence.

'Laurence put that drum down and listen to me. I do not care when your 'festival of the Absurd' is, I do not care a jot about your performance. My job is on the line because of somebody in this room and I want to know who it was. Read the data, type in the data, print off the sheet and put the sheet in an envelope – that is it. How difficult can it be? But no, one of 'the actors' is incapable of performing such a straight forward task and as a result my neck is on the line.'

Jefferson heard another voice.

'Are you absolutely sure that it was someone in this room Kenneth?'

'Did you or did you not do the schools from N to S?'

Jefferson could hear murmurs of 'Yes Kenneth.'

'Thank you and tell me do St George's College and St George's Cross begin with S?'

'Yes Kenneth.'

'Thank you. So would you say it was unreasonable for me to presume that the person that managed to swap those two schools results around might be in this room? The person who managed to give one of the worst schools in the country the results of one of the best schools in the country might be in this room.'

Jefferson's stomach lurched and he strained towards the

air vent to make sure that he could hear the next words. There was no response. Kenneth continued.

'Good. Now I want to know who it was. I want the guilty party to make themselves known. Who is it that cannot tell the difference between St George's Cross and St George's College? And if the person doesn't have the guts to own up to their mistake then frankly you can all go. Come on, you're not dealing with that cretin Tweedy now. You can't hope to bluff your way out of this. He is the least of your worries, he means nothing in this world, there are some heavyweight people who need an answer to this question and I am going to give it to them. I know the guilty party is in this room and I want a name.'

After a lengthy pause another voice began.

'This is clearly a case of the gravest magnitude to you Kenneth and if you are convinced that the guilt lies with us and there has been some error concerning the two schools of St George (and I admit from your evidence that it would appear to be the case) then I propose this; we are a company of actors, a merry band of players; we perform together and endure the highs and lows of the stage together and so it is in this spirit that I propose we fall together upon our collective sword. Like Brutus, that most honourable of Romans, we admit our fault and offer you our resignation from this most worthy of posts.'

Other voices called 'Hear, hear,' and 'well said Richard,' before silence descended on the room. The voice began again,

'We are happy and prepared to take our art elsewhere. Wherever there is a space there can be drama, wherever a person watches there can be theatre.'

There was a silence before the voice of Kenneth Andrews began again.

'Good. Now get your stuff and fuck off.'

Jefferson stood up from the toilet seat, opened the door and turned right towards LG23. As the door opened, the actors looked confused by the figure in the doorway blocking their path. Behind them the voice of Kenneth Andrews squealed impatiently,

'Come on, what's the hold up? I told you get out, now get out. I can't bear to see you a moment longer...'

He pushed through the crowd of thespians and came face to face with the chief executive of StanEd; he could not conceal the look of panic that passed over his face. His first response was to try to pull the door shut but Jefferson's size eight and a half brogue got there first and blocked the door open. He then pulled the door out of Kenneth's hand and said,

'I think we should all go back in the room and have a little chat, don't you?'

The actors and Kenneth bowed to a greater authority and shuffled dumbly back into LG23. They took their places in the circle of chairs that were still there from Kenneth's cross examination, only this time the questioner was Jefferson.

'You've made a bit of a monkey out of me haven't you Kenneth?'

'Absolutely not Mr Jefferson...'

'And before we go on may I take this opportunity to finally tell you that my name is not Mr Jefferson, Kenneth and it never has been; my name is Mr Tweedy or Jefferson, you may call me either of these but never call me Mr Jefferson again. Is that understood?'

'Absolutely sir. Now I don't know what you have heard but rest assured I can explain everything.'

'Good. So tell me, have I told Mr Montgomery at St George's College a lie?'

'Up to a point sir.'

'Up to what point Kenneth? Has his school been given the wrong results?'

'No, no absolutely not. His school has simply been left behind by the regime. On a level playing field there is no where for the educational dinosaurs like St George's College to hide.'

'So what is the lie that I have 'up to a point' told?'

'No, there is no lie sir, we have told all the parties concerned the absolute truth.'

Jefferson looked closely at Kenneth and he looked back all the time nodding his head in affirmation of the truth.

'So what was it I heard through the vent?'

'I don't know sir, what was it you heard through the vent?'

'That there was a mistake with St George's College and another St George's school and you thought someone in here was to blame.'

'Really sir, are you really trying to say that the voices that you hear whilst hanging around in toilets are anything to base a serious allegation like this on?'

'I know perfectly well what I heard Kenneth and you know what you said.'

'I simply came in here to commend the workers on the excellent job that they had done. What you may have heard was me simply recounting to these good people the story of how I had to treat a group of workers a few years ago who had not done such a good job as this group.'

'Have I told the truth to Mr Montgomery?'

'Absolutely.'

There was an element of challenge in Kenneth's eyes and Jefferson could feel his power ebbing away. It crossed his mind to threaten Kenneth with exposure to Lord McLeish but he wasn't sure what exactly he would be exposing. A voice interrupted his thoughts.

'That's not strictly true is it Kenneth.'

The circle of people turned to the eldest man in the room. Laurence Chevallier was standing up and now moved to the centre of the circle. A gasp went up from the other actors and Kenneth hissed 'shut up,' at him.

'No I shall not 'shut up' Kenneth, I shall not be gagged. You come in to our place of theatre and insult our craft, pouring scorn on our efforts to enlighten the darkness that is life without the arts and now we are expected to remain silent, no better than shameless conspirators, as you spin a web of treacherous lies to this honourable man, this Brutus figure of our world.'

'Sit down you demented old queen,' hissed Kenneth before turning to Jefferson. 'Sir, you cannot for a moment believe the rantings of this sad and deluded man. He talks of himself as an actor when what he does for a living is man the phones for this examinations board; as you yourself have seen sir, on your tour.'

'I am an actor,' cried Laurence Chevallier, 'I am an actor.'

The first of the rest of the circle to stand was Jean Plowstraight. She went and stood next to Laurence and pronounced, 'I am an actor.' In turn each of the group joined their fellow players with the same call to arms until the entire company stood before Kennth Andrews and Jefferson watched as the colour drained from his already pale face. In the ensuing silence Laurence stepped away from the group and turned towards Jefferson.

'I am the guilty party. I am at fault, they were my schools and I wronged them. I am responsible for the situation that this truth wriggler so strenuously denies. You must understand Mr Tweedy that this work is tremendously monotonous and I may have drifted away temporarily to thoughts of my performance in the forthcoming 'Festival of the Absurd.' For that I proffer you my sincerest apologies but I say with an unstained heart that this man behind me is a liar and a cheat.'

The actor threw an extravagant gesture over his shoulder and then turned smartly and glared at the seated Kenneth. Jefferson stepped forward and asked again,

'Did I lie? Has Montgomery's school been given the wrong results?'

The words never left Kenneth's lips but as every eye in the room watched him, he slowly nodded his head.

Jefferson turned and thanked Laurence and then asked the actors to return to their seats. He walked to the door and locked it; he then returned to the circle and took a seat.

'Now Kenneth, you are going to tell me every single thing that you know about the goings on here at StanEd and please don't leave anything out because we've got all day.'

chapter thirteen

Lord McLeish had read all the articles in the Sunday Papers and looked back over the headlines:

CARR IN THE DRIVING SEAT

SEX TAPE HEAD WHIPS THE OPPOSITION

CARR DRIVES COMPREHENSIVES FORWARD

SUPER HEAD CARR IN POLE POSITION

He absentmindedly stroked the head of Angus his black Labrador and watched his wife pruning some roses in the garden. He looked again at the pictures of Emma Carr that filled all the Sunday papers and it crossed his mind that she wasn't unattractive in a teacherly sort of way. She didn't look completely at ease in the pictures but that was part of her charm.

Patricia came in from the garden and put the secateurs and her gardening gloves on the side. She then poured herself a glass of real lemonade and looked at her husband.

'What are you reading?'

'Oh I was just looking at the coverage of this St George's Cross stuff, you know the comprehensive that got those results.'

'Oh yes I read about her this morning. It's an extraordinary business isn't it? The paper said the school was failing a couple of years ago and now she's turned it round. She seemed nice as well.'

'Yes she does, doesn't she.'

'What's her name?'

'Carr. Emma Carr.'

'Oh yes that was it. Well, good for her.'

'Yes good for her.'

'Oh darling, what did Jefferson want on the phone earlier?'

There was the briefest of delays in Lord McLeish's response but his wife appeared not to notice.

'Oh some stuff about the wedding.'

'Well why didn't he ask me?'

'Well I thought you were busy and I happened to be able to answer it. Something about the writer of a particular hymn.'

His wife looked at him.

'And there was some other work stuff he wanted to ask about; nothing for you to worry about.'

His wife finished her lemonade and went back out into the garden. Angus followed her with his rolling gait and Lord McLeish watched them before going upstairs and calling Kenneth Andrews.

In Balham, Jefferson looked at the phone number written on his hand and reflected on his phone call to Ailsa. She had been more than a little surprised to find him calling at such an unseemly hour but his rare sense of purpose and urgency had silenced her grumblings and they had talked for over an hour. For the first time in many months their conversation made no mention of the wedding and she listened attentively as he recounted and pieced together the information garnered from Kenneth Andrews and the actors. He had also spoken to Samantha to verify some of the things that Kenneth said and also to ask her advice about how much he should reveal to Ailsa about her father's role in the business. Samantha's response was immediate and decisive,

'You've got to tell her everything; you'd be a bloody idiot not to. A girl should know; a girl needs to know.'

So he told Ailsa everything; haltingly at first and then with increasing fluency. He didn't pause to ask her opinion and she didn't ask him to stop. Only at the end did she speak, to suggest the course of action that Jefferson ought to take.

He lay down on his bed and picked up a slipper from the floor. Their conversation ran over in his mind as he threw the slipper towards the ceiling. Each time he aimed just short of the white paint and caught the slipper as it fell towards the bed. Five minutes and two slight black marks on the white ceiling later Jefferson got off the bed and picked up the phone again. He looked at the number on his hand and dialled. The phone rang five times before a voice said 'hello'.

'Hello I'd like to speak to Jacob Haliwell please.'

'Speaking.'

'Oh Jacob, this is Jefferson Tweedy, I'm the chief executive of StanEd.'

'I know you are. How are you?'

'I'm well. Listen I don't know if you remember but we met before…'

'At the syllabus launch, I remember it very well.'

'Oh good. Listen this is slightly awkward but the reason

I'm calling is because I was wondering if you could meet me for dinner tonight.'

'Tonight?'

'Look I know it's short notice but I've got something very important I need to discuss with you.'

'Can you tell me what it's about?'

'Not yet but I'll reveal all later. Shall we say 8 o'clock at The Gay Hussar on Dean Street?'

'Fine.'

'I'll see you there then.'

'Oh Mr Tweedy, could I ask how you got my number?'

'A gentleman at *The Express* gave it to me – a Roy Downes.'

'Ah and how was Mr Downes?'

'Absolutely revolting.'

chapter fourteen

J.P.P. Montgomery walked through the woods near his home, arm in arm with Lib.

'Apparently that little turd Castle has already written a letter to the governors calling for my resignation. Nigel reliably informs that it isn't the first time either but Herr Castle has rather more ammunition this time.'

'He's a repugnant little man isn't he?'

'Oh absolutely. I never like people whose ambition you can smell.'

They walked on a little more before Lib asked.

'What are you thinking of doing? Will you fight or…?'

'I don't know Lib. Could you put up with having me around the house a bit more?'

'Oh it wouldn't bother me at all, I'm never in.'

She smiled at her husband.

'Only as things stand it's all a touch untenable. The pupil numbers are haemorrhaging; the beloved parents of St George's College can't get their little darlings out of there quick enough. All the fine words of 'wanting the school to educate the whole child' and 'how much they value the extra curricular stuff we lay on at the school' are of course shown to be the most spectacular load of guff once the exam results go down the pan. One parent of a boy in Year 8 actually told me that he was taking his son out of St George's College 'because he couldn't afford to have the school's name on his C.V.' The boy is thirteen years of age. Mind you at least he was honest; some of them have been so mealy mouthed about it. You should have heard them. I've had eight boys this week alone whose parents are apparently moving out of the area on business which will enforce a change of school for young so and so. There are also a good number who suddenly can't afford the school fees and are 'downsizing their child's schooling'. One father actually used that word with me 'downsizing'; honestly Lib, where did these people come from?'

He stopped to smell a white coloured rhododendron flower and paused.

'I don't think I have much choice in truth; I've got to go, my only decision may be the how and the when.'

'You could get involved with me at the embassy, the more the merrier.'

'That wasn't quite what I had in mind, besides I think I might have had enough of public service for the time being.'

'Well have a think about it darling.'

'I shall.'

The couple walked on into the late summer's evening.

chapter fifteen

The Gay Hussar was busy. Jefferson looked around at the caricatures and pictures of political figures that filled the walls and tried to identify as many as he could; by the time Jacob Haliwell came through the door a couple of minutes later he hadn't named as many as he would have liked.

He stood up and greeted the journalist. He thought that he looked slightly fuller in the face than he remembered and asked if he would like a drink.

'I'll just have a water thanks.'

'No problem.'

Jacob sat down at the table and said,

'So is the choice of restaurant significant?'

'How do you mean?'

'Well it's famous isn't it; they used to bug the tables to find out what was really going on in parliament.'

'I had no idea. Maybe, maybe.'

Jacob smiled and looked again at the man in front of him.

'So how are things at StanEd?'

Jefferson smiled and paused.

'Interesting. So interesting in fact that I thought I'd call you to have a little chat about it.'

'Really?'

'Mmm. I'm calling upon you as my sole representative and contact in the world of the press, because I think we may be able to help each other out.'

'Go on.'

'I need some advice; I need some advice on how best to handle some information that I've got. I want the press to be involved but I'm not yet clear about how and in what way to involve them, so that's where you come in.'

'Okay. Well do you want to start by telling me the situation and I'll see what I think.'

Jefferson paused again and drank from his glass of red wine whilst Jacob sipped as his water. Finally he began.

'Do you know who Emma Carr is?'

'I do, she's the head of St George's Cross school. I did an interview with her recently about the success that the school had achieved.'

'Absolutely and do you know J.P.P. Montgomery?'

'I don't think I do.'

'Well he's the head master of St George's College which is just down the road from Emma Carr's school.'

'I know the school, I didn't know his name. I saw it when I went to St George's Cross, it's a beautiful looking place isn't it?'

'That's it.'

'So what about them?'

'They've had their GCSE results swapped.'

'What do you mean?'

'I mean that St George's Cross have been given the

College's results and the College have been given St George's Cross's results and that's why Emma Carr is in the papers and that's why Mr Montgomery will lose his job very soon.'

'By mistake?'

'Initially it was a mistake yes, but now it is deliberate.'

'By whom?'

'Well that's quite a long story.'

'And who knows about the swap?'

'Us two, a man called Kenneth Andrews whom you've met…'

'Ginger hair and rather camp?'

'That's him: Lord McLeish of Dunblane, who happens to be my fiancée's father, and a group of out of work actors who work in a subterranean room in Copperfield House.'

'Right.'

When Jefferson Tweedy finished talking an hour later he was halfway through his second bottle of red wine. Jacob Haliwell was still drinking water and writing furiously. When he put his pen down he looked up at Jefferson.

'So, what do you want to do with this?'

chapter sixteen

Belle was looking at a card when the phone rang. It had been given to her by a Year 8 pupil at St George's Cross on the final day of her teaching practice. Inside was written 'Thanx miss, your the best teacher ive eva had. lol Billie (Huggett)'. She was holding the card when she picked up the phone.

'Hello.'

'Belle?'

'Jacob, what time do you call this?'

'It's not a school night is it? How are you?'

'Tired, I've been for a job interview today.'

'Did you get it?'

'I didn't stay for the actual interview.'

'That good eh?'

'Oh yes. God it's an antiquated system.'

'I suppose. Now listen I've got something I need to talk to you about urgently. Can I come over?'

'What, now?'

'Yes, it's important.'

'You're not going to propose are you?'

'You wish love.'

'Thank God for that, I thought I was going to have to put my posh frock on for a minute.'

'See you in a bit then.'

'Okay.'

When he came through the door twenty minutes later Jacob headed straight for the kitchen table.

'Have I got something for you Belle,' he said over his shoulder, 'come and sit yourself down.'

As soon as she had joined him he began to recount what Jefferson Tweedy had told him earlier in the evening.

Belle listened hard. On several occasions she tried to interject but Jacob insisted that he would take questions at the end. For the last ten minutes she listened in intent silence. When finished, he sat back and put his hands behind his head.

'So there you have it. What did I tell you? Is that a story or is that a fucking story?'

Jacob looked expectantly at Belle who didn't answer immediately.

'Well?' he said.

'Is it true?'

'Why wouldn't it be? Yes, I think it's true. Do you really think your school could get the results it did?'

She paused and then laughed to herself.

'Leonard Baxter did get two As in English.'

'Exactly.'

She paused again. 'So if it is true; what are you going to do with it?'

'I don't know; that's what I wanted to speak to you about. The obvious thing is to do a straight expose; get the story to the right people, get Tweedy interviewed and bring the lot of them down. It's a top level scandal story – corruption at the very highest levels of education and possibly the government, etc etc. It's a perfect scandal story…'

'And who are the winners out of that?'

'Er…the winners are the public school because they get their real results back and possibly Jefferson Tweedy because he might look like a man of honour, depending on how the papers cover it. The other big winners are the truth of course and me because I get to sell the story.'

'True.'

Jacob watched her as she looked out of the kitchen door. It was dark and he could see her reflection in the glass, her eyes were slightly glazed.

'Hello?' he said.

'Hang on.'

'Look the reason I've come round to you with this rather spectacular information is not simply because I like your company but also because you've got one of those big brains; now it's not fair and indeed of no use if you're not going to chip in here.'

'Shut up Jacob, I'm thinking. Go away for a minute.'

Raising his hands in surrender, he got up from the table and poured himself a glass of water. He wandered out of the kitchen and into the living room where he began to browse through her shelves of books. He saw the copy of *Atonement* that he gave her and then saw another copy a couple of shelves up. He checked the inscription inside his gift and then checked the other copy. He felt an odd relief when he found it inscription free. He thought back to when he grandly presented it to her and admired the show of surprise and pleasure she'd managed. He leant against the wall and idly re-

read the first few pages of the copy he gave her. He was on page four when Belle came in the room; he looked up from the book.

'Well? What is the fruit of your deliberation?'

She sat down on the sofa and pointed at the place next to her. He went over and sat down. She waited for him to be seated before beginning.

'The fruit of my deliberation is that you and your friend Jefferson should do absolutely nothing.'

'Right; and this is what I was waiting all this time for was it?'

'I'm absolutely serious; you should do nothing at all to begin with.'

'Go on.'

'You've got them exactly where you want them. The power lies entirely with Jefferson Tweedy and now he's shared the knowledge with you, you share in that power.'

'Agreed and we should use that power to expose their filthy manipulation and corruption and so rectify the travesty that has taken place.'

'No, I think you should hold the power to your chest and dangle it over them while things unfold.'

'And how do you see things unfolding?'

'Spectacularly.'

'Tell me more.'

Belle leaned towards Jacob.

'Do you remember the conversation we had in the pub with Michael Harris, the head of English at St George's Cross?'

'Which one?'

'The one about comprehensive schools.'

'I do and he was saying that they're not really comprehensive schools at all because of all the other types of schools and so it's not fair to label them comprehensives etc…'

'And what did you think of it?'

'I thought it was a noble, if obvious argument, and that it was all true but he was shouting about a fait accompli. He shouts very charismatically and eloquently about it but yes, that's what I think. Everyone knows that the system is like that and unfortunately to change the system would require people to send their kid to what they consider to be a second rate school and then hope that everybody else does that as well – which isn't going to happen is it?'

'No, but I think you could do something about it.'

'Go on.'

'You leave the results of the two St George's schools as they are, so St George's Cross has 100% pass rate or whatever it is and the College has 25%, and Jefferson and his father in law and everyone else continue with the line of how the school has benefited from visionary leadership, implementation of government initiatives etc. In the mean time you saturate the press with pieces about the story. Features on Emma Carr, interviews with star performers etc; generally selling it as a bonafide educational miracle. Then you simultaneously begin a series of horror stories about St George's College, showing how archaic it is, hopelessly out of date, bloated and elitist…'

'Fall of the Roman Empire stuff.'

'You've got it and you let these run for a couple of days. After that you plant as many 'good news' stories as you can about other comprehensives from around the country and drag up some dirt on some public schools and then we sit back and let it take its course. You know what it's like in the summer, the press are desperate for stories, especially a runner like this; they'll lap it up.'

Jacob looked at the zealous glint in her eye.

'My God you're wasted as a teacher.'

She smiled and then said, 'There is of course one victim in all this.'

'Yes I was going to say, what about J.P.P. Montgomery and St George's College? They're going to be buggered by this aren't they?'

'Yes, but they've been buggering everyone else for years so it won't hurt them.'

'Well it will…'

'Look on it as a utilitarian act Jacob. Given the chance to bring equality to the entire school's system or to save one year's worth of pupils in an obscenely privileged public school, which option do you think John Pilger would take?'

Jacob paused and looked Belle in the eye.

'I'll give Jefferson a call.'

chapter seventeen

Two days later Jefferson looked out at the pack of press photographers. Lord McLeish stood before them resplendent in navy blue suit and powder blue shirt and tie. Jefferson could hear him intoning the words 'magnificent success,' and 'a wonderful tribute to the system'. He then gestured towards the wings and said,

'Ladies and gentlemen please welcome the architect of this grand design, Jefferson Tweedy.'

Jefferson walked on to the stage smiling and Lord McLeish gripped him in his double handed shake. Lord McLeish appeared to laugh at a joke that Jefferson had not heard and then patted him on the back before making his exit. Jefferson made his way to the podium. He looked directly at the sea of photographers and began.

'We are here today to celebrate a rare and glorious success. This is a story to restore our faith in the British education system and prove that we have a system that is the envy of the world.

This time last year St George's Cross School was termed a failing school by our inspection system. Its examination results were disastrous and the school and its staff and pupils were lacking in any sense of purpose or direction. Their OFSTED report placed the school under special measures and the future seemed bleak. But here we are today, one year on and the news of St George's Cross could not be more different.

Inside of one academic year, St George's Cross has moved from achieving 18% A*- C passes at GCSE to attaining a perfect 100% A*-C pass rate this year. This is a turn around never before witnessed in one of our nation's schools and I don't consider it hyperbole when I proclaim it as a bonafide educational miracle.

So we are here today to pay tribute to the extraordinary success that can be achieved through visionary management, the implementation of new initiatives – all combined with good old fashioned hard work.

Emma Carr is the name of the head teacher who took over that failing school and Emma Carr is the name of the head teacher who has turned St George's Cross into the most successful comprehensive school in the country. She slept nights at her office, she coaxed and cajoled staff through a series of ground breaking initiatives and she showed the pupils, staff and parents of that school her vision for what they could achieve. Emma Carr would not accept that her school was in the wrong catchment area, Emma Carr would not accept that her pupils were not the sort of pupils that did well in public examinations, Emma Carr would not accept the opinion of the people that told her she could not do it.'

Jefferson paused to look around at the press pack. He noticed the political editor of the BBC sitting in the second row, listening attentively, before going on.

'St George's Cross is a beacon for underachieving schools around the country. St George's Cross is an example of what can be achieved through visionary leadership and a love of your job. Emma Carr is a Super Head, she is the very embodiment of what StanEd stands for and hopes for, for our education system. Together we're looking after the children in the United Kingdom plc – StanEd and Emma Carr.'

As Jefferson finished his speech a vast banner unfurled from behind him and revealed an enormous picture of Emma Carr. Jefferson looked behind him and held his arm up towards the picture. As he did so a barrage of flashlights went off and he smiled up at the giant image of Emma Carr.

When the cameras finished, Jefferson gestured to his right and announced, 'Ladies and gentlemen, Emma Carr.' The bulbs burst into life again as Emma made her way towards the podium. She smiled calmly and waited for the cameras to stop, which they did after nearly a minute. Jefferson smiled and asked, 'Has anyone any questions for Ms Carr?'

The man from the BBC raised his hand and Jefferson nodded towards him,

'Nick?'

'Ms Carr I was wondering how it feels to be the saviour of the British education system?'

chapter eighteen

After the press conference, Jefferson walked through the shower of compliments and sat down in an office away from the main corridor. He poured a glass of water from the bottle on the table and waited.

After a couple of minutes there was a knock at the door and he called 'come in.'

Jacob poked his head around the door.

'Come in.'

'Afternoon Jefferson how are you?'

'Pretty good. So how did you think it went?

'Superbly. I thought the banner was a particularly nice touch.'

'Yes it was wasn't it? All part of Belle's plan to turn her into the pin up girl of the education world.'

'Well it was spectacular. Dreadfully spectacular but still, all publicity and all that.'

Jacob settled himself into the chair opposite and Jefferson poured him a glass of water. The two men looked at each other and drank again from their water. It was the journalist that spoke first,

'Are you still sure that you want to go through with this? Because we could leave it at that and Emma Carr gets her moment in the sun before disappearing back to wherever she goes to and that's it. And the next day the papers are full of something else and it would all be forgotten in a week and nobody would be any the wiser.'

'I know that but I want to do it.'

'You do know that once it begins you won't be able to call it back. The press has its own energy and life and they'll take it away from you.'

'That's the idea. It's nothing to do with me really is it, I'm simply...' Jefferson paused looking for the phrase he wanted, '...well Ailsa calls it hoisting them on their own petard.'

'Fair enough but you know that if things go wrong you would still be part of the rotten system and you'd go down with them.'

'Quite.'

'You could just expose the lot of them. I'll write the article and you can blow them all apart. The burnt papers, the copying of results all of that. 'I smelt it on the toilet says StanEd chief'. Jacob mapped the headline out in the air and smiled.

Jefferson smiled briefly before answering.

'But nothing would change that way would it? Well in fact it would change but for the worse; nobody would win. It would simply confirm everyone's worst fears. It's all a shambles, the comprehensive schools are rubbish and the administrators are all corrupt. Doing things this way well...' Jefferson tailed off and shrugged his shoulders.

'Did you ever see yourself as a campaigner?'

Jefferson looked up at the half smile on Jacob's face and smiled himself.

'No.'

The two men stood up and shook hands. Jacob finished his water and said,

'We'll get them going tomorrow then. We shall feed it all to the foul and rancid breath of the British press and let them pant all over it. The very best of luck.'

Jefferson nodded and watched Jacob turn and leave the room.

chapter nineteen

The headline in the *Daily Mail* read:

WHY WOULD YOU SPEND £15000 A YEAR FOR THIS?

Under the headline the paper had printed a copy of St George's College's results. Beside the article was a photograph of J.P.P. Montgomery at the races with a champagne flute in one hand and a cigar in the other. At various points during the article Montgomery was referred to as 'arrogant', 'out of touch', 'a toff' and most damningly 'posh'. The anchorage stated that he was 'unavailable for comment'. The article stated that the St George's College governor that provided the picture and quotes for the story had not wanted to be named.

The Mirror's front page was taken up by a colour photograph of three highly photogenic pairs of twins from comprehensive schools that had all scored straight A* grades in their GCSE examinations. One of the twins, a Jennifer Wood from Lancaster, was quoted as saying, 'How could I have done any better if I went to a public school? Some of my friends from primary school went to the nearest public school and they didn't do half as well as us and now their parents are complaining that they've wasted their money.'

Two irate parents told *The Times* how they were going to sue the public school that their son had attended since his results had been so disappointing. 'They practically guaranteed us straight As and now we find we could have got them for free at the school down the road.'

On the Saturday night Emma Carr appeared on the Jonathan Ross show and patted Wossy's knee after cracking a joke about him being 'a real investor in people' and 'providing value added benefit with his show'.

The following week the leader of the Opposition announced that he would be sending his son to their local comprehensive school 'in the light of the very real progress that had been made by such schools in recent years'.

On the Wednesday Jordan appeared in her bikini and told the readers of *The Express* that she had fancied her games teacher at school and that comprehensive teachers were 'fitter' than those at public schools.

A Labour minister made a keynote speech about 'bog standard public schools' and predicted the days of the paying school were coming to an end.

Two young mothers told *The Telegraph* how they had put the names of their newly born babies down on the waiting list for St George's Cross school. 'I just want the best for my little Lily,' said Annabelle Clay from Beckenham.

The Guardian published an interview with one Leonard Baxter from Tulse Hill that discussed with him his outstanding set of GCSE results and proclaimed him to be 'one of the boys that until now our education system has traditionally failed.' In the article Leonard described his results as 'phat'.

A local estate agent told *The Evening Standard* that house prices in the catchment area for St George's Cross rose by 25% in the past month and this meant a rise of between £50 000 – £75 000 in real terms on every house. He went on to say that this trend could be seen all over the country as parents battled for places at their local comprehensive school.

City analysts told *The Financial Times* that investments in stocks and shares rose in the past month as parents invested the money they had previously set aside for their child's education. 'They simply don't see it as a productive use of their capital,' said Giles Smythe of the Nagasumi bank.

The Sun's headline read 'It was *The Sun* that dunnit!' In the accompanying article the paper claimed that it had been their distribution of St George flags during the recent football tournament that inspired the children of St George's Cross to new levels of patriotic endeavour in their studies.

Valerie Bastic Styles appeared in the next day's edition of *The Sun* wearing a pair of frilly knickers and a feather boa underneath the headline:

'THE JOB COST ME MY MARRIAGE, NOW I'M LOOKING FOR LOVE.'

The Guardian ran a series of interviews with famous figures from business, science, the arts and sport that attended a comprehensive school and in an editorial urged the Labour prime minister to follow the nation's lead and move his children to state schools.

Emma Carr turned down a chance to appear on 'I'm a Celebrity Get Me Out of Here' and her place was eventually taken by Lionel Blair who said in a statement 'Mrs Carr has more important matters to take care of; I've just got to be out in time for panto in Grimsby.'

Six of the stories were planted by Jacob and weeks of coverage followed. Even Ray Gains from the *South London Advertiser* found himself with a series of bylines in the national press, feted as a local expert on 'the schools that have changed the face of British education.'

For that summer Emma Carr was the most recognised face in England and when news came of two public schools in Yorkshire closing due to lack of demand, Jacob Haliwell unearthed his picture of John Pilger and pinned it back up on his bedroom wall.

In Balham, Jefferson Tweedy called Ailsa and asked if there was any way she could catch an earlier flight home.

chapter   twenty

Nigel Rose finished another phone conversation with another parent who wished to take their child off the school roll, and sat down in front of J.P.P. Montgomery.

'Was that another rat jumping ship?'

'I'm afraid so.' He jotted the name of the child on a pad of paper and tore the top sheet off, clipping it onto his folder.

'What you must understand Nigel is that the average middle class parent is a brutally pragmatic animal and ruthless as well, utterly ruthless. Their sole concern is the welfare of themselves and their immediate kin and anything that appears to threaten their God given, financially earned right to success and comfort must be eradicated and replaced. They are the consumer Nigel and as we all know...'

J.P.P. trailed off before breathing deeply and looking at Nigel Rose.

'We've been well and truly shafted here you know that don't you?'

He then rubbed his eyes and then put his head on his hands.

'Did you see that article they did on me in *The Times*?'

Nigel Rose shook his head although he had read it.

'They made me out to be some sort of lunatic dinosaur. The mad old fool from the public school. If you start talking about people being out to get you and the system and all that stuff you just set yourself up to be ridiculed. I came across as some paranoid delusionist, one of those poor sods that have been hidden in the jungle for twenty years and think the war's still going on.'

The phone began to ring on the desk and J.P.P. Montgomery looked long and hard at it before saying,

'Well it can't be anything good can it?' and picked it up.

Nigel Rose looked on and watched Montgomery's face crumple in resignation. He began to leave the room but as he got to the door Montgomery called him back and Nigel sat for an uncomfortable minute as Montgomery finished the conversation. Montgomery finally put the phone down and Nigel tried to catch his eye.

'Is everything all right Philip?'

'Not really Nigel, no.'

'Oh.'

'That was Buffy from the stables.'

'Oh?'

'St George's Blue is dead.'

'Oh Christ. How?'

'She had a heart attack on the gallops.' He paused. 'I didn't know horses could have a heart attack did you?'

'Oh Philip I am sorry. Is there anything I can do?'

'God she was a beautiful horse. Did you ever see her?'

'Yes I came down to Epsom that time.'

'Oh yes of course you did.'

'Were there any signs?'

'Apparently not. They were out on the downs and Buffy said it was a beautiful morning and she looked in terrific shape and then, bang. No sign, no warning. The bloody jockey broke his leg as well, falling off her.' Montgomery paused. 'Buffy says that she wouldn't have suffered, which is something I suppose.'

Montgomery stared out of the window. The phone rang again.

'Fuck.'

'Do you want me to get it?' Nigel Rose asked.

'No I'll get it.'

Montgomery picked the phone up and listened briefly, 'Yes Paul.'

He then listened before saying, 'Fine I'll see you there.'

As he put the phone down he exhaled loudly.

'He is a man without a soul.'

'Who was it, Paul Jessop?'

'Yes the one and only, Paul Jessop, esteemed governor and professional hatchet man. Buffy has called him with the news about St George's Blue and he wants me to go over and see him at his place.'

Montgomery re-arranged some papers on his desk and then got up and straightened a picture on the wall,

'Do you know he didn't mention Blue once; pure business. I fear the writing is on the wall old boy.'

'What are you going to do?'

'I'm not entirely sure I shall get that choice.'

Nigel Rose couldn't think of anything else to say as he watched his friend walk around the office. Montgomery pondered aloud, 'What would Philip Marlowe have done in a situation like this?'

'I'm not sure he would have been in a situation like this.'

'No I don't suppose he would have been. Ah well, hon y va Nigel, hon y va.'

chapter twenty one

Jefferson Tweedy walked into Copperfield House and smiled at Liz on reception.

'Good morning Mr Tweedy, is there anything I can get you?'

'No I'm absolutely fine thank you Liz. Although I would appreciate it if you could send Kenneth Andrews up to see me in about five minutes.'

'No problem sir.'

He got into the lift and hummed softly as it ascended to the ninth floor. The doors opened and he headed to his office. As he walked into his room he saw Samantha bending over her desk. He smiled and said,

'Busy Samantha?'

She straightened up and pushed her hair away from her eyes. She smiled and said,

'I didn't hear you come in Mr Tweedy.'

'Ah it's the Cherokee Indian in me, no man can hear my footsteps.'

'Really? You look very pale for an Indian.'

'Yes I am. What are you doing?'

'I'm clearing my desk.'

'Oh, are you leaving us?'

'I am.'

'May I ask why?'

'You may. Barry and I have had a bit of luck. We live round the back of that St George's Cross school, you know the one that's been in the papers.'

'I know it very well.'

'I went there actually but it wasn't as good as it is now. She's been brilliant hasn't she that head?'

'She has.'

'And anyway, everyone wants to go there now don't they and all of a sudden we've got a load of people knocking on our door and asking us if we're in the catchment area for Cross? Well like Barry says 'we could piss on it from where we are,' so as soon as we say yes they started asking us if we wanted to move and all that. So we had a talk with mum, you know her she's Aggy the tea lady here…'

'Is she really?'

'Oh yeah. I wasn't supposed to tell you but it doesn't matter now I'm leaving does it.'

'I suppose not.'

'Anyway we had a talk to her and then got a few agents in and we've sold it. Do you want to know how much for?'

'Well if it isn't rude to pry.'

'Four hundred and twenty three grand.'

'Good grief.'

'We took four two three because they asked for two grand off because the survey said there's a suggestion of damp and dry rot. Me mum nearly snatched their hand off.'

'And this is because of the school?'

'Yeah all the houses are the same round us. You can't park on our street anymore, there's Land Rovers everywhere. And they're going to shut the college aren't they?'

'How do you mean?'

'You know St George's College?'

'Yes.'

'Well they lost all their pupils didn't they, so they've shut it and Cross have bought the grounds and it's all going to be one school; still called St George's Cross though. They reckon they had to move because they couldn't fit in all the people that wanted their kids to go there.'

Jefferson said, 'I didn't know that.' An image of J.P.P. Montgomery briefly flashed through his mind.

'So anyway with the money we've made on the house me and Barry can get our place in Sidcup.'

'Samantha, that's wonderful news.'

'And mum's bought a bungalow in Selsy Bill.'

'I'm sure you'll all be very happy.'

'Well mum's already happy because our Leonard's finally got off the sofa.'

'Ah yes, she mentioned Leonard.'

'Well you know he wouldn't do anything but the school's done brilliantly for him and he passed all his exams with flying colours. We always knew he wasn't stupid but you should see him now, he's like a new man. He's had his hair cut and he's already bought a suit for when he starts in the sixth form. He tells us to turn the tele down now because he's trying to read a book. I've never known anything like it.'

She put the contents of the desk drawer into her bag and smiled.

'Well that's me, I'll be off.'

'Samantha, it's been a pleasure.'

'Likewise Mr Tweedy. Am I still invited to the wedding?'

'Of course you are.'

'Right I'll see you then and you and your wife must come over to Sidcup some time.'

'We'd love to.'

'Bye then.'

She leant forward and kissed Jefferson on the cheek.

'And don't forget, always go traditional, no one wants a new fangled wedding.'

She picked up her bag, smiled and walked out of the door.

chapter twenty two

Two days later Bryn Castle and Susan Williams waited at the doors of what used to be St George's College. The workman behind them was in the process of covering the word College that hung over the school entrance and replacing it with Cross. The two teachers peered expectantly down the drive at the approach of every car before returning to their excitable chatter.

In the building behind them J.P.P. Montgomery completed the long delayed final clearing of his desk after an extended holiday in France. His departure through 'mutual consent' with the governors had long since ceased to be news in the light of the developments that followed. After the initial surge of press coverage about the two schools and all the ensuing stories, Nigel Rose presided over a haemorrhaging of the school's student base. Parents no longer bothered to dress their son's withdrawal up in unlikely excuses, they simply demanded he be taken off the school register immediately and signed off with a promise that the school would be hearing from their solicitors in due course about the issue of reclaiming the year's fees. Within a matter of weeks the school was in an untenable position for starting the next academic year and it was then that the local authority called about the possibility of purchasing the grounds for the necessary development of St George's Cross. It was Paul Jessop who brokered the deal and the remaining parents of St George's College were consulted and thoroughly approved of the idea, since the only reason their son remained at the College was because there were no spaces left at St George's Cross.

It was confirmed that Emma Carr would be the head teacher of this 'New Super School' (as the papers called it) and Paul Jessop was appointed as head of the Governors.

Nigel Rose took the early retirement package that he was offered by the new Board of Governors and the rest of the staff would be the pick of the teachers from the two schools as decided upon by Ms Carr. Belle Jones was offered a job in the new English department that would be led by Michael Harris and she accepted the post without hesitation.

In his old office, Montgomery paused to look through a cricket score book that he had found in his desk drawer. His name appeared as one of the two umpires listed at the bottom of the page and his eye fell on the name of a recently appointed New Labour backbencher who managed to score three runs for the college in 1989 against Broadham College. The same boy had surfaced in many of the national newspapers recently celebrating the demise of the public school system. Montgomery reflected that rarely could you trust a boy who had no idea how to play a decent forward defensive stroke.

Out of the window Montgomery could see Castle and Williams chattering like hyenas and he decided that there wasn't much here that he wanted. He picked up the black bin bag that the caretaker gave him and proceeded to empty the contents of all of the drawers into it. He then swept the pads and pens from the top of the desk in as well before tying a knot at the top. He placed the bin bag at the front of the desk and then took down the picture on the left wall. It was a painting of St George's Blue in her first competitive race. He remembered the summer's day at Epsom and the joy of her gliding home to victory. She looked magnificent with sinews straining and ears pricked up and Montgomery smiled and tucked the picture under his arm. Some talking drew his attention to the window again and he looked up and saw Castle and Williams hurrying down the school drive. From the other wall he took down a painting of the school's playing fields and with a picture under each arm he left the office and made his way towards the lush playing fields and then on towards the St George's Road.

Paul Jessop, head of the Governors for St George's Cross, opened the door for the school's new head teacher. Emma Carr stepped out on to the drive way and stood in front of the gothic building that she saw so often from her office window. She looked up at the turrets and then turned and offered her hand towards the car. Her son Luke held his hand out and joined her in front of the building.

Bryn Castle and Susan Williams stepped forward,

'Good afternoon head teacher we're delighted to welcome you to the extended St George's Cross. We've all heard such a lot about you.'

All of the group smiled and Paul Jessop put his hand gently in the small of Emma Carr's back,

'Now Emma, where would you like to see first? Your office or Luke's classroom?'

'Oh I think we'd like to look around the junior school first wouldn't we Luke?'

Paul Jessop smiled and said 'very good,' before leading the way into the glorious old building. Bryn Castle and Susan Williams stepped back to allow the head teacher and her son through, nodding slightly as they passed. They looked behind them and saw a group of boys in hooded tops and caps standing together on the corner of St George's Road. The boys were talking with their backs to the college; Bryn Castle and Susan Williams followed their new head teacher into the building and shut the doors behind them.

chapter twenty three

When Jefferson Tweedy picked up Ailsa from Gatwick airport he was delighted to see that her flight was delayed. He had fully intended to catch the 3.25 train from Victoria but missed it due to his taxi being stuck in traffic on Piccadilly. Once on board the train he read an article about himself in *The Evening Standard* that proclaimed him 'The Saviour of British Education' and featured a pleasingly flattering picture. The article also mentioned his imminent marriage to Ailsa and featured a quote from Lord McLeish of Dunblane saying 'I'm delighted to be acquiring a son-in-law like Jefferson.'

Once inside the terminal he bought a bunch of flowers and made his way to arrivals. He had been waiting at the barriers for twenty minutes when the passengers began to make their way through from the flight. He watched them all arrive and depart and checked the board again to make sure he was in the right place. As he looked down from the board Ailsa walked through the screens and Jefferson broke into a smile. She wheeled her suitcase behind her and he thought she looked terrific. He stood where he was and Ailsa dropped her suitcase behind her. They stood in front of each other and she asked,

'So how have you been darling?'

'Not too dusty, yourself?

'Oh mustn't grumble. It's nice to be home.'

'Still want to get married?'

'I suppose so.'

'In which case may I take your luggage for you?'

'That would be charming Mr Tweedy.'

'Not a problem. And how was the flight?'

'Late.'

'Good; so was I.'